"What's unacceptable?" Miranda asked her aunts. "What's scandalous?"

Aunt Sibelle pointed. "Hiring this man as your secretary, of course. He's young, handsome, fit."

"Virile," Aunt Olivia added.

"Indeed, madam," MacGregor said. "Guilty as charged."

Her aunts gasped. Miranda didn't know whether she was shocked or amused, but this did cause her to really look at Andrew MacGregor. He noticed her perusal and stood up straight, with his arms held at his sides. Her aunts were correct, Miranda realized, as an unexpected rush of heat washed over her. Despite the glasses, the baggy suit, and the dreadful hair, Andrew Mac-Gregor was quite—fit. His height and broad shoulders alone were quite impressive. He had a strong, square jaw, and there wasn't a hint of meekness in what were not so much icy blue, but chilly gray eyes. As for the virile . . .

"You'll do," she said, and wasn't quite sure what she meant.

Other **AVON ROMANCES**

GYPSY LOVER *by Edith Layton*
KEEPING KATE *by Sarah Gabriel*
A KISS BEFORE DAWN *by Kimberly Logan*
A MATCH MADE IN SCANDAL *by Melody Thomas*
RULES OF PASSION *by Sara Bennett*
SCANDALOUS *by Jenna Petersen*
STILL IN MY HEART *by Kathryn Smith*

Coming Soon

THE BRIDE HUNT *by Margo Maguire*
A FORBIDDEN LOVE *by Alexandra Benedict*

And Don't Miss These
ROMANTIC TREASURES
from Avon Books

THE LORD NEXT DOOR *by Gayle Callen*
A MATTER OF TEMPTATION *by Lorraine Heath*
THIS RAKE OF MINE *by Elizabeth Boyle*

SUSAN SIZEMORE

Scandalous Miranda

AVON BOOKS
An Imprint of HarperCollinsPublishers

This is a work of fiction. Names, characters, places, and incidents are products of the author's imagination or are used fictitiously and are not to be construed as real. Any resemblance to actual events, locales, organizations, or persons, living or dead, is entirely coincidental.

AVON BOOKS
An Imprint of HarperCollins*Publishers*
10 East 53rd Street
New York, New York 10022-5299

Copyright © 2005 by Susan Sizemore
ISBN-13: 978-0-06-008290-1
ISBN-10: 0-06-008290-9
www.avonromance.com

First Avon Books paperback printing: December 2005

Avon Trademark Reg. U.S. Pat. Off. and in Other Countries, Marca Registrada, Hecho en U.S.A.
HarperCollins® is a registered trademark of HarperCollins Publishers Inc.

Printed in the U.S.A.

10 9 8 7 6 5 4 3 2 1

For Elizabeth Jean Murray,
in memoriam.
Mom, thanks for the doves,
the Dunnett, and the privilege
of being there.
Love, Susan G.

Prologue

Italy, 1881

Visiting Italy was supposed to be every Englishman's dream, but he wasn't here on holiday. Besides, Andrew MacLeod was Scottish, and it was too hot by half for his somber tastes. The sky was a far-too-perfect bright, cloudless blue. The difference between light and shadow stood out too sharply on the rocky landscape. Painters might find the play of colors all very interesting, but it irritated his eyes. One thing he needed right now was clear sight. Though he preferred glasses for reading, his long vision was sharp as a hawk's. It came in handy in his work.

He didn't completely trust the information he'd been given. He didn't completely trust the hill bandits that were supposedly under his command today. He didn't completely trust the natives of this tiny village perched on this scenic, rocky hill. But then trust didn't come easily to Andrew MacLeod after all these years in Her Majesty's service. He'd been accused of having cynicism in his blood, like a disease, but he found it more of a tonic than poison. At times cynicism was the only thing that kept him going. It was his duty to kill a man today. If all went well, a traitor to the British Empire would be identified and disposed of without the bother of a trial, without scandal. And without exposing any flaws or foibles in the men who ran the Empire. The man Andrew waited to kill was a murderer himself, though at a distance. He was a bureaucrat in the foreign office who had sold secrets that led to the deaths of hundreds of soldiers and civilians in the lands the British protected.

The problem was, Andrew had no idea what the man he was going to kill looked like. He had been given no name. He knew only the location where the traitor was going to pass documents to Britain's enemies. He hated not having all the facts. He hated having to depend on a hill bandit named Dante for the successful completion of such a delicate assignment.

He allowed none of this irritation to show. He waited on the hillside in the growing heat, still as a stone, infinitely patient. He'd wait as long as necessary to get the job done. Andrew MacLeod always completed his assignments.

Finally, two of Dante's scouts reported to the bandit chief. Dante came to Andrew. "Two parties approaching the grove," he said.

"Get your men into cover."

The grove was where artists and foreign travelers climbed to appreciate the view of the medieval walled city in the valley below. It was a lovely spot to rest and have a picnic beneath the shade of ancient olive trees. There were plenty of places where a man could fade behind trees, boulders, and other concealment.

Andrew moved to kneel behind an ancient broken wall. A dust-covered vine, its leaves limp from the heat, spilled over the wall, added a bit more cover. He was oblivious to the sweet scent of the foliage and the birdsong coming from a nearby tree. Within moments he caught sight of a group of men coming down the path from the next village. From the opposite direction, a man in a large, floppy hat came up the road from the valley. The hat covered the man's face. He also carried a canvas rucksack and used a walking stick. Andrew watched the man's approach and took careful aim at the traitor's heart. A bead of sweat rolled down Andrew's back, sending a chill like a finger tracing down his spine. He ignored discomfort as he waited for the lone hiker and the group to meet. He wanted proof of information being passed before he took the traitor down.

For the first few moments everything went as planned. Then a woman appeared, walking briskly across the olive grove.

Where the devil had she come from?

Men began to shout and come out of their hiding places. For some reason Dante and his ruffians took her appearance to mean that they were being ambushed. The approaching group of men thought the bandits were attacking them. Everyone was armed. Even the traitor's walking stick turned out to be a concealed rifle.

Shouts and shots rang out, and the whole situation went violently to hell.

Chapter 1

Passfair Castle
Kent, England, 1882

"I am used to always having my own way."

Andrew looked over his metal-rimmed glasses at the woman seated so stiffly behind the library desk and replied, "So am I, Lady Miranda."

One of her eyebrows went up, but otherwise not a flicker of surprise or annoyance showed on her serenely composed face. "Really, Mr. MacGregor? And how is that possible?"

"I am a man," he answered. "That is the way of the world."

He waited calmly, to see how this arrogant reply from a man she was interviewing for a position in her household would affect this lady of power and privilege. There was a stillness in her bearing he admired, but the firmness of her jaw and the fire in her hazel eyes spoke of temper and endless amounts of trouble. A strong woman. He had nothing against strong women, but they were the bane of a man's existence if he let himself become involved with them. It was his fate to become involved with this one. It didn't mean he had to do it on her terms.

Lady Miranda DuVrai Hartwell had a strong spirit. She was famous for it. But Andrew saw hints of frailty about her, despite the stubborn will that kept her upright and calm in the face of his effrontery. She was thin, and not because of any artifice of a tight-laced boned corset. Her cheeks were hollow, and her high cheekbones more prominent than they should be. She was pale, and there was a thinness about her lips that spoke of pain being ruthlessly ignored. He knew her age was thirty. Still young, yet there was a streak of silver in her otherwise jet black hair, rising in an arc over her scarred left temple. She'd made no effort to hide the small, round scar. It might have been polite to not look at her temple, but Andrew was not polite. He briefly looked, but kept any feelings or comments to himself.

"The way of the world," she finally said. "You will find that I go my own way, Mr. MacGregor."

"Will I?" he asked. "So you find my qualifications suitable for the position."

Miranda distinctly did not like Mr. MacGregor. That alone should be enough for her to end the interview and continue searching for a more amenable male to fill the position. Unfortunately, liking the man she sought was not something she'd put on her list of requirements. She needed intelligence, competence, scholarship, and good character. What she did not need was a toady or a sycophant, and Mr. MacGregor had certainly shown no signs of any servile eagerness to please. He didn't even act as if he wanted the position. He seemed quite relaxed as he sat in the deep leather chair across from her desk. His long legs were stretched out on the Persian rug, his long-fingered hands resting on the chair arms. He sat with an almost unnatural stillness that was still somehow as graceful as an alert hunting cat. He regarded her with a somewhat predatory boldness, as well. It was as though she were the one being examined, as if he were deciding whether he would take her, rather than the other way around. This made him not only annoying, but intriguing. He also came with the highest of recommendations.

"Lady Phoebe Gale has told me—"

A knock sounded on the library door, interrupting her. The door opened before Miranda could call out that she did not wish to be disturbed. She was not surprised when the two people who would have entered no matter what Miranda wanted opened the door and came in. Little, plump Aunt Sibelle entered in her usual brisk fashion. Aunt

Olivia right behind her, tall, thin, gaze darting about in open curiosity. The pair of them were shameless, interfering biddies. They were twins, though they didn't look it a bit. Both wore black, as usual, for they seemed to be perpetually in mourning. It was usually for one of the family's numerous distant relatives, but now they wore black in respect for the passing of a local lad. Sibelle brightened her black bombazine with lots of lace on cap, collar, and cuffs. Olivia favored so much jet bead jewelry that she rattled when she moved.

Miranda rose as her aunts came into the room, and Mr. MacGregor laconically did the same. The women immediately concentrated on the tall man now standing before the fireplace. They studied him with the raptorlike eyes of confirmed spinsters.

"What do you think, Olivia?" Aunt Sibelle asked her twin sister.

Olivia pursed her mouth and shook her head. "Impossible. Won't do at all."

Sibelle nodded. "Even with the glasses, and that dreadful suit, it simply can't be disguised."

MacGregor glared at the women over the top of his glasses. "Madam—"

"What magnificent eyes," Aunt Olivia declared. "Like hot blue ice."

"Hot ice? Olivia, really, that is impossible," Sibelle said.

"What are you two doing?" Miranda demanded of her aunts.

Aunt Olivia finally looked her way. "Totally unacceptable," she proclaimed. "There's already enough gossip about your wandering off to foreign lands. It's not proper."

"It certainly didn't help that you came home with a bullet hole in your head," Aunt Sibelle added. "It was scandalous."

"And no doubt painful," Mr. MacGregor spoke up.

Miranda wasn't sure if his dry tone warranted a grateful look or not. It did elicit a smile from her. She did not admit to anyone that it was indeed painful, or that it was still painful. Her head hurt most of the time, and she had learned to ignore it—most of the time. The scar throbbed, but she resisted the impulse to touch it. That would put to the lie her insistence that she was completely recovered.

"What's unacceptable?" she asked her aunts. "What's scandalous?"

Aunt Sibelle pointed. "Hiring this man as your traveling companion, of course. He's young, handsome, fit."

"Virile," Aunt Olivia added.

"Indeed, madam," MacGregor said. He nodded his head to them. "Guilty, as charged."

Her aunts gasped. Miranda didn't know whether she was shocked or amused, but this did cause her to really look at Andrew MacGregor. He noticed her perusal and stood up straight, with his arms held at his sides. Her aunts were correct, Miranda realized, as an unexpected rush of heat washed over her. Despite the glasses, the baggy suit, and the dreadful hair, Andrew MacGregor was quite—fit. His height and broad shoulders alone were quite impressive. He had a strong, square jaw, and there wasn't a hint of meekness in what were not so much icy blue, but chilly gray eyes. As for the virile . . .

"You'll do," she said, and wasn't quite sure what she meant.

"You're hiring him?" Aunt Olivia questioned.

"She is," MacGregor answered.

"You can't!" Aunt Sibelle declared. "You simply can't run off with this man."

Miranda wasn't planning on running off with a man. She was planning on running to one, but she wasn't telling anyone about her true intentions. "My travels were interrupted last year," she said. "I intend to resume them. You were the ones who insisted that I shouldn't go alone." She gestured toward MacGregor. "This is my solution. You have no reason to complain."

"Which won't stop them, I'm sure," MacGregor put in. "I know all about meddling aunts. My family has an endless supply of them."

"Well, that's something we have in common," she murmured.

"Meddling!" Olivia squawked. "Young man—"

"Excuse us," he went on, stepping between Miranda and her aunts. He moved forward. "Lady Miranda is very busy at the moment." He herded them back without the women seeming to notice that they were being ejected from the room.

When they were gone, and the door closed behind them, he turned around and said, "There's something to be said for a large male presence."

"Especially when dealing with maiden ladies unfamiliar with the breed," Miranda answered. "They have no idea how to react." It was a rude thing to say about her aunts, but they had been rude first.

"Breed?" He asked, an eyebrow raised sarcastically. "Are you seeking a sheep dog, as well as a secretary, factotum, and assistant in composing your memoirs?"

"Yes," she answered. "I am seeking a man of many talents." She gestured toward the documents on her desk. "The glowing recommendations, as well as your educational and employment history, are as nothing compared to the impression you have just made on two of my three aunties. They are tigresses, Mr. MacGregor. Dangerous, and difficult to defend against."

"Had I known you needed protection from tigers, I would have packed more firepower, Lady Miranda."

"Never fear," she answered. "There's a gun room in the castle full of any weaponry you might require. Mind you, I won't have you shooting my aunts. You'll have to learn how to charm them instead."

He adjusted the glasses on his hawklike nose. "Will I?" he asked. "You will find that charm is not listed among my accomplishments."

"You'll have a few weeks to learn it," she assured him. "There are many preparations to be made, and I have promised to attend several functions in London in the near future. There's a speech you can help—" Her words were cut off as a blaze of pain swept through her head. What had been a throbbing ache turned into blinding agony. The world around her went dark, and Miranda was falling, falling—

Hands came around her arms, strong, yet gentle. "Don't struggle, cara." The voice was a soft, purring rumble, the language Italian-accented English. "Lie still. The pain is better when you lie still."

"Where am I?" she asked. She knew she'd asked this many times before. She didn't know if he never answered, or if she could not remember the answer. She was lost in darkness, with only the voice to comfort the confusion and pain.

"In my village," he answered. *"In my house. You're safe here. You're with me."*

"Where am I?" Miranda asked. She knew she was lying down. She felt the warmth of a nearby fire on her face. The wave of pain had receded, and she was being held, tenderly. Strong arms surrounded—"Dante?"

"Lady Miranda?"

The man's voice was as deep as Dante's, but the accent was Scottish rather than Italian. There was concern in his tone, but without the warmth or compassion that had comforted her in the darkness.

Darkness. Oh, bother.

She opened her eyes and found that vision had returned. The pain was better, and she was lying on the carpet before the library hearth. She remembered MacGregor. Her head was propped in his lap. She realized he must have caught her when she—

"Fainted. I fainted again. Bloody hell."

"Lady Miranda!"

He went stiff with shock, his muscular thigh going rock hard beneath her head. "Please don't drop me if you're going to bolt from the room because of my swearing," she requested.

"I would not abandon a woman in distress," he replied. "But mind your language in the future."

Miranda sat up, very slowly. She kept her gaze on the flames dancing in the hearth, drinking in the warmth that was nothing like Italian sunlight, but would do for now. Dante used to take her out into his garden to drink in the scent of sun-warmed earth and herbs, to feel the warm breeze on her skin. She'd been desperately ill, but it had still been wonderful.

That was then. That was for the future. It was to-day she must deal with. She heard MacGregor rise to his feet behind her. "Don't call anyone," she said, knowing he was going to ask if she wanted him to. "I'm all right now."

"You're sure?"

She turned around and looked up at him. She tried to keep her tone light, not to sound as if she was pleading when she asked, "You aren't going to refuse employment because of a minor fainting spell, are you?"

Andrew wanted out. More than anything else, he wanted to bolt, to run from this woman and never see her in pain again. Duty, of course, would not permit such craven behavior. Damn duty to hell. He damned Phoebe Gale to hell as well. But of course that was nothing new. He'd always known Aunt Phoebe was a cold-blooded old witch.

"I'm out of it, woman," he told her. "I have better ways to spend my time. I won't take any more assignments." He hated himself, what he'd become, but he'd be damned even more than he already was if he'd let

Phoebe Gale know he was anything but bored with the life of a secret agent.

"One more," she said, calm and superior as ever. "It isn't over yet. You got the girl into it, only you can protect her now. You can't walk away from an unfinished assignment. Go down to Kent. Do your duty. I've made the arrangements already."

Of course she had. He'd raged, he'd protested, but here he was. Miranda wanted him to stay.

For all that Miranda tried to seem unconcerned at her own disability, he saw the fear in her eyes. "I'm not going anywhere, Lady Miranda," he told her. "My skills are yours to command." He held out a hand to help her to her feet. "For as long as you need me."

Chapter 2

"For as long as you need me." Miranda sighed.

"What did you say, my dear?"

Miranda was embarrassed to realize she'd been speaking aloud. But she couldn't get MacGregor's words out of her head as she dressed for dinner. It was ridiculous, really, to be so affected by his statement. It was not as if he'd been promising her the moon, or anything. It was not in his power to give her the moon, and he was certainly not the person she wanted such promises from.

She also realized she'd been staring dreamily into her dressing table mirror. Her heavy black hair swung around her shoulders as she turned from the mirror to answer her aunt Rosemary's question.

"I seem to be suffering from an overactive imagination this evening."

16

Lady Rosemary Edgware was seated on a chaise longue near the fireplace. A large sight hound rested at her feet. Its miniature cousin was curled in Rosemary's lap. In her fifties, Rosemary was the youngest of Miranda's three aunts. Unlike the twins, who were spinsters, Rosemary was a widow. Childless, she had returned to Passfair to be with her family after her husband's death. Rosemary was a cheerful, sensible woman with a sharp eye for business and the world at large. As a career officer's wife, she'd traveled throughout the Empire, and loved it. She'd always encouraged Miranda's own wanderlust and sense of adventure.

"Better an overactive imagination than a headache," Aunt Rosemary said. "You really are over those dreadful headaches, aren't you?"

Miranda gave a slight shrug and a smile, rather than actually lie. At least she wasn't in pain at the moment. And she was sick of being treated as an invalid. Sick of being carefully watched over and coddled. "I need to fly free, Auntie," she said. "I've been home far too long."

"We went up to London only a month ago. You seemed to enjoy yourself."

"I did."

This was an outright lie. Miranda hadn't enjoyed the lectures, salons, and exhibits she'd attended, but had kept up the pretense to serve her purpose. She had made one new friend, and that had been pleasant. Lady Phoebe Gale was proving a lively correspondent, a wise confidante, and a very helpful person. Having made Lady Phoebe's acquaintance was a godsend.

But for the most part people had stared, offered sympathy, and asked questions. She'd braved it all, ignored scandalized whispers, and thankfully hadn't had a fainting spell in public even once. In fact, despite frequent headaches, the pain hadn't overwhelmed her for some time. Not until today.

Miranda turned back to look in the mirror as she pinned up her hair. "I intend to leave for the continent soon. That is why I hired Mr. MacGregor today."

"Against your other aunts' advice."

"It wasn't advice, it was . . . it was an appalling scene, actually."

"So Olivia and Sibelle said. Though they blamed you for being a willful, headstrong girl, blind to every propriety when you want your own way."

"I have the occasional blind spot," Miranda said. She couldn't help the irony, but hoped her aunt didn't recognize it. "I have taken Mr. Mac-Gregor into my service in the hope that my family will be reassured of my safety on my travels."

Aunt Rosemary petted her lapdog for a while, then added, "They say you're attracted to him."

Miranda whipped around so quickly on her seat that it made her dizzy. "They saw me with the man for thirty seconds . . . How could they possibly think—?"

"You're blushing. You don't do that often."

Miranda waved a hand in front of her face. "I am flushed with annoyance."

"Of course. And you would have me believe you were thinking of climbing the Matterhorn while you were staring so dreamily into the mirror just now—and murmuring sweet nothings."

"Murmuring sweet—!" Miranda took a deep breath and got herself under control. She finally saw her aunt's faint smile. "You are teasing me, madam."

"A bit, but you are flustered. I haven't seen you flustered in years. Not since Malcolm . . ."

Miranda hated the way her aunt trailed off, as though Malcolm were some sacred, forbidden subject. Once upon a lifetime ago, when her father had disapproved of him, and Malcolm's father had disapproved of her, there had certainly been a *Romeo and Juliet* quality of dissension on the subject of their being in love.

"Malcolm brought out all sorts of romantic yearnings and melodrama, Auntie." She smiled. "But his death didn't make my life a tragedy. Don't act as if it did."

Though watching Malcolm slowly die of consumption had certainly drained hope for love and fulfillment out of her for a long time. She didn't discuss Malcolm often. It disturbed her now to realize that she didn't think about him very much anymore. She supposed her aunts thought the loss of Malcolm Rivers was the reason she lived the life she did.

"I didn't bury my heart with him."

"Yet you haven't married," Aunt Rosemary said. "You haven't looked at a man in over a decade."

Miranda laughed. "Of course I've looked. I haven't seen anything I've liked. At least not well enough to bring home."

"Mr. MacGregor is in your home."

"As my secretary."

"Is he as handsome as the twins say?"

"I suppose so," Miranda conceded. "In a taciturn way."

"Taciturn describes personality, dear. I'm interested in physical attributes."

Miranda recalled broad shoulders and a sensual curve of lips that softened MacGregor's stern expression. And she remembered gentle hands and competent strength. She needed strength. And hated needing it. It was likely that she was going to make the man's life hell because she hated needing him.

Miranda picked up a hairpin and began the process of arranging her hair. "If you want to peruse the man's physical attributes, Auntie, you'll have the chance in a few minutes. He's joining us for dinner."

"There are words for men like you," Lady Sibelle told him.

Andrew looked down at the plump, elderly woman who stood too close to him. They were in a huge, drafty medieval hall in the center of Passfair Castle. Staircases on either side of the hall led to different wings of the building. One part of the house was modern, the other dated from the Middle Ages. There was a minstrel's gallery above one end of the room, over the carved doorway that was the main entrance to the castle. There was a huge fireplace on the other end, with doorways on either side. The fire in the grate did little to warm the cavernous hall. Family portraits in many styles from many centuries took up every available inch of wall space. There was also a sprinkling of ancient weapons, armor, and shields amid the pictures. Banners with heraldic devices hung from the high rafters. Freestanding suits of armor stood at attention beside the staircases. Dogs were curled up on colorful rugs scattered here and there on the stone floor.

Lady Olivia was seated on a couch by the fireplace, working on a piece of needlework. Andrew was stationed in a spot where he could keep an eye on both staircases and the doors. They were waiting for the mistress of the house and yet another of her aunts to join them before dinner.

Aunt Sibelle had chosen to spend her time bedeviling him. She'd been peppering him with questions for a quarter of an hour. He'd merely nodded or shaken his head until now, but he couldn't stop himself from responding to her current accusation.

"Men like me? Yes," he answered the old lady, "but I doubt a person of breeding, such as yourself, would know those words."

His answer was meant to put her off, but instead she put a hand over her lips and giggled. "Of course I don't know any improper language. I've never read novels, or those awful newspapers they print in London. But I still think you're an adventurer."

"Just so," he answered. "My experience as an adventurer is one of the reasons Lady Miranda wishes me to serve her."

Lady Sibelle blinked pale blue eyes at him, obviously trying to work out if what he'd said contained any double meanings. Fortunately, she was saved from thinking of a reply by Lady Miranda's appearance at the top of the new wing staircase. The old lady's features lit at the sight of the young woman. "Miranda, at last! Isn't she lovely?" She flashed him a hard look. "Don't answer that, young man."

He had no intention of responding. Whatever he thought of Miranda Hartwell was a matter to be kept strictly to himself. He didn't even want to think about it, about her, and had succeeded for much of the time during the last year.

However, seeing her gracefully descending the staircase, dressed in a dark red gown that set off her pale skin and black hair to perfection, set his head momentarily to spinning. He was almost unaware of moving, but he was waiting at the bottom of the stairs when Miranda stepped into the room. The man he was pretending to be should not do this. It was not Andrew MacGregor's place to approach his employer in such a manner. Miranda did not know that he was really Andrew MacLeod, and that he was here to protect her.

But even as Andrew MacLeod he had no business being forward with her. He had no right. Especially as Andrew MacLeod.

He wanted to reach for her hand, but he made himself step back instead.

Miranda could not help but notice the panther-like grace and speed with which MacGregor moved. There was something not quite right about him, but he was certainly a pleasure to watch. She was not surprised when he tamped down his natural energy and took a diffident step back at her approach. He wasn't a man used to being in a subservient position. She knew that from reading his references, but she also recognized his fiercely independent nature from the way he moved and spoke, and the masculine energy that radiated from him. He was not what he seemed, she'd known that almost from the moment he stepped into her office. His credentials were impeccable, his manners were not. This should have made her wary of him, but it intrigued her instead.

"What *are* you doing here?" she couldn't help but ask him.

"Escorting you in to dinner," he answered. He glanced at a grandfather clock set beside a nearby suit of armor. "Whenever the dinner hour might be."

"It may be a while," Miranda apologized.

"Something awful happened," Sibelle spoke up.

"She's not referring to the cook burning the roast, I'm afraid." Aunt Rosemary said, following Miranda into the hall.

"Cook isn't even here right now," Sibelle said. "She's poor Harry's aunt. And the housekeeper's his mother. The butler's his uncle. Miranda's personal maid is his sister. They're all gone. Gone."

"Gone?" MacGregor repeated. "Who is Harry?" He spoke with a commanding sharpness that set Miranda's senses buzzing.

"Harry Blount," she answered automatically. "The head coachman. The Blount family have been retainers at Passfair for generations." Miranda had known Harry all her life, he was only about five years older than she was. The teenaged Harry had been a victim of Miranda's childish adoration, and the formality of their adult relationship had never completely extinguished her fondness for him.

She had spent the last several days trying to keep herself too busy to think about his death. Dealing with MacGregor had provided a welcome distraction, until now. Miranda decided to let her aunts finish this part of the conversation.

"He was found drowned in a ditch," Sibelle offered. "The poor lad, leaving a wife and two children."

"Who will be taken care of," Rosemary said. "Not that a pension will make up for the loss of a husband and father. Fortunately, the family is large and close, and that will be of some comfort to her and the children."

Andrew had not been idle since arriving at Passfair. Between being shown to his quarters and being called down to the hall, he'd had a look around. He had noticed that there were not as many servants about as was usual for a wealthy establishment like Passfair Castle.

"Your staff's been given leave to attend the funeral," he concluded.

"We'll all be attending the funeral," Miranda said. "His family's gathered together in the village to mourn their loss."

"Hence the lateness of the meal," he added.

"Well, the cook's helper is talented in the kitchen, but slow and careful," said the woman who'd come down after Miranda. "And she's short-handed, so we must be patient."

He nodded politely. "Of course." A pair of dogs had followed the woman, and the animals were currently sniffing his trousers. Andrew stood patiently still for this.

"Juno, Apollo," the woman said. "Mind your manners." The dogs looked at her, then obediently wandered off. "You would be Mr. MacGregor," the woman said to him. Her look was frank, assessing, but without the suspicion he'd encountered in the others. "I am Lady Rosemary. Come along, Sibelle." Then she put her arm through Lady Sibelle's and led her toward where Lady Olivia sat.

His attention hadn't been off Miranda for a moment, but now he let himself look at her. "We've been left without chaperones."

She shook herself, as if clearing her head, before smiling thinly at him. "Not for a moment," she answered. "They're watching us like hawks. A rather nearsighted hawk in Aunt Olivia's case, I'm afraid. But never fear, we *are* being watched. And we will bear my aunts' scrutiny until such time as they are convinced that you will make an excellent traveling companion for me."

"Then we will leave for the continent," he concluded. "And not a moment before."

"Just so. I'm impatient to be off, but I gave them such a scare the last time that I don't dare upset them again. I don't *want* to upset them again."

"Your family is very important to you."

"Very. They are all I have."

"Aye, I understand that."

"They are to be protected at all costs."

"Aye," he repeated.

She turned toward the center of the hall. "Walk with me, Mr. MacGregor."

"As my lady wishes."

"I hope you find your rooms comfortable," she said as he fell in step beside her.

"Let us say that I find them instructive" was his dry reply.

She flashed him a surprised glance. "Instructive?"

"I find history fascinating, so being assigned a room that I am told once housed King John—and where the bedding appears to not have been changed since—proves to be quite a history lesson."

Miranda laughed. She was quite beautiful when she laughed. "They put you in the old wing?" She spared a quick look toward the women. "I wonder which auntie ordered you put up in the ruined part of the house?"

"Trying to drive me off, are they?"

"Will they succeed?"

"Not a chance."

"Good. But I'll still have your things moved to more suitable quarters." As they talked they reached the other side of the huge room. They came to a halt, and Miranda gestured at a row of portraits hanging above a massive sideboard. "Meet some more of the relatives."

Andrew perused the pictures, of varying quality and from many eras. "Ancestors, you mean?"

"Just because they're dead, doesn't make them any less family," she answered. "See the couple in that painting? It's probably a reproduction of a reproduction, but those are the founders of the line."

The couple in question wore medieval garb. He was tall and thin, with a square jaw and heavy black hair. The woman was small and curvaceous, pretty, but she squinted a bit.

"She looks a bit like Lady Sibelle," Andrew said.

"She is Lady Sibelle. The first of the family with that name, but there have been dozens since. This Sibelle is said to be the granddaughter of Henry II by one of his mistresses. He's Sir Stephen DuVrai,

Norman knight, and first or second Baron DuVrai, we're not sure which anymore. I have his hair."

Andrew looked from the knight in the old painting to the woman beside him. But for the lightning streak of silver, her hair was black and shining as a raven's wing. He beat down the mad impulse to reach out and touch it. He already knew how soft and heavy it felt against his fingers.

"You do indeed have black hair," he said.

"If you believe in ghosts, you might run into Stephen and Sibelle in the old part of the house. They're quite friendly."

"I have no interest in ghosts, even friendly ones."

"They're part of the family. Family is important."

"That I'll agree with."

"Do you have a large family, Mr. MacGregor?"

"Aye," he answered.

"Good."

"Why good?" he asked, though he knew it was best to keep any personal information out of the conversation. Of course, he could lie to her. He should lie to her. After all, he was not who he said he was. He was here under a false name, under false pretenses. Lying to her should come easily; it had before.

"A man with a large family, with ties like I have to my family, might understand me better."

"It is not my place to understand you, my lady."

If she noticed his cool tone and stiff demeanor, she ignored it. She gestured to another painting, of another square-jawed man. This one had a heavy mustache and green-hazel eyes. "That's my father. A man both wise and foolish, kind and despotic. A typical father, I suppose. Was your father a hard taskmaster, Mr. MacGregor?"

"My father died when I was a lad," he answered—more truth! Good God, what was he doing? "My brother raised me."

Miranda did not know why she was speaking intimately with MacGregor. It was not like her to be so open with either information or her feelings. She'd learned to hide much of herself away over the years. Discretion, even secretiveness, was important for a woman who chose to live unencumbered, unattached, but still fully in the world. She'd grown even more closed in and private in the last year. She had told no one what happened, had told no one about Dante. She kept the pain and weakness hidden as much as she could. She hadn't talked to anyone about anything for a long time.

She didn't know if she was opening up to MacGregor. She certainly shouldn't be babbling at him like this. It was not proper. Propriety was supposed to be important between them. Still, there was something about him that drew her out.

She saw that the answers he gave her made him uncomfortable. She guessed that he was not used to talking about himself, either. He was reserved, a typically dour Scotsman.

Their gazes met for a moment, and an intense connection flashed between them. This sensation did not require words. MacGregor took a step closer to her, then caught himself and looked away.

After a tense moment passed, he broke the crackling silence with a gesture, and asked, "Who's this in the third portrait?"

Miranda ignored her racing heart, but had to clear her throat before she could focus on the painting and speak with reasonable calmness. "Oh, that's my third cousin Cecil. He is the current Baron DuVrai."

"A wastrel, a fool, and a troublemaker," Aunt Rosemary said, coming up behind them. "Pity the family title went to him instead of our Miranda."

"He was the heir to it," Miranda said. She looked back at the picture of her father. "The title was legally his after Father died."

"Fortunately, your father saw to it that the title and a stipend was all Cecil received. I never have been able to stand that boy."

"The boy's nearly forty now, Auntie," Miranda pointed out.

"Dinner's ready," a hard, harsh voice announced from the dining room doorway.

"Who's that?" Miranda asked, as they all turned to look at the servant.

She was a thin woman, with steel-gray hair, sour features, and an air of utter confidence.

"A temporary housekeeper," Lady Rosemary answered. "Your new friend in London heard about the Blount family tragedy and sent Mrs. Swift down to help out."

"How kind of Lady Phoebe," Miranda said.

"Yes. How kind," Andrew said, staring hard at the woman. He held his arm out to Lady Miranda. "Let us go in to dinner." It was a command, rather than the request it should have been. She put her hand on his arm and let him escort her anyway.

Chapter 3

❦

"**W**hat the devil is my brother's housekeeper doing at Passfair?"

The woman standing so truculently in the doorway of Andrew's new bedroom gave a most unladylike snort. "I'm on holiday," she answered.

"Oh, really?" Andrew questioned. "Are you in
the habit of spending your holidays working for
some other employer? Come in here," he added.
"And close the door."

"Now you're finally showing some sense," she
said. She stepped inside and silently closed the
door. "It's not wise to discuss our sort of business
in public. You work better cold, lad," she added.
"So put your temper away."

He hated that she was right, and that he'd had to
be reminded of how to act on an assignment was
galling. He'd been spoiling for a confrontation

since the moment he'd seen Mrs. Swift, and had barely managed not to openly glare at her through the evening meal. He'd excused himself as quickly as possible after dinner, and Mrs. Swift had appeared as he left with the perfectly legitimate excuse of showing him to his reassigned quarters. Ominous silence had reigned until they were alone.

"I am here for the same reason you are," she told him. "The assignment is to protect Lady Miranda."

"That is my assignment," he corrected.

He had never liked Phoebe Gale, for all that he admired her abilities as a spymistress. She served the Empire and the queen, and had since she was a young woman. She'd brought her niece Hannah into the world of espionage when Hannah was in her teens. Somewhere along the line, Hannah had found Mrs. Swift, a woman of dubious background with the skills of a master criminal.

Hannah Gale had met Andrew's brother, Court MacLeod, when he was a soldier stationed in the East, and she was on an assignment for Lady Phoebe. That encounter had eventually resulted in Court's marrying Hannah, their being fruitful and multiplying, and all the MacLeods of Skye Court becoming involved in the Gales' secret service work.

Phoebe used them all ruthlessly, though they were kin by both blood and marriage. She used everyone to the best of their abilities, and she'd discovered Andrew's talents early. She'd had him trained by the greatest weapons masters in the world. It had been exciting, until he began to put his deadly skills to work.

Every day he'd been on the path Phoebe set him on, a bit more of his soul died, until he was practically hollow. Even when he tried to quit, she'd managed to draw him back into the game.

He resented that, but even more, he resented Mrs. Swift's sudden appearance on the scene. "She sent you to watch me, did she? Is she concerned I've lost my nerve? My edge?"

Swift shrugged her thin shoulders. "She didn't mention any concern about you to me. But you don't look good," she added.

"I am fine." His tone was steely cold.

Swift was never impressed with anyone, and ignored his dangerous attitude now. "Your assignment is to protect the woman," she told him. "I'm here to find who's trying to kill her."

"*If* anyone is trying to kill her."

"Lady Phoebe's certain that the Hartwell woman's sudden reappearance in society has come to the attention of the traitor. He fears she could identify him."

"She didn't see him, I'm certain of that. I didn't see him, either. The man got cleanly away."

"*He* doesn't know she didn't see him. He probably felt safe enough after he escaped, but then word began to spread about Lady Miranda's encounter with Italian bandits when she came to London to give a talk about it. Lady Phoebe's certain the traitor will figure out Hartwell's a witness."

"I know all this, woman. What I still do not know is why you are at Passfair."

"What I don't know is why the coachman was found dead in a ditch three days ago," Swift answered. "Might have been an accident. Might have been a way to disrupt the household. The fewer people about, the easier to move around unseen or unchallenged."

"Ah." Andrew nodded. His mind neatly clicked over the possibilities. "Perhaps someone working for our traitor was inserted into the household staff. It would be safer for our man. There's no need for the traitor to show himself when he can get someone else to commit murder."

"Lady Phoebe wants her man. She'll not stand by and let a henchman do his dirty work."

Andrew disliked the unspoken reference that Miranda Hartwell was being used as bait in a trap, but he let it go. His job was to make sure no harm came to her, and he intended to carry out that assignment. With his life, if need be.

"So, you are here to sniff out anyone the traitor might have sent."

Swift gave a curt nod. "You can't work belowstairs, but I can. You stick close to Hartwell's side—and keep your mind on business," she warned. "I'll snoop and sniff and let you know what I find. And get this house in order," she growled. "The aunts are mad, the servants spoiled and undisciplined. And all those dogs—" She shook her head. "These people need a firm hand."

If there was one thing Mrs. Swift had, it was a firm hand. Andrew had memories of her cuffing him on the ear a few times as a lad for proof. Actually, he agreed with Swift's assessment that the Hartwell women were decidedly odd. Coming from an odd family, he should know.

"Do what you can with them," he said. "Good night," he added.

Mrs. Swift exited the room without bothering with any reply, other than to close the door a bit more firmly than necessary.

"Lemons." She sighed, and took a deep breath as the fruit was waved beneath her nose. "I love the smell of lemons."

"I know," Dante answered. "That's why I brought them to you. Fresh picked, and warm from the sun."

She remembered how he had put warm, damp cloths scented with lemon water on her eyes and forehead in the first days when the pain was excruciating, and the darkness terrifying. She was growing stronger now. It warmed her heart that Dante still brought her lemons, simply to please her. She held out her hand, and he dropped the fruit into her palm. The scent and texture was so rich that she had no trouble imagining the vibrant, bright color. Dante had brought her out to the garden, sitting her in a chair by a rough wooden table. She was learning to appreciate textures, scents, and sounds. Birds were singing in the trees. A donkey brayed in the distance. Dante took a seat beside her, and she was acutely aware of his size, his shape, his clean male scent. There was nothing more comforting, and yet disturbing, than being close to the man who'd rescued her.

She put her hand on his arm. His sleeves were rolled up, and she was acutely aware of the sinewy muscle she touched. It was quite improper to be so familiar, but Dante did not shy away from the contact.

The weakness from her injuries made her something of a prisoner here, yet she had never felt so free.

"You like it here," he said.

She sighed. "Yes."

"I like it here as well."

He sounded wistful. Miranda wondered why she found his tone disturbing.

"Perhaps it's wrong for me to be so—comfortable— here." With you, she thought.

"It is good that you're comfortable now. I remember how frightened you were at first. How sick and weak. I almost didn't help you," he added. "Please don't

think I'm kind." He put his hand over hers. "I am a dangerous man," he reminded her. "A brigand. I kill people."

"So you say." She smiled. She knew he did not want her to speak of gratitude, of his compassion, or even of how she enjoyed being with him. "You are a fierce brigand," she agreed. "But you grow the nicest lemons I've ever smelled."

"So you say," he answered. She sensed him leaning closer to her. "I like the way you smell."

There was a roughness in his voice that was a little frightening, and very compelling. She could not keep from turning her face to his. She felt the sun on her skin, and light began to grow before her eyes.

As her vision returned he bent to kiss her. She saw his face a moment before his lips touched hers.

Miranda awoke furious. The dream consisted mostly of vivid memory, but it was still a dream, and nothing at the end was right.

She had never seen Dante's face. She had never felt the touch of his lips, even though the feel of them was on her mouth now. She touched her mouth and sat up, staring into the darkness of her room. The candle she kept lit by her bed had gone out. She did not fear the dark, she would not let herself fear it. She just didn't particularly *like* the dark after the weeks she'd spent being blind.

She did not get up and relight the candle. Instead she stared into the shadows, and tried to erase the face that had appeared at the end of the dream.

She had very little to remind her of the man who had saved her and nursed her. She remembered his voice, his touch, his smell, the texture of his clothing, the texture of his hands, his strength and his tenderness. Everything she knew of him was sensory impressions. She held them close, and precious. She hated having these memories polluted in any way, even by dream images she knew to be completely false.

That her imagination had substituted Andrew MacGregor's face for the real Dante while she dreamed was quite unacceptable. Quite infuriating. Miranda was outraged, even though it had only been a dream. Dream or not, she refused to go back to sleep, for fear of the dream returning. She was not going to allow her mind to substitute a recognizable person for the dark form and voice that was all she knew of her rescuer. Dante was a mystery, and she wanted the mystery. At least until she could return to Italy and find him in the flesh.

Mr. MacGregor was not a substitute for anything or anyone. He was a means to an end. She had no idea what dreaming of him as Dante meant, but she didn't like it.

Refusal to sleep meant she had to do something. Rather than stay in the dark, Miranda got out of bed and left her room in favor of the library.

"What are you doing in here?"

It was a good question, and a fair one, especially coming from the owner of the castle.

"Reading your journal," Andrew answered, then looked up from where he sat behind Lady Miranda's desk to confront the lady herself.

He hadn't expected her to be in her nightgown, with her dark hair loose around her shoulders. She looked lovely, soft and vulnerable, even though her expression flashed with anger. He couldn't blame her for her outrage. He couldn't stop his gaze from skimming down her body, enjoying the strong suggestion of rich, womanly curves covered by only the white embroidered material of her gown.

Lady Miranda stood quite still for a few moments before she said, "Stop that."

"Reading your journal?"

"Looking at me."

"You are dressed for being looked at."

"I'm wearing a nightgown."

"So you are. A fine one, it is. Though it's not proper attire for socializing."

"I am not here to socialize."

"You shouldn't wander around dressed like

that. Not with a man in the house. What would your aunts say?"

Lady Miranda did not shrink away for modesty's sake, nor did she flee the room in embarrassment at being seen in such a state of undress. "What's a man doing in my library?" she demanded, coming toward her desk. "What are *you* doing in my library?"

"My job," he answered calmly, aware of her unbound breasts swaying gently as she moved. "You did hire me to help you with your memoirs." He closed the leather-bound journal and tapped it with his finger. He managed to concentrate on her face. "Interesting stuff."

Interesting indeed, but he knew from firsthand experience that much of what she'd written about her trip to Italy the year before was fabrication. She hadn't mentioned anything about bandits, or being shot. According to her account she had injured her head by falling and hitting her temple on a rock. She claimed that the wound had caused her to lose her memory for a few days, days spent being nursed by kind villagers who had no idea who she was or where she came from until she regained her senses.

There was a certain amount of drama and adventure in this version, but no hint of the true melodrama of the situation. He admired her restraint, and was also unreasonably disappointed by it. It was almost on the tip of his tongue to point out that she hadn't mentioned anything about Dante.

Perhaps she didn't want to remember Dante.

And that was for the best, now, wasn't it?

"The library was not locked," he pointed out. "I could not sleep, so I came looking for a book. The journal was on the desk. Since it is source material for your memoirs, I saw no harm in reading it."

Miranda disliked the man's logic as much as she was disturbed by his bold stare. She couldn't quite manage to refute either. After all, she was the one standing in her library barefoot, dressed only in her nightclothes. Perhaps a gentleman should avert his eyes or excuse himself and flee, but Mr. MacGregor did not seem to have any genteel qualities. For a noted scholar he was certainly a rough-and-ready sort—which was exactly what she'd been looking for. She would have no use for a secretary of average temperament. So she had no one to blame for his bad manners but herself. At least he'd looked his fill, then stopped. The way he'd looked at her told her that he was not indifferent to the sight of a woman.

"I couldn't sleep, either," she admitted. Rather, she knew full well that she could sleep, but she wanted no more dreams involving Andrew Mac-

Gregor. "Facing you in the flesh is quite difficult enough."

"What?" He rose to his feet, finally showing a bit of manners in the presence of a lady.

"Nothing."

Andrew ignored his puzzlement. "As you wish, my lady."

He stood and watched while she turned from him and perused one of the bookshelves near the fireplace. He leaned against the desk, crossed his arms, and waited. He didn't suppose she was aware that the firelight rendered the material of her gown nearly translucent. This gave him a tantalizing, shadowed view of her trim legs and nicely rounded bottom.

When Lady Miranda found a book she wanted, she turned back to him and said, "Good night."

He nodded, then followed her when she marched stiffly to the door.

She noticed him once they were in the cold, dark corridor. "What are you doing?"

"Escorting you to your room."

Though the hallway was dark, her glare was so strong, it was very nearly tactile. "Whatever for?"

"It might be dangerous."

"Dangerous? In my own home?"

He put his hand on her arm, and felt her shiver despite the warmth of the contact. "Pretend we are somewhere else. An inn in some primitive land, perhaps, where it will be my duty to escort you wherever you wish to go. You need to get used to the idea of my being by your side." She had gone stiff as he spoke. "You need to learn to trust me," he added, and waited.

And I need to learn to be trusted. He could barely admit to himself how frightening a transition it was, to be guarding a life rather than planning to take it away.

Gradually, her muscles began to relax. In the dark he was aware of her scent; the cool air accentuated the heat of her body. Andrew stayed still, fighting the urge to move closer, and the longing for her to lean against him. A reassuring hand on her arm was all the contact he could allow himself no matter how tempting the softness of her skin.

Miranda realized that she'd closed her eyes, and had become attentive to nothing but MacGregor's touch and the sound of his voice. It was too much like being blind again, and for a chilling moment, it terrified her. He terrified her. But the terror passed, and the logic of his words reassured her.

Gradually she became aware that her bare feet were freezing as she stood on the cold wooden floor. And that the chill air had caused her breasts to become heavy, and her nipples to stir and stiffen. She hadn't noticed the chill before now, or her reaction to it.

"Very well," she said. "You may escort me."

She set a brisk pace, but the long-legged Mr. MacGregor certainly had no trouble keeping up with her down the hall, up a staircase, and down another dark corridor. Miranda was far too aware of his large presence, though he moved with astonishing silence.

"You are wearing shoes, aren't you?" she finally asked as they approached her door.

"Shhh," was his reply. Then he drew her to a sharp halt.

Andrew felt Miranda's quivering outrage, but she obeyed his demand for silence. While she kept still, he looked carefully around. He could not claim to have actually seen anything more than a movement of shadows out of the corner of his eye. He had sensed a presence, and trusting his senses had saved his life more than once. Saving Miranda's life was what was important now.

The route they'd traveled had not been completely dark. The occasional window let in faint moonlight. A gaslight, turned down very low, was placed at the top of each stairway. There was enough light to cast deep shadows. Though he had heard nothing, Andrew was certain of movement within the shadows. Perhaps it was nothing more sinister than a servant on a late errand. Or one of the nosy aunties checking on Lady Miranda.

"Which door is yours?"

Miranda gestured, and he led her to the wide door in the center of the hall. He could just make out the elaborately carved woodwork that framed the door, and what was likely a baronial crest above the lintel.

"Obvious, when you think about it," he murmured, and reached for the carved crystal door handle. "In you go," he said, and pushed her into her bedroom. He would have liked to come inside and give the room a thorough search, but he doubted she'd let him go that far on such short acquaintance. If she raised a ruckus about having a man in her room, the aunts would be sure to appear. The ensuing chaos would surely scare off any danger, for now, but it would also result in his dismissal. Then who would be there to protect Miranda tomorrow, or the day after?

"Enjoy your book," he said once she was inside. When she whirled to face him, he added. "Lock the door."

Then Andrew closed the door and went to search the shadows. Instincts could be tricky, and the balance between trusting them and succumbing to paranoia was difficult to maintain even for the most experienced agents.

Andrew was extremely experienced. The parts of his mind that automatically watched, listened, felt for the tiniest clues were all insisting that someone else had been in the corridor with them. He prowled the hallways of the new wing, then the old wing, and finally the misty cold of the grounds outside the castle.

He didn't find a trace of anyone in his search, but that didn't mean that no one had been there.

Chapter 4

The village church was small, and crowded to the rafters with mourners. It was a dark place, the ancient stones barely lit by a few overhead oil lamps and a row of candles by the pulpit. A small pair of stained-glass windows hardly let in the meager light from the dim, rainy day outside. Though Andrew had never met the dead man, he'd come to the funeral.

He'd had very little sleep the night before, and fought hard now to stifle his yawn. After his fruitless search of the castle and grounds, he had kept a watch on the lit windows of Miranda's room from the outside for several hours. Around dawn he'd consulted with Mrs. Swift. The housekeeper had little information about which servants might have been out of their quarters the night before, as many were still away because of the death in the

49

extended family that served Passfair Castle. When most of the servants returned today she'd be able to keep a closer watch on the downstairs portion of the household. It was fortunate for them that Lady Miranda was generously giving the grieving housekeeper the rest of the month off, leaving Mrs. Swift in charge. Her presence was useful to him, no matter how annoying. Being annoyed was a minor price to pay for any assistance in keeping Miranda safe.

Stop thinking of her as Miranda, he warned himself. *She's the assignment. Do not allow it to be personal.* Andrew sighed. *It's a little late for that, isn't it?*

He tried to stop thinking and concentrate on the moment. Ostensibly he was in the church on this wet and dreary morning out of respect. He loathed the hypocrisy of it, having been the cause of too many funerals himself. But where his assignment went, he was obliged to follow.

Miranda sat surrounded by aunts in the family pew at the front of the chapel, a large black bonnet obscuring her features. He stood in the back, near the church door, memorizing each face as he took a slow, careful look at the people around him. Was it a trusted servant waiting to harm her? Or was there a stranger lurking somewhere in the environs of Passfair waiting for his chance? Was there more than one?

He took note of two men who glanced Lady Miranda's way more than once. Neither of them looked particularly furtive, nor did either of them have the look of a professional killer about him. He would have recognized one of his own kind. Still, one did not need to have years of training and experience to commit murder for hire, though it did help one get away with it.

Andrew disliked the holes in his conscience that allowed him to have such a cynical thought in a church, and during a funeral.

What would Miranda think?

And what would it matter?

Miranda had to fight hard not to yawn. She sat up straight in her seat, kept her expression somber, and cursed herself for not getting enough sleep. Her fears of the dream returning had made a certain amount of sense to her last night, but in the daylight she thought her logic bordered on madness. She was tired when she should be sharp. It was disrespectful to Harry, and to his family, for the lady of the manor not to be able to give her full attention to the sad event. Even when they were children, as soon as he was old enough to understand about social position, Harry had always insisted on propriety. She'd thought of him as a friend and playmate, but she knew he always thought of her first as Lady Miranda. What would Harry think of Andrew MacGregor? She could picture his protective scowl at the Scotsman's impertinence. That made her smile a little.

All through the eulogy and the sermon her respectful thoughts about Harry Blount kept drifting treacherously back toward Andrew Mac-Gregor and their meeting the night before. The book she'd chosen was a new volume by an American writer, a fascinating story of two boys who'd exchanged places with each other. One was a king, the other a pauper, and the game of hidden identities they played was a dangerous charade indeed. The notion of someone hiding his true identity was oddly disturbing to her. She found herself imagining MacGregor in the dual roles. A part of her seemed to think that man was not what he appeared.

She forced her thoughts back to the present. Between dreams and the fancy of her sleep-deprived imagination, she was concentrating far too much on her new employee.

She had found being near him last night truly disturbing. Not what he did, or even how he did it . . .

But there'd been a certain undertone to their words, and the walk back to her room. A sense of danger, a sense of . . . eroticism?

Nonsense. Neither of them had made the slightest overture in that direction. He had touched her only to guide her steps. She'd allowed it out of courtesy. If she had not dreamed of Dante touching her, and if Dante in the dream had not looked like MacGregor . . .

She shook her head, and blinked, and realized that her head hurt and her sight was a bit fuzzy.

Despite her discomfort Miranda made herself concentrate on the vicar, though the sermon went on and on. When he requested that she say a few words, she took a deep breath and made her way to the pulpit. She was used to public speaking, but not under such circumstances. She dreaded facing the mourners, but she was the lady of the manor, and duties such as this came with the privileges of the position. That was the difficulty, really. Her fondest memories of Harry were of playing together in the stables and running wild across the grounds a quarter century ago. But he would not think it appropriate for her to reminisce about such things in front of the Passfair community. So she honored his memory by talking about his love for his family, his lifelong service to Passfair, and how much he would be missed by everyone in their community.

She did not think Harry would begrudge her the silent tears she shed as she spoke. He would understand that at moments like this she felt the full significance of her position as lady of the manor. The combined love, duty, pride, and responsibility that she felt for her people could be overwhelming. Her cousin Cecil had inherited the title and was continuously resentful that he had been denied the family estates. But Miranda knew full well that the arrogant nobleman would never stoop to address a group of peasant servants in a spare country church. Cecil did not understand that these peasants were also members of the family, that this place was rich with hundreds of years of tradition.

Andrew saw the look of love on Miranda's face as she addressed the mourners. He hated how a fist tightened around his heart at the sight of her so openly showing affection. He wondered how many of these people deserved her affection. He certainly did not.

God, but there was nothing more morbid than a Scotsman with a guilty conscience!

Knowing that, and because she was safe for the moment, he slipped out of the church as Miranda began to speak.

"You left the funeral early, Mr. MacGregor."

"Indeed, I did," he answered, looking up at her over the rims of his glasses.

Miranda did not know why she brought this up. Possibly it was because the silence in the library had grown on her nerves. She wished she'd said something else, for now her secretary knew that she'd been aware of his presence at the funeral. He had not been at the burial, or at the breakfast for the mourners in the hall afterward. The truth was, she should not have noticed. She'd known the man but a day, but her awareness of him was already far beyond normal.

She'd found him waiting in the library when she'd finally been able to retreat to this private sanctuary. She'd been annoyed that he was there, almost more annoyed than she had been to walk in and find him there the night before. But it was logical and right that MacGregor be in the library. She could not scold him or order him out. This was the place where he was supposed to be. She'd hired a secretary. She had no right to dismiss her secretary for being dutiful.

She would simply have to learn to share her retreat if she was going to find a way to leave it and fly free once more.

"Does your head ache?"

She focused on MacGregor. "Why do you ask?"

"You are frowning, and your brow is furrowed. I thought you might be in pain."

"Not at the moment."

"Then you are annoyed at something."

She couldn't help but smile a little at this accurate assessment. "Not really," she said. "Not exactly."

"I see."

"You don't."

He smiled at her retort. "You are annoyed with yourself," he said.

"Really?" she questioned. "How can you tell?"

Of course, the moment she asked, she wished she hadn't. And of course, he had to answer her.

"There's a look in your eyes that is altogether too grim, but I do not sense this grimness is turned on me. Rather, there's an inwardness about your mood. My assessment is that you take a great deal of pride in your self control, but feel that you are not as in control of yourself as you should be. Self-control is an admirable trait. But you also fear that showing your emotions makes you vulnerable. This is understandable, but chastising yourself for showing any emotion, any vulnerability, will make you constantly annoyed with yourself." He had a challenging gleam in his eye, as if daring her to deny the truth of his assessment.

She laughed. She should have been angry, but oddly enough, the man's impertinence touched her quite differently than it should. "You have me dead to rights, Mr. MacGregor."

"I always offer good advice," he answered. "Though I admit that I do not always follow my own good counsels."

Miranda leaned forward, lessening the distance between them across the width of the desk. "Why is that, Mr. MacGregor?"

"Good advice frequently has no bearing on the emotional inclinations or needs of the person being advised."

"One knows what one should do," she said. "But what the devil difference does that make?"

"Precisely," he replied. "A person's past history, regrets, recriminations, thwarted desires, guilt—these things prey on the mind. They are not so easy to abandon with the application of a little good advice."

"How true," she agreed. Then she looked at him closely. For a moment she was caught by his gaze, and saw a brief, devastating glitter of anguish in his usually cool blue eyes. It both shocked her and drew her to the man.

Miranda fought a sudden longing to reach across the desk to touch him. To comfort? Console? It was not her place. There was more than the width of the desk between them. There was the matter of rank, and her responsibility toward him as her employee. Their relationship needed to be more informal than average, but she was tempted toward impropriety.

"This will never do," she said, and sat up straight. "I asked you to meet me in the library this afternoon to begin work on a travel book." She grew irritated as she remembered that he had started the work already, by reading her journal without her permission. She couldn't recall if she'd reprimanded him for this impertinence last night. The events of last night were almost like one long fever dream. Any sense of being out of control could not be borne.

She kept her spine straight, her head lifted proudly. She tried not to look at him, but through him, past him. If she looked at him, she feared her gaze would linger on his firm chin, and the sharp planes of cheekbones; on the sensual slash of mouth that softened his otherwise ascetic features. Her tone was imperious when she said, "We waste valuable time with such—"

"Fraternization," he supplied.

She barely managed not to glare at him, but her reply was a crisp "Quite."

She was quite right, Andrew thought. Their behavior was too personal. Far too casual. It was his fault. After all, he had set the tone when they first met the day before. Perhaps the problem was that it was not their first meeting, though Miranda did not know it.

Didn't she? At least in some unconscious way? He sincerely hoped not.

What did she know? This was not the first time he'd asked himself the question. He wasn't the only one who wanted the answer. What Lady Miranda Hartwell remembered about the day she'd nearly died was of vital importance to Andrew's assignment to protect the Empire. It was also vital to the man who had gotten away. He knew that a year ago her memory of the incident was a complete blank. Even though he'd coaxed and prodded, and carefully assessed her responses, he was fairly certain that she hadn't lied to him. Not during all the time they'd been together.

Now though, a year later, perhaps the memories were coming back. She was healed, or nearly so. He remembered how she would wake up screaming, but not remember why. The terror must have receded by now.

It was time for a proper interrogation.

It was not as if he was going to tie her up and force her to answer his questions, but question her he would. Even if this caused her some mental pain, his duty required it.

"There are several entries in your journal from last year that will need to be expanded for the sake of publication," Andrew told her.

Miranda remained cool and stiff, and all business. "No doubt many entries will need expanding. I am not as good at keeping a proper diary of events as I should be. The entries I make are more sensory impressions and memory aids than anything else." She folded her hands before her on the wide desk. "If you would begin at the start of the journal entries, I will dictate more complete descriptions."

That was all very good and logical, but if they

went through her memories of the last year that way, it could be weeks before Andrew got to the information he needed.

He did not dare say, *Miranda, I know where you lied.* For then she would want to know how he knew. The why and how he could not confess. His secrets must be kept, for the sake of the safety of the Empire. And for the sake of his cover identity, of his pride . . . and even of his heart.

"I think we should start with the most problematical area," he countered.

Her brow wrinkled. "Problematical?" Then she took a sharp breath. "I think I know what you mean."

He picked the worn, leather-bound journal off the desk and thumbed through it. Andrew had read these entries over and over the night before, and could have found the pages instantly. But she already looked annoyed, and he saw no reason to arouse her suspicions by instantly thumbing the book open to the page he wanted.

"Here we are," he said when he reached the first false entry. He held the book up and read, " 'I was told of a grove in a village above the town that gave a spectacular view of the valley.' " Andrew put down the journal, and picked up a notebook and pen. "Annotation to page twenty-two," he wrote as he spoke. With his gaze on the paper, and the writing instrument poised, he asked, "The name of the town, the valley, and the village?"

Miranda remained silent for a long time, but Andrew did not look up. He waited. He was an expert hunter, with the gift of patience. And he always knew how to stalk his prey. This first question was seemingly innocuous, but was a bit of bait to draw her out.

"It was in Tuscany," she finally answered.

He dutifully wrote down the word. "The names of the town and village? What was the landscape like? Was the view worth it? How did you reach the village? What was the weather like?" He glanced up, looking at her briefly over the tops of his glasses. "Your readers will wish to experience the place through your eyes." She winced, and he hurried on. "Through your words."

"My eyes," she repeated, and bit her lip. She put a hand up for a moment to shade her eyes.

He knew the expression of fear that flashed across her face. He knew it all too well. He knew she was reliving the helplessness, remembering the pain. He pretended not to notice.

"Sevina," she answered. "I made my way there from Pisa."

"A long and tiring journey, no doubt."

She gave a curt nod. "Very."

"You traveled alone?"

"Not exactly. I made the acquaintance of a young married couple while in Pisa. They had an estate west of Sevina. I made the journey as far as the town with them. We parted company after they saw me settled at a hostel that was part of a large convent complex. It is the mother house of some holy order, I believe. They take in travelers out of charity, and to raise funds. It was spartan, clean, and much more proper than staying at the town's inn. They were scandalized at a woman traveling alone, of course, but very kind."

"You stayed in Sevina how long?" He looked at her, and asked carefully, "Did you meet any other foreigners while you were there?"

The question took her by surprise. She relaxed a little, tilting her head to one side. "Yes, I did encounter a few other visitors to the town. I'd forgotten."

"English?"

"Yes." He watched her as she concentrated, her gaze somewhere off in the distance. "There was a hunting party, I believe. We never actually met, but I saw them at a distance a few times. They had a great many horses, guns, dogs, and guides. Someone told me that the English gentlemen were going up into the hills to meet another party coming from Rome, I think. Something about hunting wild boar. I remember hearing the hunters' voices in the town square while I visited the medieval church. It was such a hot day." She touched the base of her throat and nodded. "Yes. They were English. Only we English stand out in the full blaze of the sun at noontime."

"Yet you preferred the cool shade of the church."

"Ah, but I'm an eccentric maiden lady known for behaving like the natives wherever I go."

"Which saves you from distress in such a warm climate as Italy."

"Well, I didn't behave like the natives once, and—" Miranda's mouth closed abruptly.

"And—?" Andrew coaxed.

"Nothing."

He was aware that she'd gone pale, that her jaw was tensed. He ignored her distress. She'd already given fresh information. There might be much more hidden away that she didn't even know she knew. "How long did you stay in Sevina?"

"Too long," she answered. She gave the smallest of shrugs. "Not long enough."

"I don't take your meaning."

He wrote her words down anyway, in a quick, concise shorthand code devised by his niece Beatrice. Beatrice was young, and would probably accuse him of badgering Lady Miranda if she knew of this conversation. He would reply that he wasn't badgering, he was interrogating, which was much worse.

"You left the town to go up into the hills," he reminded her. "For the view."

"Yes," she answered after a while, through gritted teeth.

"Was it a nice view?"

"No."

"But wasn't the view why you—?"

"I do not recall the view. I don't remember anything."

He thumbed through the journal, and read aloud. " 'Fell and hit my head on a stone.' " He gave her a level, searching look. Her aunts knew she had been shot. The discrepancy was the opening he needed to drive a wedge into the armor of her memory. He kept his voice soft, but commanding. "Is that what happened? Do you recall the day? The hot sun. The sky a bright, burning blue. Dark birds circling overhead. The silvery leaves of the olive trees, the branches gnarled like old men's hands. The stony track, and the scent of goats and donkeys."

Miranda was still as a statue, her eyes closed. Her breathing was ragged, and she nervously moistened her bottom lip with the tip of her tongue. He knew that her awareness was focused on the images he evoked with his words. It was a form of seduction, and a form of torture, for he needed her to relive the most painful moment of her life. A kinder man would not put her through this.

"And the sound of voices," he went on. "Voices in the distance, people on the stony track. What happened, Miranda? Who did you see?"

Miranda leaned toward him, her expression strained.

The library door opened before she could speak. Miranda's eyes flew open. Andrew twisted, fast as a cat, toward the door, reaching for a weapon inside his coat. His automatic reaction was halted when he saw the maiden aunts bustling into the room.

"Have we interrupted a séance?" Lady Olivia asked.

"Were you trying to raise a ghost?" Lady Sibelle chimed in.

"You're pale, Miranda," Olivia added. "Did you see a ghost?"

Andrew cursed the old women for the interruption, and himself for not locking the door. "Don't you ever knock?" he asked. Olivia gave him a critical look.

Miranda took a deep breath and forcibly banished the images of the hilly Italian countryside MacGregor had put into her head. She did not want to go back there—not back in time, at least.

She ignored her aunts and glared at her secretary. "What was that about?"

He spread his hands before him. His expression was mild, and vaguely embarrassed. "I was attempting a technique for enhancing the memory that I have read about," he answered. "A harmless experiment."

"It didn't feel harmless," she snarled back. There was a dark place inside her where she didn't want to look. She didn't want to remember. "I fell and hit my head on a stone," she insisted. "That's all that happened."

"So you wrote in your journal," MacGregor said. "But the details are still missing. Your readers—"

She slapped her palm on the desktop. "My readers may go to the devil."

"Miranda!" the shocked old women gasped as one.

She turned to her aunts. "What do you want?"

Aunt Sibelle sniffed in affront.

Aunt Olivia was much calmer. "We came to see how you are doing, my dear." She waggled a finger at Miranda. "This is no day to close yourself up away from your people, not so soon after seeing a member of the household buried. There is no time to be working."

MacGregor's little "memory exercise" had left her shaken to the core. There was a nightmare inside her trying to get out. She intended to keep the nightmare at bay. Perhaps what was trying to get out was a dark, ugly memory. Well, she didn't want to know. She'd had quite enough of pain and darkness and loss to last a lifetime. Perhaps facing the dark was the best way to conquer it—but she didn't want to. She wasn't ready.

She became aware that her head hurt. She blamed MacGregor for that as well, and gave her blasted secretary a dark look. He met it with a totally unreadable expression. She didn't know why she was interested in what the man thought in the first place.

"You are quite right," she told her aunts. "It's stuffy in here, and I want away from books."

"Good," Aunt Sibelle said. "I've always said this library is haunted. All these books stir up . . . things. They've made you eccentric."

"We're all eccentric, dear," Aunt Olivia put in. She fixed her attention on MacGregor. "Aren't we, young man?"

"I, for one, am exceedingly eccentric," he answered.

"I want tea," Miranda announced. "In the downstairs parlor." She came around the desk and walked toward the door, gathering her aunts up with a look. She wanted to get away from her *eccentric* secretary.

They followed, but much to Miranda's annoyance, Aunt Olivia said, "Come along, young man. We're having tea."

Miranda woke the next morning feeling anything but refreshed. She had one blissful moment when she opened her eyes, when all she knew was simple relief that she could see her own hand on the bedclothes. Then, in quick succession, came the memories: her coachman was dead, her new secretary was dangerously attractive—and possibly just dangerous—and she was *not* looking forward to working more on the Italy book even though she had a publisher nagging her that she'd promised to get it done. Keeping one's promises was *important*, even if there were times when she wanted to forget the whole affair.

Speaking of potential affairs, whatever was she going to do about her secretary? And where on earth had that naughty thought come from?

She considered simply staying in bed for the day, but eventually her rumbling stomach drove her out of her bed and her room. She had to admit to herself that it was nice to feel hungry for a change, but she resented the need to venture out into the house. With Harry's relatives still in mourning, she had no interest in disturbing the servants. She decided that she could steal a quick breakfast from the kitchen and retreat again to the safety and privacy of her rooms.

Or so she thought. The imperious Mrs. Swift appeared in front of her before she could reach the kitchen. The mistress of the manor was informed by the substitute housekeeper that a *proper* breakfast would be served in the small dining room shortly. She hinted darkly that allowing Lady Miranda to carry off so much as a scone would be a betrayal of Mrs. Swift's sacred duties.

Miranda imagined defiantly snatching some tidbit, but running through the house trailing messy handfuls of poached eggs or kippers just seemed too undignified.

So she ceded the round to Mrs. Swift, and braced herself for a meal with her aunts and Mr. MacGregor.

To his credit, MacGregor had been subdued during tea yesterday. He had not pursued his disturbing memory-enhancing techniques any further, for which she was grateful. He could not know the depth of her discomfort at discussing Sevina—her journal made no mention of Dante, nor would her book, so there was no need for MacGregor to learn the truth about that part of her travels.

She supposed she might eventually have to tell her secretary something of the real reason for their trip to Italy. But not until they were safely away from England, and not unless she needed his help to track Dante.

MacGregor looked more than competent to take on Italian hill bandits as he stalked into the small dining room shortly after Miranda. His hair and jacket were as unkempt as they'd been the day he arrived, but there was a sense of coiled energy in his movements that reminded her of a hunting cat.

Before either of them had a chance to say anything, Miranda's aunts all noisily bustled in together, with a trail of dogs large and small following behind.

"What have you two been up to?" Aunt Sibelle demanded immediately.

Miranda was in no mood for foolishness this morning. "I for one have been turned away from my own kitchen and am suffering from a lack of coffee," she snapped. "I cannot speak for our guest, but I hope he has not been treated as poorly."

Miranda took some perverse satisfaction in her twin aunties' matching expressions of affront. But Aunt Rosemary just smiled quietly, and Miranda felt her frustration begin to soften. Aunt Rosemary could bring perspective to almost any situation.

Once they were all eating, MacGregor took it upon himself to restart the conversation.

"I must say, Lady Miranda, that I admire your bravery," he said.

For a confused moment she thought he was talking about Italy, and couldn't understand why he was bringing it up again. But then he continued, "Mrs. Swift strikes me as a most intimidating person. I don't think I would have the courage to face her this early in the morning."

"She is quite aggressively efficient," Miranda agreed, grateful for this safe topic.

"Nonsense," Aunt Sibelle interjected. "How can either of you expect to fight off dangerous foreigners if dear old Mrs. Swift frightens you?"

Andrew decided to ignore, for the moment, the discussion of whether there was anything *dear* about Mrs. Swift. "I was merely making conversation, madam," he said instead.

Olivia spoke up then, but Andrew wasn't sure whether she was defending him or contributing to the criticism. "You saw his references, Sibelle," she said. "He's spent lots of time with foreigners."

"That's what worries me," Sibelle replied ominously.

Lady Rosemary was busy feeding small pieces of sausage to the dogs at her feet, and did not seem inclined to come to his rescue. Miranda was staring morosely into her coffee. She looked drained.

"Lady Miranda, would you like to go for a walk?" he asked abruptly.

Her eyes widened as she looked up, as if startled that he had addressed her. "I had planned to rest," she demurred.

"Nonsense," he said, deliberately echoing Aunt Sibelle. Miranda's lips quirked in acknowledgment.

Andrew, of anyone, knew the temptation to waste time on brooding. But it would be healthy for her to get some fresh air. And, he admitted to himself, a walk would also provide an opportunity to pursue yesterday's interrupted interrogation.

"The weather is much improved since yesterday," he continued, "and the exercise will be refreshing."

"I think it over-generous to say that the weather is improved," Miranda replied.

"I am from Scotland, my lady. Kent is a paradise in comparison."

"I see your point. Compared to Scottish weather, this is a mild and beneficent day. You do have a point. I have spent far too much time indoors lately."

"That's because you've been ill," Aunt Olivia pointed out sternly. "And you're certain to catch something else dreadful if you go wandering about in this mess."

The small dining room had three large north-facing windows, and the heavy curtains were drawn back to reveal the morning's misty gray light.

"We'll be out and back in no time," Andrew promised cheerfully. "Just long enough to get the blood flowing." And, with any luck, the information. He felt certain that getting Miranda out of these stifling surroundings could help loosen her memory.

Miranda was feeling more lively already. "I'm convinced," she said, raising her hands in surrender. "Shall we meet by the garden door in fifteen minutes?"

She deliberately addressed the question to her aunts as she pushed back her chair and dropped her napkin on the table. All three agreed, though Aunt Olivia—and MacGregor—looked less than pleased about it. Miranda had felt a strange flutter in her stomach at the thought of going for a walk alone with MacGregor, and quickly suppressed it. She was still annoyed about his little memory trick from yesterday afternoon, and it would be ridiculous for her to *want* to be alone with him.

They all processed back to their rooms to change, and Miranda dawdled before returning downstairs. She waited long enough to allow Aunt Sibelle to try on and discard three different dresses, and was pleased to find the others all waiting for her when she arrived at the garden door.

The garden door did, in fact, lead to a garden, which Miranda had always found somewhat disappointing, given the peculiar standards of Passfair Castle. She wished it could lead somewhere more exotic, like the tiny secret passage on the third floor of the old wing.

The outside air was cool and crisp, and a sharp breeze rattled the leaves of the trees. Miranda shivered a little in her wool jacket, but the chill of the air in her nostrils seemed to focus all her senses. Their footsteps crunched on the gravel path as they strolled among the elegant arrangement of hedges and trees. Olivia and Sibelle started bickering about something, and the dogs ranged ahead, looking for rabbits to chase.

MacGregor walked quietly by her side, apparently admiring the groundskeepers' work. Miranda found herself thinking of his grip on her arm, that first night when he'd escorted her to her rooms from the library. His grasp had been firm and supportive and gentle all at once, and had reminded her that she'd barely been touched by any man at all since . . .

Dante. It all came back to him. MacGregor was a mere distraction.

She sighed, trying to think of something polite to say. Trying to banish the memory of standing next to MacGregor in nothing but her nightdress.

Andrew sensed that it was time to get the conversation going. The cool breeze had brought some color to Miranda's cheeks, and he could smell the rain coming on again. She had not worn a bonnet, so the breeze stirred the raven's-wing dark hair. This drew his attention to the white streak that began above her scarred temple. Guilt tried to distract him, but he firmly set it aside.

"I read your book about New York," he offered. "On the train from Oxford." He had read it first six months ago, but she didn't need to know that.

Her eyebrows raised in surprise. "Really? I'm

impressed you found a copy. What did you think?" she added, looking up at his face. Her hazel eyes were bright and amused, challenging him. "Of course you must say that you liked it."

"Because you pay my salary?"

"Oh, no! Because you are a gentleman who knows that authors have delicate sensibilities."

"I would—almost—never lie to you, Lady Miranda."

"Almost? That does make you sound like an honest man."

"As much as I can be. I really did enjoy the book," he said. "You have a historian's eye for detail."

"I'll take that as a compliment."

"As well you should. I am a stern critic."

"Some might say an observer of contemporary life ought to avoid sounding like a historian."

"Writing about history is no different from writing about the present," he said. "Only your sources are sometimes less easily accessible."

"And there are certainly parts of New York City that are not easy to access," she agreed. "There are some slums that even make London's East End seem safe and cheery."

"Yet I was surprised how little you discussed the lives of the upper classes," he admitted. "I should have thought someone of your—"

"Enormous wealth," she supplied.

"—social standing," he continued doggedly, "would have spent most of her time among the elite. Yet you wrote just as much about the immigrant street life."

"As much as I could. Yes, my publishers were a bit alarmed at that, as well. But at least some of my readers enjoy it, and I can be quite persuasive."

He knew she could, at that. She was becoming more animated now, her steps and gestures gaining energy. He stuffed his hands deeper into his pockets as they came around the lee side of the castle and the wind picked up. More wisps of her black hair came loose to blow around her face, and she raised one slim, gloved hand to brush them away. She was truly a gorgeous creature, Andrew thought. Her poise, her wit, and the steely determination he knew lay just beneath the surface made her incredibly attractive. *And she is not only my employer, but my charge*, he admonished himself quickly.

She continued talking, raising her voice a little over the blustering wind. "I don't travel just to meet people like myself who happen to speak different languages, you know."

"No more than I would restrict my studies to university scholars of the past," he agreed. "I would find it incredibly dull." Though a monograph on the history of espionage might be rather interesting . . .

Miranda grinned, pleased that he understood. The outdoors suited MacGregor. He seemed at ease, striding along at her side, as though the energy he kept leashed within the walls of the castle could finally be allowed expression. Rather like Aunt Rosemary's hounds, actually. She smiled again, and resisted the sudden temptation to scratch MacGregor under the chin. He really was a gorgeous creature, with all that lean muscle and those alert, intelligent, icy blue eyes.

She was getting distracted again.

But MacGregor himself brought her mind back to Dante when he commented, "So I expect you'll want to focus this next book somewhat on the villagers you spent time with."

"I expect so," she agreed. She did have plenty of material from before Sevina. But she really didn't expect to work on this book much before going abroad again. After she found Dante—and she *would* find him—she might or might not have more interesting things to write about.

Her thoughts of sitting in Dante's arms in a sun-drenched grape arbor were interrupted when she felt the first few drops of rain on her face. Her aunties had been lagging a short ways behind them, but now Aunt Sibelle and Aunt Olivia rushed over together to insist that they all return inside.

"A bit of wind can be bracing," Aunt Sibelle an-

nounced, "but you'll catch your death of something, standing out in the rain."

Miranda knew that her aunts needed to see her
taking care of her health if they were to let her
travel again without a fuss. They had walked far
enough to be closer now to one of the new wing
entrances than to the garden door they'd left. The
aunties were now ahead of Miranda, MacGregor,
and the dogs, bustling toward the comfort of
warmth and dryness. She noticed that MacGregor
removed his glasses as the rain picked up, but
other than that he still seemed perfectly comfortable. The dogs were still playing, and seemed to
barely notice when the damp air began to coalesce
into raindrops. The four of them were still a few
yards from the heavy oak door when the heavens
opened and the storm began in earnest.

With unspoken consent they all ran the last few
paces, Miranda laughing as she held her heavy
skirts with one hand and covered her head with
the other. They tumbled into the castle together, a
tangled mass of wet dogs and wet people.

The dogs shook themselves, spraying water
over the waiting aunts. Olivia and Sibelle glared in
unison at their younger sister because of this offense. Miranda thought they resembled a slightly
mismatched salt-and-pepper set.

Aunt Rosemary was unfazed, as usual. "Come

along," she addressed the hounds. "We'll go find a nice fire to dry you off."

The twins then turned their doubled frowns upon Miranda and her secretary.

Miranda felt she ought to say something. Mac-Gregor was wiping the lenses of his glasses before putting them back on his face. He had removed his hat, and the damp ends of his graying hair were plastered to his skin. He seemed lost in thought, gazing into the middle distance, and she noticed that steam was starting to rise off his damp jacket.

She smiled suddenly. "This is rather typical of Scottish weather, is it not?" she asked him.

His attention snapped back to her, and he grinned. "Aye," he drawled.

Her heart fluttered a little at his smile, and she felt a blush rising in her cheeks that had nothing to do with coming in from the cold outside. Disconcerted, she mumbled something about changing clothes and hurried out under the protective eyes of her aunties.

Chapter 5

"I must say that the last five days have been entertaining." Aunt Rosemary's voice interrupted Miranda's reading.

It was very early in the morning, and she'd chosen to take her breakfast in the garden parlor because the room was so little used. She'd brought in the morning mail and a book to keep her company. It was called the garden parlor because its windows faced a patch of overgrown weeds that had long ago been an herb garden. According to tradition the garden was haunted, and it was said that to disturb the ghost would bring ruin on the house.

Personally, Miranda believed the legend had been made up by a lazy gardener, but she'd never gotten around to ordering the garden cleared. It wasn't as if the estate didn't have plenty of other well-tended landscaping, as well as a few other broken-down places that the family passed off as follies, but were really ruins.

Besides, the small windows in the parlor were about as ancient as the garden, thick diamond panes of mullioned glass that let in some light, but only a faint, distorted view of the outside. There were no gaslights in this room, either, so oil lamps, candles and sunshine were used to light the room. Today an oil lamp alone provided illumination, with little help from the gray daylight. A damp breeze was leaking in, as the window casements were also ancient, and they sagged. There was a fire in the small grate at one end of the room that added some warmth, though the chimney did smoke a bit. The furniture consisted of a trestle table and benches that some ancestor had raided from a particularly ascetic monastery back during Henry VIII's day. The room was actually quite uncomfortable. It was the place where Miranda went when she really wanted to be alone, for her aunts liked their creature comforts.

She'd settled in contentedly, if not comfortably, when Aunt Rosemary had tracked her down. Her annoyance had deepened when her aunt sat down on the bench opposite her and ordered Mrs. Swift to bring more tea and a great deal more food than Miranda had any intention of eating. Now her meal was finished, but for the tea she was drinking, but she lingered with a book at the table. Miranda kept on reading *The Prince and the Pauper*, and rudely ignored her aunt's presence. That is, until now, when Rosemary tried again.

"Yes, very amusing," she persisted, smiling at some private joke.

Miranda finally glanced up. "What has been amusing?"

"Watching you and Mr. MacGregor dancing around each other like a pair of courting hedgehogs."

Miranda frowned at her aunt. "That isn't funny."

"I didn't say it was funny. I said it was amusing. The funny part has been watching my dear, dotty sisters orbiting around the pair of you like small, confused moons." Rosemary broke a piece of bacon in half and fed it to a hound leaning against her chair.

For a moment, Miranda almost complained about the dogs being underfoot, but that was silly. She just wanted something to be irritable about. The hounds were always underfoot, had always been, for centuries. The dogs were part of family tradition. There was too much family tradition. Sometimes it weighed her down to the point where she had to escape for a while. It was a big part of her wanderlust—but she always came home.

She needed to wander now, to get away. She was

being crowded, surrounded. That's why she'd tried to find privacy in the garden parlor, for all the good the attempt had done her.

"You are correct about Aunt Sibelle and Aunt Olivia constantly keeping me company," she conceded to her most sensible aunt. "You are incorrect in comparing me to a dancing hedgehog."

"You *and* Mr. MacGregor."

"I cannot speak for Mr. MacGregor's prickliness." Miranda realized how that sounded when her aunt snorted with laughter. She waved a hand at the other woman. "You know what I mean."

Miranda considered what Rosemary had said about her other aunts. It was true that Sibelle and Olivia had made complete nuisances of themselves since MacGregor's arrival. But Miranda didn't completely resent being so closely chaperoned. Frankly, MacGregor's attempt to fill in the details of her trip to Sevina disturbed her. He had not brought up the subject of the journal while her aunts were present. Though it was work she knew needed to be done, she was grateful for the respite.

She resented what he'd done to try to make her remember, but despite his almost mesmerizing method she could not complain. He had only been doing one of the things she'd hired him for. All he'd intended was to help her remember, but dark, amorphous fears had been stirred up instead. For days her dreams had been full of ghastly images that she could quite recall upon waking. She really resented that she'd woken up screaming once.

There had been nothing unconventional in her dealings with Mr. MacGregor in the last several days. He had helped her prepare a talk for an upcoming salon in London. He'd complained about her writing and speaking style, and her posture. She was too stiff, he'd said, and proceeded to grasp her around the waist and pose her like a doll until he was satisfied.

He had listened to her practice the pianoforte once without comment or complaint. She played for her own enjoyment and did not usually like to have an audience, but he'd entered the music room so quietly that she hadn't noticed his presence until she was finished.

He'd been utterly charming and deferential to Sibelle and Olivia. They tittered like girls at his comments on her speaking style. Miranda protested that she was no actress, but a scholar, and he said everyone was an actor no matter what else he did. The aunts had contributed comments when he'd asked for suggestions.

"My sisters are beginning to like MacGregor," Rosemary said. "They just don't trust the two of you together yet."

"I didn't expect them to accept my plan to travel with a male companion easily."

"Oh, I don't think they would have minded if you'd chosen an elderly gentleman."

"Which would have defeated my purpose. I need someone who can take care of himself, not someone I have to worry about." Miranda smiled at the mental image of her bringing a white-haired, elderly gentleman evening tea in some exotic port of call. She shook her head. "MacGregor is irritating, but I'm sure he can fetch his own tea."

"I fear the twins are beginning to think him sweet."

"He isn't sweet to me."

"But he is . . . attentive. He watches you like a hawk, dear. The girls notice such devotion."

"Devo—"

"In fact, they can't talk to me about anything else."

Miranda shook her head. "They thought the man was out to seduce me before they even met him. They're being fanciful."

"Yes. But now they're starting to like the idea."

"That's because he's been paying more attention to them than he has to me in the last several days."

Rosemary tilted her head to one side. "That sounded waspish, dear. Are you feeling a bit jealous?"

This brought Miranda's head up with a snap. "Jealous? Don't be ridiculous."

She must have sounded far more angry than she was, because the dog turned toward her, putting itself between her and her aunt. The DuVrais were a protective breed.

Miranda laughed. "Maybe it's not a man I need to travel with, but a couple of good dogs."

"They aren't very good at taking dictation," Rosemary replied. "Which I suppose MacGregor is."

"I'm not sure. He made me rework the notes for my speech. I haven't actually tried dictating anything to him."

"Why not?"

"The twins, of course. Do you think I could actually get them to keep quiet long enough to get any real work done?"

"Then shoo them away, and lock the door behind them if you really want to work."

Miranda wasn't sure she really wanted to. Thoughts of being alone with MacGregor disturbed her, on several levels. Maybe this wasn't going to work out. Maybe she should dismiss him, find some deferential, mild-mannered gentleman. Maybe it was a mistake . . .

And why the devil was she second-guessing herself? She'd always had such a strong personality, always been so sure of herself. Before someone shot her in the head and left her to die. If Dante hadn't found her . . .

"My dear, are you all right?"

Miranda discovered that her eyes were closed and her hand was at her scarred temple. She put her hand on the table and looked at her aunt. "Fine. I'm quite fine."

"Of course," Rosemary said, and took a sip of tea. "You do not suffer from headaches anymore."

Miranda picked up her book and began reading again, rather than respond to the challenge in her aunt's tone. The journey home from Italy had not helped her injury, and she'd spent a good portion of the last year feeling unwell. The safety of Passfair and her aunts' love were exactly what she'd needed then, but now they felt stifling.

She barely noticed when Mrs. Swift came in with a fresh pot of tea. She did look up when Rosemary reached over and picked up the letter on top of the pile of correspondence.

"Oh, dear," Rosemary said. "Not Cecil's solicitors again."

"Yes," Miranda answered. "I'm afraid so."

Rosemary looked at the paper rather than reading it. "What is he demanding this time?"

"The usual. That his client was cheated out of his inheritance. That I surrender all claim to the family estates, etcetera, and so on."

"Preposterous!"

"Yes."

"And quite rude. Why do Cecil's lawyers insist

on pestering you when you have Mr. Shaw and his law firm to deal with the matter? Not that there should be a matter to deal with."

"Because Cecil's solicitors still have it through their thick heads that I am a weak, fragile woman that can be bullied and badgered." She took the paper from Rosemary and put it back on the stack. "We're in for another round of threats and lawsuits, I suppose." Miranda sighed. "In the end Cecil will accept a cash settlement and leave me alone for a while. Though he will probably require that I make a personal appearance first."

"You should send this letter to Mr. Shaw immediately."

"Yes. I suppose." Miranda thought about it for a moment, then smiled. "Perhaps I'll send Mr. MacGregor up to London with it. There are a few other errands he can run for me as well."

Maybe a few days away from MacGregor would give her time to get her thoughts in order about the man.

"Don't think I haven't had my eye on you," Mrs. Swift said, and slammed Andrew's bedroom door behind her. She marched across the room and put the breakfast tray she carried down on the small writing desk with a force that rattled the china and silverware. Tea slopped onto a pile of papers.

Andrew whisked the papers away and shook

the tea off them. "I do not need your eyes on me, madam." When he looked at her she was standing in the middle of the room with her arms crossed. Her usually severe expression was more sour than usual.

"You're going to tell me to mind my own part of the assignment. I am." She shook a finger at him. He remembered her doing the same when she caught him stalking her favorite laying hens when he was fourteen. He had not been intimidated then. He was not intimidated now.

Andrew raised an eyebrow. "If you know what I am going to say, then I won't bother."

"Cold as ice, aren't you?"

"I try."

"Well, I'm colder. I see clearer. That's one thing you're not doing at the moment, seeing clearly. You've got eyes for the girl. Hot eyes. You've got the same look Court has for Hannah."

Andrew did not like being compared to his overly romantic brother. Overly romantic and overly dramatic. Andrew did not approve of drama in personal relationships. He wasn't quite sure he approved of personal relationships.

"Mrs. Swift, I hardly think—"

"That's right." She gave an emphatic nod. "At least you admit that your mind's not on the job. Not for the last few days, anyway," she conceded before he could protest. "Lady Rosemary's right, you and the girl are dancing around each other like courting hedgehogs."

Andrew bridled at the woman's impudence. "You've been eavesdropping on Lady Rosemary's conversations?"

"Of course."

Of course she had; it was part of her job. Whatever gave Miranda's sane aunt such a notion? "There is no courtship going on," he assured Mrs. Swift. "I haven't even been alone with Miranda for nearly a week. You have no idea how frustrating it has been to be constantly chaperoned." He realized how that sounded as she raised an eyebrow sarcastically. "You know what I mean. While I am with her, I can protect her, but since we are never alone, I cannot question her."

"The sisters are pests, all right."

"But they do add a layer of protection. A killer will want to get Miranda alone. Make her death look like an accident."

"That's how you'd do it."

He gritted his teeth, but nodded. He'd stayed close to Miranda each day, and kept watch on her room most of each night, but hadn't given in to the impulse to break in and continue interrogating her. "I'm sure she recalls more about what happened than she realizes. It would be helpful if I could get a description of the traitor from her."

"Then get her alone."

"It's not that easy."

"You haven't been trying. You've been enjoying playing your role. You've enjoyed spending time with the lass. Don't think everyone hasn't noticed—except maybe you and the lass."

Andrew hated being lectured like this. Very well, he'd concede that he enjoyed Miranda's company, but that was all. He'd made her laugh a few times in the last several days. Didn't he owe her something besides pain?

No.

All he owed her was protection until such time as the traitor who wanted her dead was apprehended. What he owed his country was finishing the job started on the hillside above Sevina. Then he was through, gone, out of the espionage game. What he truly owed Miranda was to leave her alone.

Andrew took a deep breath and returned to business. "What about the servants? Any threat from belowstairs?"

"There are two new men working on the estate," she answered. "One's a retired army man that's returned to his home village to work in the gardens. He's from one of the families that's served the estate for generations."

"Does that automatically make him trustworthy?"

"Hardly. He's been away a long time. People change when they go to foreign parts."

Andrew did not argue with this observation. "You having his army records checked?"

Her answering sneer told him that this was a ludicrous question.

"What about the second man?"

"Works in the stables. Replaced the dead coachman. Showed up in the steward's office with excellent letters of recommendation. Rather like you," she added. "I figure his papers could be as false as yours. I'm looking into it."

Andrew did not point out that most of his documented history was quite legitimate. He was an archivist and researcher, when he wasn't off in foreign parts shooting people, and worse. He had shown up at Passfair with a false last name, and definitely under false pretenses, but his credentials were sound.

"Point them out to me when you get a chance. And let me know what you find out about them."

She nodded. "Another thing," she said. "If you're going to get the girl alone, you better do it fast. Find out what she knows. And talk her out of sending her secretary off to London, while you're at it. Can't have her bodyguard running errands, now can we? Eat your breakfast before it gets cold," she added, with the same sort of rough affection he'd had from her when he was an adolescent.

Chapter 6

It was Lady Rosemary who provided the diversion Andrew needed to spend time alone with Miranda. He couldn't help but think she did it on purpose. Possibly simply to irritate her sisters.

This morning the twins came into the library as usual, bringing their embroidery and tatting and settling down by the fire to keep watch on their niece's virtue. He greeted them with a kindly smile despite his annoyance at their presence. They beamed back. Miranda merely glanced their way and sighed before going to her desk. He went to his chair. The pattern of the day seemed set.

Then Lady Rosemary swept in, a pair of hounds at her side, and announced, "You do realize that you have a stable full of the finest horses in Britain dying of boredom, don't you, Miranda? Get up, girl, and go for a ride. Do it for the sake of your closet full of riding habits as well as for your fancy horseflesh. You're too thin, and they're in danger of getting too fat. For an active woman you hardly get out of the house these days. I don't think you've set foot outside since that ridiculous walk in the rain. No wonder you're all pale and pasty." She gestured imperiously. "Off with you, I say." She glanced slyly toward her sisters. Olivia had stood; Rosemary gestured her back down. "And take Mr. MacGregor with you. A strapping lad like him needs exercise."

"But," Sibelle began, "it's not—"

"Proper," Andrew finished. He was delighted at this sudden chance. "A ride would do us good, my lady," he said. "We'll certainly be doing a great deal in the future."

He followed Miranda's glance to her elderly aunts. They were looking alarmed, but they stayed put. Apparently they were not up to taking to the saddle to carry out their chaperoning mission.

Miranda smiled and looked at Andrew. "We do need the exercise. Thank you for mentioning it, Aunt Rosemary. Come along, Mr. MacGregor. Meet me at the stables. After I've changed, I'll give you a history tour of our little corner of Kent."

She swept quickly out of the room, and he followed, closing the door firmly behind them.

In the stable he kept careful watch over the

groom who saddled the horses while Miranda made a point of meeting and talking to her new employee. Andrew assessed the man as well. He was a big fellow. His face and hands bore the knots and scars that told Andrew he'd done a lot of bare-knuckle boxing. The fighting might be a sporting hobby, or the fellow might be a street tough. His manner was polite enough toward Miranda, but Andrew noted that the man gave her a long, hard stare when she turned away. Andrew didn't like the look. In fact, any man boldly looking at Miranda infuriated him. If he didn't have that right, neither did anyone else.

Andrew made sure to keep between the other man and Miranda until they were mounted and on their way. He'd make a point of getting the man alone and having a talk later. Whether the man worked for the traitor or not, Andrew would warn him off.

They rode away from the stables and through the old courtyard. The horses' hooves struck loudly on the ancient paving stones. "No surprise visitors at Passfair Castle," Andrew observed.

"Indeed not," Miranda answered him over the noise. "Of course, the only time any enemy ever breached the defenses was during the Civil War. The Roundheads had very good cannon."

"Hurray for the New Model Army," he replied.

She gave a mock frown. "Needless to say, my family were Royalists."

"I'm sure you would have made a dashing Cavalier, my lady."

"I rather fancy I would," she said. "I can see myself in boots and buff coat. With lace cuffs and collars over my armor, and wearing one of those fancy, floppy hats over flowing curls."

"You'd have looked fetching in such masculine attire."

She laughed, and he knew it was because she was aware that the riding clothes she wore were ever so much more severe than the seventeenth-century masculine costume she'd described. She was dressed in dark red wool, decorated in black piping. Severe or not, the closely tailored jacket set off her waist and bosom beautifully. She sat sidesaddle on her dark gray mare with an assured grace that was as captivating as her womanly form.

She noticed him looking at her and asked, "Am I doing something wrong?"

"Hardly. I was noticing how well you ride. I thought you hadn't been on a horse for a while."

"I haven't." She patted the animal's dark neck. "Some things the body remembers."

"Yes," he agreed, though his body was remembering how to make love to a woman.

"I'll be sore in the morning."

"A hot bath should help," he answered.

"No doubt a good soak will be welcome."

It was a mundane conversation, yet the words struck Andrew as far too intimate. Miranda must have thought so as well, because she blushed and looked away for a moment.

They rode on in silence out of the courtyard and a short distance along the gravel drive that led to the estate entrance. Miranda turned her horse toward a thick woods on the other side of a large pond. The morning was bright and cloudless, with a fresh breeze tempering the warmth of the sun. There were birdsong and bright blossoms everywhere. The stream that fed the pond burbled merrily, and diamonds of sunlight sparkled on the water. It was altogether a lovely day.

He took careful note of his surroundings, making himself aware of places where a person could conceal himself. He and Miranda were hardly alone on the property. Gardeners and other servants going about their business were scattered around the grounds. Any one of them could pose a danger to Miranda's life.

"Those trees look ancient," Andrew said as the horses splashed across the stream. There was more shadow than sunlight in among the trees they approached.

"Quite ancient," Miranda answered. "Some of those oaks were here before the Normans. I promised you history." She finally looked at him again. "Would you like to see a proper ruin?"

"I have been in the old wing of the castle."

She smiled. "This place is even older than the bedroom Aunt Sibelle first assigned you."

"So it was Lady Sibelle's doing."

"She likes you better now."

"Does she indeed?" he asked, with mock skepticism.

"She's really sweet," Miranda went on. "So's Olivia. They're the ones who need protecting, even though they think I'm the one who does."

"I admire how you defend your family." He hadn't meant to voice his opinion, or to make her blush again. "I do not understand why you want to leave them. Or the pleasant surroundings of Passfair. What makes you want to roam?" he asked. He shouldn't ask, this was no business of his. She should tell him so, would, and that would be the end of it.

Instead she answered, "I never meant to be the way I am."

Neither did I, Andrew thought.

"What happened?" he asked.

"My father . . ." She shook her head. "There were bad memories for me here. Perhaps I ran from them at first. Then I discovered I appreciated home more when I'd been away from it for a while."

"Aye. I understand that."

She gave him a searching look.

"Why return to Italy?" Andrew changed the subject before she could question him about his home and family. He had always been brusque and taciturn, but with her he seemed to have few defenses against a tongue that wanted to tell her everything. "Surely you will be running to bad memories there."

Miranda wished the man would stop pestering her about Italy, both what had happened in the past and her plans for the future. Still, she felt compelled to answer. "Perhaps I simply wish to say thank you to a friend."

"Perhaps you should send this friend a letter."

"No. I don't think so. He probably can't even read."

An eyebrow quirked high above the rim of his glasses. "He?"

Miranda frowned and urged her horse ahead of his. "Never mind, Mr. MacGregor."

Andrew closed his eyes for a moment when Miranda was past him. *Thank him? Dear God, thank him! If she only knew.*

His soul crawled with bitter shame, but Andrew quickly closed off his reaction. Cold as ice, was his reputation. Ice was what he had to put over the memories and the wounds, and the ice burned.

It was quiet inside the woods. Even the sound of

the animals' hooves was muffled by the dead leaves and moss that lined the little-used path. Sunlight filtered obliquely through the trees, leaving much of the place in deep shadow. It was cooler in here, even though the foliage blocked much of the brisk breeze.

The silence made her very aware of the man riding behind her. She was aware of the easy grace and sure command with which he rode. For a scholar he was certainly a fine horseman. She wondered where he had acquired his skill. She was more aware of how fine he looked in the saddle than she was of his expertise. Riding showed off the strong muscles of his thighs and the width of his shoulders. His brown hair shone in the sunlight and made her aware of the hint of healthy tan in his skin. The virility of the man was not toned down out here the way it was in the drawing room and library. She wondered if he was aware of the change.

They rode along single-file in silence until the path widened into the clearing where a spring bubbled up and a tiny stream trickled back into the woods. The ruin sat in the middle of the clearing, surrounded by tall grass and bluebells.

Miranda brought her mare to a halt, and MacGregor came up beside her. "This is it," she announced, gesturing toward the tumbled-down wall, and the square, two-story tower. "The first place my family built when they moved to England."

"Moved to England?" he asked.

"From Normandy." She grinned at him. "We moved in sometime after the Battle of Hastings and made ourselves at home."

"Ah, yes," he answered. "My family did something similar when they *settled* in Scotland."

"Viking invaders in your ancestry, eh?"

"The Isle of Skye was settled by Vikings. And what are the Normans but domesticated Vikings?"

"True. So we both have to control our natural impulses to raid, pillage, and burn?"

He cocked an eyebrow at her. "I know I do, Lady Miranda."

There was a look in her secretary's eyes that half convinced her that he wasn't joking. It sent a bolt of sensual heat through her as well. The reaction was so strong, it made her dizzy. She had to turn her head away and take several deep breaths to get herself under control. Her body was still tense and tingling a few moments later when MacGregor dismounted and came to help her off her horse.

His hands were on her waist before she could protest that she could do it herself. She found herself looking down helplessly, almost as if in a dream. First at his large, competent hands. She wanted those hands on her, and not just on her waist. From his hands, Miranda's gaze drifted to his upturned face. His mouth was so beautiful, especially compared to his strong jaw and the sharp planes of his cheekbones. She wanted his mouth on hers. The longing came over her like sudden madness, like wildfire.

She had never wanted like this before. Not Malcolm. Not even Dante.

"Dante."

When she whispered the word, a shudder went through MacGregor. His arms jerked, and instead of helping her down, he pulled her off the horse. The mare shied, and Miranda reached out instinctively. She found herself with her arms around MacGregor's shoulders, and his around her waist. Her body was crushed against his. Her breasts stirred as she was pressed against his chest. His thighs molded to hers. Their position was very nearly compromising.

And very exciting.

Miranda made no effort to escape. She didn't want to be anywhere else. The heat of Mac-Gregor's skin permeated her, hotter than the Italian summer heat, burning away reason. His scent was intoxicating, male, familiar, overlaid with a civilized hint of soap and bay rum shaving lotion. Every other scent, sound, and sensation disappeared in her intense awareness of the man holding her.

Andrew's heart pounded as though he'd run ten miles. Every muscle was tense and singing with his sudden desire. Miranda was so easy to hold. She was light as a feather, fragile as a bird. A firebird, a phoenix that could burn him to ashes. All he could do was hold her, and tremble with the terrible need to do more.

She moved, just a little, fitting herself closer, pressing her hips to his, arousing him further. How could that be possible? The woman had inflamed him since the moment she—

Miranda turned her face up to his, and Andrew stopped thinking. His lips brushed hers gently at first, but a whisper of a taste would not do. He put his hand behind her head and drew her into a deep, hard kiss. Hairpins flew as he buried his fingers in her silky, thick hair. She moaned against his mouth, the hungry sound echoing his need.

Miranda held tightly to Andrew, her knees were weak and her head dizzy with the kiss. *Pillage and burn*, she thought. Neither of them seemed able to control those impulses now. This was wrong, impossible. Any moment now she was going to come to her senses and pull away. But her mouth clung to his, and her hands grasped tighter. The tension coiled in her belly, and fire raced in her blood.

She heard the first sharp crack and whine that

followed, but it didn't register as a sound outside her roaring, raging needs. But when Andrew threw her to the ground, she instinctively knew why he'd done it.

Then the roar of a second shot pierced the air.

Chapter 7

For an instant she was back on that blood-drenched hillside with the roar of weapons in her ears and the stench of gunpowder in her nostrils. Fear overwhelmed lust, and all she wanted to do was run.

But Andrew held her down, then pulled her up and began to drag her toward the shelter of the broken wall. She fought him for a second. She tried to claw. She would have screamed if fear hadn't clogged her throat.

Then she focused on the man's grim, determined face, and panic was replaced by the realization that she was not the only one exposed to the danger. Andrew was as much a target as she was, and fighting him was doing neither of them any good.

A third shot sent stone chips and chunks of moss flying off the tower.

Miranda stopped struggling and went still in Andrew's arms. It took a moment longer to find her voice. "Let me go. So we can run."

He released her, then grabbed her hand, and they sprinted behind the wall. The horses had startled at each shot, and now huddled together at the edge of the clearing. Once Miranda was out of the line of fire, Andrew dove at the nearer animal and grabbed its reins. Another bullet zipped past him. He noticed that he'd grabbed his own horse, not the one with the sidesaddle. This complicated things, but he dragged the frightened animal back to where Miranda crouched.

Another shot was fired from the woods, this one sounded closer than the others. Miranda's horse finally bolted from the clearing. He had to keep a firm grasp on his own horse to stop it from following.

"Poachers!" Miranda said when he knelt beside her, the reins held tight in his hand.

He looked at her, searching for signs of panic. He saw fear in her eyes, but it was overlaid with very determined anger. It amazed him that she was not utterly hysterical, but it appeared she was made of far sterner stuff than he'd imagined. The woman had the backbone of a MacLeod.

"Not poachers," he replied. "Someone's trying to kill you."

Her eyes went round with shock, which instantly faded, to be replaced by anger. She nodded. "I see. I suppose it was only a matter of time before he did something like this."

Andrew was surprised at her easy acceptance of her peril. Who was she talking about? He wanted to grab her by the shoulders and question her, to find out what she really knew about the incident at Sevina. There was no time for that now.

"Hold the horse," he ordered. She took the animal while he cautiously peered over the jagged top of the wall. He was furious with himself for letting his vigilance slip for even a moment. How could he have allowed her to stand in an open area like that? The woods gave excellent cover, and Miranda had been as vulnerable to attack as a person could be. That she hadn't been killed by the first bullet was a miracle. If he'd been the one firing the shot, Lady Miranda Hartwell would already have ceased to be a problem for anyone.

The thought of having been the marksman nauseated him, the disgust hit him like a hard blow.

He'd put her in danger. He'd had no right to kiss her, and look what had happened.

"What do you see?"

He tucked his glasses in his vest pocket, and then drew a gun, all the while carefully searching the trees for any movement. They were sheltered enough here, with the old tower to their backs and the wall in front of them. Their position limited the assassin's area of attack. They were sheltered, yes, but not safe. Getting Miranda to safety was what mattered.

"I don't see anyone," he answered after a few more seconds of searching. He knelt back beside her. "He may have fled."

"Or he may be waiting until we move," she answered. "Don't try to protect me with half truths, MacGregor."

He gave a curt nod. She was right. "Can you ride astride?" She nodded. "If I put you before me on the horse?"

"It would be easier to ride behind."

"Where you can be shot in the back," he answered, blunt as she'd ordered him to be.

"You're the one whose back will be vulnerable if we ride."

"That's what I'm paid for, lass," he answered. "Come on."

She balked. "I'm not paying anyone to take a bullet for me. Especially not you."

Her words stung like fire. "Then call it an act of gentlemanly chivalry," he answered, and grabbed her arm with his free hand.

She dropped the reins, and the horse tried to bolt, but MacGregor swung up onto the saddle before the animal could get away.

He controlled the horse with his knees, stuck

the pistol in his belt, then reached down and hauled her up in front of him. Then he gave the horse its head and let it do what it wanted to do. It ran, and Miranda's hair flew out behind her like a long black cloak.

In the last several minutes her life had changed significantly. She'd been thoroughly kissed, and the man who kissed her carried a gun. She knew she was not altogether rational when she found herself wondering where MacGregor hid his pistol since she'd been pressed close enough to him to be aware of his arousal, but hadn't a clue that he was armed until he drew the weapon.

Someone had shot at them, right here on the grounds of her own property. She'd been attacked in the one place she'd always believed utterly safe, utterly boring. The place she'd spent years running away from in search of adventure.

She'd lost her independence in Italy. Now she wasn't even safe at home.

Why was her life so out of her control?

This was no time to consider all that had happened in any logical way, but all the lust, fear, and surprise boiled in her, and she was wild with them. She held on tight and closed her eyes. She was aware of MacGregor's arm around her, of her back wedged solidly against his chest. She was aware of speed, and air rushing over her. Her muscles were tense, and her ears strained for the sound of another bullet being fired. She waited for the impact and the rush of hot blood.

Andrew knew how hard it was to hit a moving target and rode as straight and hard down the path through the woods as he could. There were no more shots while they were in among the trees, and he grew even more confident when they reached the carefully tended grounds of the estate. He was glad when people stopped their work to stare and point at the mistress of the manor scandalously riding astride, and the horse running hard. The more commotion the better. It was far easier for a murderer to get caught if the act was committed in public, so few assassins took the risk of killing in the open.

Andrew kept going until he drew the horse to a halt in the castle courtyard. There he slid Miranda to the ground. "Get inside," he ordered her. "And stay there."

As he turned the horse, she called out, "Where are you going?"

"Hunting," he answered, and rode off.

Miranda stared openmouthed as Andrew raced away. Her aunts, who had an instinct for finding anything out of the ordinary, came flocking out of the house in the few moments it took Miranda's shock to turn into anger.

"How dare he?" she demanded. "Who the devil does he think—"

"What's going on?" Sibelle demanded. "Miranda, you look a fright." She put a plump hand on Miranda's arm. "Your dress is stained. And your hair! What did that man do to you?"

Miranda brushed her aunt off and began to march across the courtyard, her riding boots striking hard against the cobblestones. All three aunts, some servants, and several dogs followed in her wake.

"Where are you going?" Rosemary demanded.

"After him."

"Where's he going?"

Miranda did not want to disturb anyone by announcing that someone had tried to kill them. "After a poacher," she answered. She looked around, and saw Mrs. Swift. "Inform the steward that there's a stranger hunting in the woods. Have him send out the gamekeepers."

Mrs. Swift gave her a strange look, but nodded and hurried off without a word.

Miranda kept on walking. The crowd followed her to the stables. "I need a fresh horse," she shouted.

Grooms scurried to obey.

"But where are you going?" Olivia asked.

"After MacGregor."

"But we need to talk to you about Mr. Mac-Gregor."

"Later." She was getting one of her wretched, awful headaches, but she was determined not to let it stop her. This was her land, her emergency. She would not allow that man to order her to stay out of harm's way.

Besides, he might need her.

"Take the dogs," Rosemary said as a fresh horse was brought up. At least Rosemary didn't try to stop her. The dogs were excellent trackers and fierce protectors. Miranda nodded and mounted the horse. She and the dogs were off after Mac-Gregor a second later.

Andrew stood from the edge of the ditch as he heard the horse approaching. He'd picked up the dead man's rifle, so he held it up, waiting for the rider to crest the small hill beyond the last of the hops fields. A pair of the white and brown hounds appeared first, moving toward him like ghosts. One of them bayed, then the other took up the noise.

"Hush," Miranda called as she came into view. "You've found him, now be quiet."

The dogs moved back to flank the horse, waiting in silence for the next command. It occurred to Andrew that the spoiled canines might have some practical uses after all.

As she reached him, Andrew lowered the weapon and stood in front of the body.

"What are you doing here?" he demanded. "I told you to stay safe."

"You found the man who shot at us?" she asked.

"He's dead."

Miranda refused to be shielded. She nudged her mount a few feet forward and looked over Andrew's head at the body lying half on the bank and half in the shallow muddy water.

"I found him floating facedown."

"Did he drown?"

"No. There's a bullet wound in his head."

She looked at the rifle in Andrew's grasp. "Did you—"

He gave a slight headshake. "Never kill a man you want to question," he answered. "It defeats the purpose."

"I see."

"Neither is it helpful for you to gallop about in the open when someone has recently been shooting at you."

"But that's just what you did," she retorted. "Are you all right?" She got off the horse. "How did you find him? What happened? Who is he? No, wait." She took another look around Andrew. "That's the new man from the stables." She turned her attention back to Andrew. "Why was he shooting at us?"

"And why did someone shoot him?" Andrew countered. "That question I can answer. He was working with someone else. The other man decided to cut his losses and make his own escape when this one bungled the job."

"Bungled the—" Miranda rubbed her temples, then looked back at Andrew. She was squinting, as though the light hurt her eyes.

"Headache?" he asked.

"How do you know any of this?" she demanded. "How can you tell there was an accomplice?"

"I found his tracks." Andrew took her to her horse and helped her mount, then got on his. "You shouldn't be here." They rode back toward the hops fields.

"I'm not delicate." She looked back down the hill. "Or squeamish. We must call in the authorities. There will be an inquest." She sighed. "And another scandal to be whispered around my name. Well, a man's dead, so I shouldn't worry about raising a scandal. His killer needs to be found."

"Yes," Andrew agreed. "Before he tries to kill you."

"You said this accomplice ran away."

"He might come back."

"I doubt it," she said confidently.

"Why do you say that?"

"Because the man who tried to have me killed is

a complete bungler. And he likely hired the cheapest assassins he could find."

Andrew's protectiveness toward Miranda turned to annoyed suspicion. He recalled her earlier comment about knowing who wanted her dead, and it infuriated him. Why hadn't she reported this knowledge to the authorities sooner?

Before he could ask, they encountered a pair of gamekeepers coming through the field. Miranda got off her horse to talk to them, and Andrew followed. He stood silently while she gave instruction on finding the body and sending for the authorities. Andrew fumed the whole time, suspicions about Miranda's involvement with the traitor growing by the second.

Chapter 8

After the men were gone, Andrew grabbed her by the shoulders without meaning to do it. The dogs growled, but Miranda waved them off.

"Stop that," she demanded.

"You didn't protest when I grabbed you before. This is for your own good," he went on. "No prevaricating, woman. Tell me what I need to know. Who's trying to kill you?"

"Cecil," she answered. She gave an unhappy sigh. "It must be him. He's such a fool."

"Cecil?" Andrew thought hard, and brought up the memory of his first night at Passfair, when Miranda showed him all the family portraits, one of a man called Cecil. "Your third cousin. The current Baron DuVrai." He let her go and took a step back. All his anger dissipated with the realization that she hadn't been playing him for a fool. He also had to fight the knowledge that touching her at all, even in anger, was too much temptation. "What makes you think your cousin is trying to kill you?"

"Someone tried to kill me," she replied. "And he's the only one who would profit from my death."

Not the only one.

He almost told her her true danger then and there, but that was not the way of undercover work. Secrets were not for sharing, especially not state secrets. State secrets were not his to tell. Nor could he reveal to her the secret that *was* his.

He would never have seen Miranda again if Phoebe Gale had not insisted on it. Of course, he hated to admit it, but he'd given in to the old woman's emotional blackmail because he had desperately wanted to see Miranda again. But he would never have acted on this desire on his own. He was strong enough to leave Miranda alone—or so he'd thought until he kissed her.

Where was the ice people always said was in his veins in that wild moment?

By silent mutual consent, they began to walk side by side, leading the horses along a path between fields. It gave them a few more minutes to be alone together. Andrew dreaded the chaos that awaited when the aunts would descend on them upon their arrival back at the castle.

"I hope we can keep this quiet," Miranda said

after they'd gone a little ways. "The man's murder must be investigated, of course. Justice must be done, but Cecil can't be brought into it."

"For the good of the family name," Andrew agreed. "I understand."

"You don't understand at all," was her tart answer. "For the good of the family, yes, but mostly not to upset Sibelle and Olivia. They'll attach themselves to me as permanent bodyguards if they think I'm in danger. It's hard enough trying to escape them having brought you into the picture." She stopped and turned to face him. For a moment she couldn't seem to look at him, then she lifted her head and looked him in the eye. "Thank you," she said. "Thank you for risking your life for mine."

He started to tell her it was his duty. The words came out, "My pleasure."

Though he could have bitten his tongue, he was glad to see amusement and interest in her eyes. The fear did not quite disappear, but she continued to hide it fairly well. If he had not known her so well, he might not have known how deeply affected she was by the events of the day.

"I'm delighted you enjoyed yourself, Mr. Mac-Gregor."

"I hope I will not face that kind of enjoyment again."

She touched a finger to her lips. "Speaking of enjoyment . . ."

"Let's not speak of it," he countered.

Humor continued to spark in her eyes. "Why not?"

"Because it should not have happened. You have my sincerest apology."

"Why? Do you think you kiss badly?"

"Miranda." He found he had moved closer to her. He cleared his throat, and took a step back. "Lady Miranda."

"You use my title as though it creates a wide chasm between us."

"As it should. What I did was wrong."

"What we did. The interest was mutual."

"You should be shocked at my—our—behavior. You should be ashamed."

"Are you?"

"Utterly."

"I'm no green girl, Andrew. I've been kissed before. Not for a few years, I admit, but the sensation this time was more pleasant than I remembered." She gave him a thorough look up and down. "Haven't you been kissed? And if you haven't, you should get out of the library more often. Do you always carry a gun?" she asked before he could respond.

This was a question he could answer easily. "Yes."

"Even while working?"

"I have tutored some rather rambunctious

youngsters," he answered. "You've no idea how handy a pistol can be for keeping their attentions."

She laughed, and he wondered how she would take it to know that he was only partially joking. His brother had many children, and those children had been trained in many esoteric skills. Andrew was the family weapons master.

Miranda knew that it was foolish of her to be talking about kissing with MacGregor when there was a dead man who had tried to kill her lying in a ditch. But remembering the way she'd felt in his arms was infinitely better than thinking about what happened afterward. She'd been shot once, and that had been the most frightening thing she'd ever experienced. She'd been blinded, and powerless, and right now she had a headache that was part of the aftermath of that awful day.

She was not going to let this be another awful day. She had not been hurt. She held on to the knowledge that she was all right, or the fear could paralyze her. She might start bawling like a child and cry hysterically to the heavens that it was unfair, that she didn't deserve this. She already knew that life was unfair, there was no use complaining about it.

To keep away the fear she concentrated on the one thing good that had happened. Oh, to have kissed her secretary was wrong, and there would be consequences, but it had felt so very good at the time.

"Of course, it will not happen again," Mac-Gregor said, as though reading her mind.

She took a deep breath. "Of course not," she agreed. They mounted their horses and rode on in silence.

There was propriety to maintain. There was rank to maintain. One did not carouse with one's servants, at least honorable people did not. She tried to live an honorable life, even if she wasn't as proper as a woman of her station was supposed to be.

And what about Dante?

She'd spent nearly a year pining for her Italian bandit. Her plan, impractical and romantic as it was, was to return to the Italian countryside and find the man who'd saved her life and nursed her so tenderly. After she found him—what then?

She'd never kissed Dante.

She very much wanted to kiss MacGregor again.

She'd never thought of herself as fickle or flighty. In fact, between Malcolm's death and meeting Dante she'd been courted enough, but totally uninterested in any man she met. She hadn't so much resigned herself to being a spinster, but had reveled in her independent heart.

Now here was MacGregor, the one man she

should not care for, the one she'd determined to have a businesslike relationship with, and—

"Miranda!"

Aunt Sibelle's voice shook Miranda out of the twisting labyrinth of her thoughts. Looking around, she noticed that they were nearly at the entrance to the castle. She also saw that Mac-Gregor had put his glasses back on, and his expression was perfectly composed. He looked as if they were just returning from a pleasant ride in the countryside.

How she envied him his cool aplomb. She tried to emulate it when she reached the house and was surrounded by her relations as a groom led the horses away.

"What an awful day you've had, my dear," Olivia said, drawing her into a tight embrace.

It's been a worse day for the dead man, Miranda thought as she was passed from aunt to aunt for quick hugs. Then they turned her around and marched her ahead of them into the house, across the great hall and up the stairs. It was almost as if they'd practiced the maneuver. Miranda managed one look back at MacGregor as she mounted the stairs. She saw that he'd been waylaid by Mrs. Swift.

Much to her surprise the aunts did not march her to her room. No maids were called. No hot baths were ordered. No one flashed a bottle of smelling salts under her nose or asked her if she'd like a glass of water. Instead the library door was locked behind them, and she was told to sit down. Aunt Olivia handed her two telegrams and a letter.

"Read these," Aunt Rosemary ordered.

Then they all stood back and waited while she did.

"Young man, do you know that you are the reason she fainted? Fainted dead away."

Andrew looked down at the plump woman who guarded Miranda's door as fiercely as any of the castle's dogs. He was completely honest when he answered, "I am deeply sorry to have caused Lady Miranda any distress."

"We thought you would do, you know. We really did."

"Do for what?"

She stamped a foot. Her round face grew pink. "You know very well what."

It was not long past dawn, and he had not had a very restful night. He'd been confident enough to leave Miranda safely ensconced in her rooms, knowing that her family hovered protectively around her. He and Swift had concentrated on questioning everyone at Passfair on what they knew, what they'd seen, what they'd heard about any threat to Miranda in recent days. He'd gone to the village and sent coded telegrams to London with a report, and also asked for inquiries to be made about Cecil, just in case the current Baron DuVrai was somehow involved in a plot to kill Miranda for her inheritance. He'd organized a search for the murderer of the stable hand, and answered many questions from the local authorities. With all that done, he'd snatched a few hours' sleep.

Now, here he was ready to take up his duties as bodyguard once more, only to find his way blocked by a small, elderly woman intent on berating him. He was tempted to pick her up, set her aside, and batter down the thick door to Miranda's room. The need to see for himself that she was safe was an almost physical drive.

"Lady Sibelle," he began, "if you would please—"

"Get out of your way? Oh, no, young man. I'm afraid you have to go." She shook a finger at him. "How dare you play her false? We were beginning to have such high hopes for you."

"False? I—"

"You seemed so good for our girl. You made her smile in that dreamy way a woman doesn't realize she's doing when she looks at the right man. And you had that soft look in your eyes when you gazed at her when you didn't think anyone was looking. And you could talk to her about all those odd things that interest her."

Andrew did not know where Lady Sibelle's

tirade was going, but he couldn't help but say, "Odd? Lady Miranda's interests are not odd."

"Not to you. That's the point. You deal together very well. You got our hopes up."

"It gratifies me that you now approve of me as Lady Miranda's traveling—"

"It's more than that. It always has been, and you know it."

He did, but all he said was "I need to see Lady Miranda."

The old woman stayed where she was, keeping herself and the door between him and her niece. He supposed the door was thick enough to block out the sound of their conversation.

"You will not see her!" Sibelle proclaimed. "Not under any circumstances, especially not under false ones."

He stepped closer, aware that he loomed menacingly over the short woman. "What are you talking about?"

"About your marrying my niece. Not that we could possibly allow that now. What are you? A fortune hunter? Something worse? Did you try to kill our girl?"

"Madam, I—"

"Or did you arrange yesterday's fright to make her trust you completely? Oh, you are wicked, Mr. MacLeod. Truly wicked."

Andrew was so taken aback by the kernel of

truth in some of her accusations that it didn't register for a moment. When the word did register, all he could do for a moment was step back and stare.

"Don't look so surprised, young man. We are not complete doddering old fools, you know."

"Apparently not" was all he could answer.

"We have our ways. We wanted to find out if you were from a good enough family for our girl. It's shocking who some people marry these days, Americans and other foreigners, and tradespeople. We couldn't let Miranda go that far, but we thought that if your family was at least scholarly or from the clergy, that would do. So Olivia wrote to an old beau of hers that holds a chair at Oxford. He recognized your accomplishments and description, but not your name. So he made inquiries of other gentlemen he thought knew you. The answers came back yesterday. *Mr. MacLeod,*" she added with an angry sniff.

Andrew had never been more chagrined in his life. How could a pair of little old ladies who lived in seclusion in the countryside have penetrated so easily into his real life? No, they knew nothing of the *real* Andrew MacLeod, but it still should not have been so easy to have found out about the quiet life he led when he was not working for the Crown. How could one letter to an "old beau" have brought him down so easily? Well, the academic world was a small one, and he had never worked undercover inside the country before.

If word of this got back to his family, he would be a laughingstock. Not that his reputation among the MacLeod family mattered at the moment.

He took Lady Sibelle by the arm, and gently but firmly set her aside. He knocked on Miranda's door while the old lady squawked in protest.

"Don't bother," Swift said, coming up behind him.

He whirled to face the housekeeper. "Why not?"

"Because the coach that took her to the train station just came back. She's on the way to London."

"London! When someone's trying to kill her? What's she doing going to London?"

Swift's habitual glower deepened. She took his arm and pulled him out of Aunt Sibelle's earshot. "That's your job to know, lad," she said. "I couldn't very well follow her, could I? I set one of the local constables to watch her back, but I think you best go find out what she's up to. Maybe you'll even be able to catch the train."

Chapter 9

Phoebe Gale looked from the calling card in her hand to the young woman her butler had just shown in. As the parlor door shut, she said, "How nice to see you again, Lady Miranda."

Miranda Hartwell gave a stiff nod. Tenseness radiated from her like sound from a tuning fork. She was pale, and her lips were set in a narrow line. She was clearly attempting to hold very strong emotions in check.

It made Phoebe wonder just what Andrew had done this time. He'd always been a difficult lad, but so very gifted.

"Please have a seat. I'll send for tea."

Miranda was in no mood for the trappings of polite society right now, but she was cold and her head ached fiercely. A cup of tea might actually help. She took a chair near the fireplace and man-

128

aged to keep still and silent while Lady Phoebe rang for a maid and gave instructions. It was raining fiercely outside, another storm like the one in Kent—was it only last week? London's sooty air was saturated with water, making the downpour very unpleasant to move through. She'd taken a hansom cab from the train station to Lady Phoebe's town house. A brief dizzy spell before she found the cab stand outside the station left her prey to the elements. She didn't know how long she'd been disoriented, but her skirts were splashed with mud, and her shawl, bonnet, and gloves had been soaked before she got her bearings. She was too angry and determined to allow a little dizzy spell keep her from her goal. Still, she'd been glad when she was able to hand her damp things to the butler who showed not a flicker of emotion that she was not dressed for an afternoon social call.

She was aware that her dirty skirt hem was staining the room's pale floral rug, and was not in the least bit guilty about the mess. She had been in this room several times, and still found the overwhelming femininity of the place disconcerting. There were flowers everywhere. Fresh flowers in crystal vases, flower prints on the walls, china flowers on shelves and tables, flowers embroidered on pillows, and flower-printed upholstery and wallpaper. Floral tiles surrounded the fireplace, and the white mantel was carved in a tulip pattern.

Miranda's gaze drifted up to the mantel, which bore numerous photographs and painted miniatures in gilded frames. She had seen the pictures before, but took no notice of them until now.

The most ornate frame held a photograph of Queen Victoria in her younger days. The queen had never been a beauty, but the expression of fierce pride on her face suited a monarch very well.

Among the other photographs and paintings was a family portrait of a couple with a great many children ranging in age from nearly grown to a babe in arms. Miranda was not sure from this distance, but she half believed that she recognized the nanny holding one of the younger children on her lap.

Miranda looked sharply at Lady Phoebe, who waited patiently in the chair opposite her. "Is that Mrs. Swift in the picture?"

"Yes," came the calm answer. "I hope she's working out for you until your own housekeeper recovers from her tragic loss. Swift has been a trusted member of my niece's staff for many years."

Of course, she'd forgotten that Swift had been sent by Lady Phoebe! Just as MacGregor had been recommended by this woman. Perhaps there was nothing sinister about Lady Phoebe's acts of helpfulness.

The tea was brought in and placed on the table between them. Miranda studied the older woman carefully as Lady Phoebe busied herself with cups and saucers, cream and sugar. The woman moved with precision and grace. She smiled and made small talk that needed no reply. She appeared to be everything a woman of her class and era should be. Her hair was silver, her cheeks were pink, her eyes held a lively sparkle.

Miranda had known Lady Phoebe Gale by reputation before she ever met her. Lady Phoebe was the daughter of an earl. She had never married, and had led a life of genteel scholarship in the days before women were allowed to attend university classes. She had traveled widely in her youth. Lady Phoebe sponsored salons, supported scientific and cultural societies, organized charity events, and was altogether a paragon of all the virtues Miranda admired.

Miranda had been flattered when Lady Phoebe sought her out when Miranda first appeared in public again after her long convalescence. They had hit it off immediately. They had so much in common, so much to talk about!

"I've always thought you were the epitome of everything I wanted to be."

Phoebe looked the girl in the eye over the top of her teacup. "Oh, no, I am the last person you want to be like."

The Hartwell heiress looked at her suspiciously, as though waiting for a speech about how a woman really wasn't meant to live alone and all that other romantic balderdash. She could tell that Miranda hadn't come here looking for any sort of sentimental musings. Phoebe wasn't sure what the girl was looking for, but she suspected it had something to do with Andrew's assignment. And where was Andrew?

"I am hard, cold, and ruthless," Phoebe went on. "That is where my life of freedom has led me. Where will yours lead you?" she inquired. She took a sip of tea, then put the cup down. "And how is Mr. MacGregor working out?"

The young woman's hazel eyes blazed, going almost green with anger. "MacLeod," she said. "His name is MacLeod."

Genuinely surprised, Phoebe sat back in her chair. "Really? Are you sure? All these Scottish names sound so alike."

"I am not sure of many things at the moment," Miranda answered. "Other than that you sent that man to my service under false pretenses. Oh, and that someone is trying to kill me."

"How rude."

"Perhaps I am, but I want an explanation."

"I meant how rude that someone is trying to kill you. How's the tea?"

Miranda remembered that she held a cup in her hand, and drained it quickly. "It's cold."

"Rather like the hard facts of life."

Miranda poured another cup for herself, and drank it down in one long gulp. "I prefer things hot," she said, and set the cup and saucer down forcefully enough to rattle all the dishes on the table.

"Don't waste your passion on me," Lady Phoebe answered. "If you are furious with Mr.— MacLeod, is it?—confront him."

Of course that was precisely what she should have done, Miranda knew that very well. She hated that her courage had failed her, but that was the truth of it. The thought of facing MacLeod terrified her.

It was not that she was afraid of him. It was that she feared what she might do. She had never known such white-hot passionate anger. She feared herself in this state. She did not want to whirl out of control. She'd had too much of that already.

"Why did you place MacLeod in my service?"

"My dear, I merely recommended him—"

"Don't patronize." Miranda held up a hand when Lady Phoebe would have continued. "You recommended MacLeod. You sent Swift to manage my house. One of my servants died before they arrived, but I suspect their presence had something to do with that death."

"That seems an odd conclusion."

"Yes. But I've always had a knack for seeing patterns. At least when I'm not ill."

"I sent MacLeod to protect you."

Miranda appreciated this admission. "But that is not the only reason, is it?"

Phoebe had not expected the young woman to be clever, discerning, and tenacious. Lady Miranda had a reputation for being reckless and headstrong, and had gotten herself in deep trouble for it when she ran off to the continent by herself. When Phoebe had sought Miranda out to use as a means to an end, she'd found a woman subdued by her bad experience, but also chafing at the bit to return to roaming the world. She had not thought Miranda Hartwell was in the least bit practical, but apparently Miranda had a stronger core than Phoebe had guessed.

Phoebe was a bit puzzled at how to handle the young woman. The parlor door banged open before she had much time to think. She rose to her feet as Andrew MacLeod marched in. She was not particularly surprised to see him.

"You look like a drowned rat" was Phoebe's first comment to her niece's brother-in-law, and one of the finest agents she had ever trained. "Did you come to drip on my rugs?"

He glared, which was his usual way of looking at her. "Don't start on me, woman," he complained. He took off his rain-spattered glasses and tucked them in a pocket. "I've had a hell of a day."

"Would you like tea?"

Andrew stripped off his coat and handed it to the butler who'd come silently in after him. "Yes. With whisky in it. I've lost my charge," he added, duty-bound to report despite any embarrassment it caused him.

The chair where Miranda sat faced away from the door. Where Phoebe stood she blocked the view further. Andrew's mood and wet state dulled his senses for a moment longer. Phoebe watched as he sharpened, as his shoulders squared and his head came up, as he turned into the pure hunter she had trained and nurtured, and perhaps used too ruthlessly over the years. He had the look of a hawk to him, with his high-beaked nose and sharp eyes.

His hawk's gaze focused on Miranda as she stood up and mirrored his gesture of straightening her shoulders and proudly lifting her head. Phoebe sat down and waited to see how this pair dealt with each other.

"Why the devil did you run off?" he demanded.

"I left you a letter dismissing you from my service, Mr. MacLeod." She gave him one hard look before her gaze slid from his. "What I do is none of your affair."

No preliminary greetings, Phoebe noted, no wasting time asking each other what the other was doing in Phoebe Gale's house.

"I never did work for you," Andrew told Miranda.

"So I suspected," she answered.

He spared a glance for Phoebe. "What have you told her?"

Phoebe spread her hands out before her. "What do I ever tell anyone?"

"Never the truth."

"You know how I feel about the truth. It's so *malleable*. So dependent on point of view."

"I would like to hear the truth," Miranda said.

Phoebe noted how the young woman addressed her rather than Andrew. She noted how Miranda's fists were balled, how pale she was, and how she quivered with outrage. Miranda Hartwell might very well resemble a wet hen at this moment, but she was in truth the fiercest of creatures imaginable; a woman who felt scorned, wronged, and humiliated.

"Heaven help you, Andrew MacLeod," she murmured, and crossed her palms on her lap.

"Why don't you tell Miranda some truth," she added. *You're better at it than I am*, she thought, *though you don't think so.*

"Your life is in danger, Miranda," he said. "That is the truth. You have to trust me to keep you alive."

Miranda finally turned to look at Andrew MacLeod. She made herself *look* at him. Tough as nails, she decided. Hard-edged and dangerous, full of secrets.

"Why should I trust an impostor?"

"Because I am very good at what I do."

"And what is it you do?"

"Whatever needs to be done. Whatever I must to complete an assignment," he answered without hesitation, without any shame. Without any expression at all. "You are my assignment."

She had always suspected he was not what he seemed. She didn't know why she didn't act on that suspicion the moment she met him. She should never have allowed him near her. Too near. God, but she could still feel his body molded to hers, and the press of his lips, the taste and smell of him.

No doubt that kiss had meant nothing to him. She'd let herself be vulnerable and open with him, but—

"I believe you," she told him. "But you haven't

said another true word to me, have you? You have some agenda of your own." She gestured toward the woman watching them. "Some agenda of hers. You have no interest in—"

"I saved your life."

"Did you? What really happened yesterday?"

"Too much for your nerves to take, obviously. Or you wouldn't be behaving hysterically."

Phoebe winced at the man's words, and tone, and shook her head. "If you wish to throw something at him, my dear," she told Miranda, "I really dislike the porcelain dogs by the grate." She then sat back to see what would happen, for she was beginning to wonder if she had not seriously underestimated Lady Miranda Hartwell.

Miranda glanced toward the statues by the fireplace. "I'll keep them in mind."

She had never thrown anything at anyone before, but being called hysterical by this superior, supercilious male was almost grounds enough to behave as though she was. She could imagine him ducking as she hurled things at him. But tempting as that sort of scene was, it was not what she wanted.

"I want information," she said.

Andrew ran a hand through his wet hair. He was tempted to tell the woman exactly what she wanted to hear. Before he gave in to temptation, the butler came back into the room and handed him a crystal tumbler a quarter full of fine single malt whisky. Andrew tossed down the drink as though he indulged in it regularly, and waited while the smoky liquid warmed him.

He longed to step closer to the fire, but that would mean coming closer to Miranda, which he feared would be a dangerous move. He was in a fine, high dudgeon now, but what if he should accidentally touch her? Or see a tear shining in her eye? He was a fool for the woman. Which was why he should never have taken this assignment. Never mind that he owed her; she deserved the best protection there was. Normally he would be the best.

Once the whisky had spread its fire through him, Andrew returned to the fray. This time he spoke to Phoebe Gale. "She wants information."

"I heard her," Phoebe answered. A long silence followed while Phoebe offered no more.

"You've been in danger for more than a year," Andrew finally told Miranda.

Miranda thought for a moment, then touched the scar on her temple. "Not from Cecil," she concluded, and sighed. "That's a relief."

"Your life is in danger," Andrew reiterated, speaking slowly and clearly, as if to a child.

"I know," she answered. "But I'd much rather have a stranger trying to kill me than a family member."

"I disagree," Andrew said. "From a professional standpoint, family members are easier to catch."

"How true," Phoebe contributed.

Miranda continued to concentrate on him. "This has to do with what happened in Italy, doesn't it?"

"Why do you think I've been trying to get you to remember what happened during the ambush?"

"I remember what happened," she answered tartly. "I refuse to think about it, that is a different matter."

"Blacking it out won't save you."

"Don't talk to me about blacking anything out!" she shot back. "The blindness I suffered was . . . dreadful."

"I am well aware of that," he answered.

"And how could you be?"

He could not meet her suspicious gaze. He ignored the question. "You have a talent for sketching," he reminded her. "I've seen the drawings in your journal."

"Doodles," she said. "Hardly a talent."

"Enough to draw a picture of the man in the grove."

"The man who shot me?"

"You did not see the man who shot you."

She gasped, and Andrew very nearly bit his tongue at this slip.

"I've thoroughly investigated the incident." He

hurried on with an edited version of the details. "I know the rough details. An English traitor was in the village to pass documents to a foreign agent. These people were attacked by bandits."

"The villagers were attacked by the foreigners," she corrected. She blushed. "Or so the person who rescued me said."

"Whoever fired first doesn't matter," he countered. He didn't want to tell her that her sudden unexpected appearance had been the catalyst for that day's chaos. "What matters is that the traitor got away."

"He may have seen your face," Phoebe said. "At least discovered who you are, and thinks you may have seen him."

"I didn't."

"Are you sure?" Andrew asked. "How can you be sure if you won't let yourself think about it?"

She shook her head. "No, I don't want to think about it. The nightmares are bad enough, full of shadows and screams. You have no idea what those dreams are like."

He knew exactly what they were like. Only his nightmares were frequently filled with accusing faces and voices. "You have to face the monsters to be free of them," he said, and felt like the worst hypocrite in the world. "You didn't panic when you were shot at yesterday. That's a fresh memory, and you are handling that well enough—other than haring off like a fool when you should have stayed put under my watchful eye."

Instead of the outraged response his outburst probably deserved, she said, "It was foolish of me to leave—for here you are and I'm forced to face you anyway."

"And what is wrong with facing me?"

"You betrayed me!"

"I am working undercover for the government to protect you. How is that a betrayal?"

Miranda bit her lower lip. It was very hard not to remind him of how they had come together in a passionate kiss only moments before being attacked. Her insides were still on fire with the memory. It was this fire that burned her now, fueled her temper to an almost uncontrollable pitch.

She certainly wasn't going to discuss anything personal in front of Lady Phoebe. Perhaps it was best not to discuss it at all. Hadn't they agreed already not to discuss it? At least they had agreed that it would not happen again, and that was a bargain she was willing to keep. So there was no use casting recriminations at him for hurting her because he was a lying impostor.

"I did not run away," she said. "I came to find out the truth."

"And now you know it," Lady Phoebe said. "Andrew is your guardian. You are safe with him until the man trying to kill you is captured." She looked from one to the other. "More tea?"

"That is not the complete truth," Miranda said.

"But it's shocking enough knowledge to give a normal woman the vapors," Phoebe said. "And as much as you need to know."

"It's my life."

"You seem quite adamant about pointing that out."

"I will not be helpless," Miranda told them. "I will not be treated like a child. I will decide what I need to know. And what I need to know is everything." She glared at Andrew MacLeod. "Is that understood?"

"You're spoiled," he said, "and willful."

"I told you that when we first met. I haven't changed in a week."

"And I like you that way," he answered, "But it doesn't mean you get what you want."

She did not want to be pleased to know that he liked anything about her. She made herself turn away from MacLeod, and hated that it took such effort. She addressed herself to Lady Phoebe.

"You are a spy, an agent for the Crown."

The older woman gave the faintest of nods. There was amusement in her wise, discerning eyes.

"You are trying to catch a spy. A traitor."

"Correct."

"This traitor has eluded you for some time, but you see an opportunity to draw him out into the open. You are using me as bait, aren't you?"

"Why would you think that?" Lady Phoebe questioned.

"Because you came to me," Miranda answered. "Because you encouraged me to lecture on my travels and attend upcoming social functions. After I agreed, you sent MacLeod to me. I suspect you have started rumors about my adventures that make the traitor certain I saw him. My aunts have reported hearing all sorts of nonsense about my adventures being spread through society," she explained before Phoebe could protest any innocence. "You've set me like a canary in a coal mine to sniff out this man you want to find."

"Yes," Lady Phoebe agreed after another tense silence passed. "That is exactly how we are using you."

Miranda looked at Andrew. "You knew about this?"

He made himself look dispassionately at her. "Of course."

"But nobody bothered to tell me." She glanced from one spy to the other. She hid her disgust. She pushed aside the hurt at being used. She said, as dispassionately as MacLeod, "This man is going to continue trying to kill me, isn't he?"

"Yes," Andrew answered.

"Well, then," she said. "I suppose there's nothing for it but that we go on as we have. Only from now on," she added, "*I* am the person in control of how my life is put at risk for the sake of queen and country."

Chapter 10

⁓⁓∽∾⁓⁓

"I have it," Lady Phoebe said after a brief, tense silence. And was ignored.

She looked from the fiercely glowering Andrew to the angry young woman who was staring back at him. She wondered if they were aware of the tension that quivered like heat haze between them. Being a pair of adults, they ought to, but people did try to lie to themselves when unwanted attraction was involved. Phoebe was in favor of attraction, as long as it did not interfere with one's work or duty. She was in favor of sex. She was even in favor of romance, as long as it didn't get in the way of her goals.

She'd known it was a risk assigning Andrew to protect Lady Miranda, as he'd let his guard down with the woman once already, but an acceptable risk. Even after the Italian episode, she still trusted him more than anyone else in the service to provide the needed protection. For a year he'd castigated himself for his behavior, and hadn't yet realized that he'd shown that his humanity was still very much intact despite the years on the job. He was a grim, hard man who'd grown out of a mischievous, clever boy.

She wondered if Miranda was taken with Andrew because of his intelligence, for Miranda seemed the sort who would like a man to be as bright as herself. Or perhaps it was because Andrew was a glorious figure of a man, even if his hair was beginning to thin just a bit over his fine, noble brow. It actually added to the ascetic beauty of his lean features. There was something to the stubborn set of his firm jaw that a woman with equally strong character might be attracted to. And, of course, he exuded danger when he wasn't playing the mild-mannered librarian.

From the report she'd had from Swift, Phoebe knew that Andrew wasn't able to keep to that self-effacing character around Miranda. The idiot probably had no clue that with Miranda he could not help but behave like a peacock preening before a potential mate. Andrew had never had a clue about that sort of thing. Ask him to dispose of a group of murderous anarchists and he was up for the job. Ask him to make a life for himself and he'd look at you as if you were mad.

At least he'd look at Lady Phoebe that way. He didn't like her very much. He was about to like her even less, as she completely changed the plan she'd been about to propose and said, "You two are going to wed."

Of course they stopped staring balefully at each other and turned their outrage on her.

Miranda shot to her feet. "Really, Lady Phoebe!"

"Are you mad?" Andrew asked, stepping toward her.

"Not that I am aware of."

Phoebe calmly rang for the butler, and silence reigned for a few moments while she quietly gave instructions. Miranda sat down, Andrew backed up.

When they were alone, Miranda was the first to speak. "You are joking, of course."

"You need protecting," Phoebe answered. "You have agreed to help us lure the traitor out of hiding. The traitor must be a high-ranking government official. This means he is also a man of high social standing. It is not likely that he frequents the scientific and scholarly sorts of gatherings that you prefer."

"You can't be certain of that," Andrew said. "He found out that Miranda is still alive when she attended such a gathering."

"Only because I made sure her name appeared

in the newspapers and started the rumors about her. I've stirred things up, but only enough to get the man to send hirelings after Miranda. We need to put the girl out in the open."

"Tie the sacrificial goat out in a field where the wolf can see it?" Miranda suggested.

"Out in the open where she's also surrounded by layers of protection," Phoebe went on. "The Season is upon us, and Miranda needs to dance among the peers of the realm. She needs to show herself and be seen at all the proper parties."

"She doesn't like balls and dinner parties," Andrew said.

"I do so," Miranda countered. "Or I would if I could be allowed to enjoy myself. But I'm a disgustingly rich heiress. The money forces everyone to ignore my eccentricities, but I've always hated being fawned over because of it. I've never been able to set foot in a ballroom without being accosted by the most boring men imaginable."

"Which is another good reason for you and Andrew to become engaged. Not really engaged, of course," Phoebe finally added, as Andrew MacLeod looked about ready to explode. She found his outrage amusing, but there was really only so much teasing the man should be subjected to. Besides, there was an assignment to get on with, and she required cooperation from both of them. "As your fiancé, Andrew has every reason and right to be at your side. At your side he is the best defense you can ever have against danger. Besides, he is a fine dancer."

"Madam," he complained.

"I've made sure all the MacLeods can manage in polite society. They'd be a gang of hairy Highlanders otherwise."

"Nonsense," he complained again.

"Also, being betrothed to this fine fellow will eliminate most of your would-be suitors fawning over you when all you want is a waltz and a glass of champagne."

Miranda raised an eyebrow. "Most?"

"There will be a few men who ignore Andrew's claim on you. Fortune hunters can be most persistent. And the man who wants to kill you might insert himself into this group."

Miranda noted Lady Phoebe's use of such equivocal terms as *can* and *might*. She disliked this lack of precision, but realistically had to suppose that espionage was not a science. There was no exact formula for catching a villain, was there? "This is a game," she said. "The pieces and players are human beings. You all don costumes and disguises."

"We," Lady Phoebe corrected. "You are a player now, which you claim to prefer to being a pawn. To fulfill your role you need to play at being in love with Andrew. And he with you," she added, looking sternly at MacLeod.

A maid entered and left a small jewel box with Lady Phoebe before either of them could respond. Phoebe looked through a selection of rings. "This will do," she said, and tossed a sapphire ring toward Andrew. He caught it with his usual sharp reflexes, then looked as though he wished he hadn't. "That ring belonged to my mother," Phoebe told Miranda. "I'd planned on leaving it to one of my numerous great-nieces, but if you two should decide to formalize the arrangement, consider it my wedding gift to you."

"We are not going to formalize any—!"

"Stop complaining, MacLeod," Miranda cut him off. She stood and marched up to him. "I've agreed to play the game." She held her left hand out to him. "You and I know it's not real and it's never going to be. So put the blasted thing on me and let us begin."

"I have a town house of my own," Miranda pointed out as they waited for the door to be answered.

They were in Mayfair, at a very fashionable address. Her own London residence was in the same neighborhood, but several streets away, and not nearly as large and impressive as this mansion.

"This will be safer," Andrew replied.

"You are going to continue using that as an excuse, aren't you?"

"It is not an excuse."

The man had been stiff and cold and formal since finally acquiescing to Lady Phoebe's plan. Miranda did not know why his demeanor disturbed her. If anyone should be sulking, it should be she.

He gave her a sideways look. "You are enjoying this."

"Nonsense."

After all, the rain was still pouring, although the fresh bonnet and cloak Lady Phoebe had loaned her helped quite a bit. She was about to enter a stranger's house under false pretenses. She was still very annoyed at Lady Phoebe's using her, lying to her, and then saddling her with a false fiancé because she'd agreed to serve her country. Even with MacLeod as protector, someone was still trying to kill her. She was not having a good time.

All right, she was, but she knew she shouldn't be.

It was as if he could read her mind. He turned toward her and shook a finger at her. Rainwater dripped off it as he lectured. "Having an adventurous nature has nearly gotten you killed once. Just because you think you are punishing me by going along with this—"

The door opened before he could finish. "How good to see you, Mr. MacLeod," the butler said. "Please come in, and I will inform Lord Martin and Lady Harriet of your arrival."

"I had a message from Aunt Phoebe to expect houseguests," Lady Harriet Kestrel said after they'd been shown into a sitting room and introductions had been made. "But she didn't say who or why."

"Your great-aunt is too fond of secrecy when it's not required," Andrew answered.

"You shouldn't be so mean to Aunt Phoebe. It isn't nice."

"I am not nice."

Lady Harriet looked him over critically as he stood by the closed door, and said, "Uncle Andrew, you look like you have a poker stuck up your backside."

Miranda did not know whether to gasp or to laugh. So she sat quietly in her chair and looked between the uncle and the niece. She found it hard to believe that Andrew was old enough to actually be Lady Harriet's uncle. Of course, she knew next to nothing about MacLeod and nothing at all about the woman who was now their hostess.

She glanced at the long-limbed, dark-haired man seated on the sofa next to Lady Harriet. He was smiling at his wife as though she'd just said the most clever thing in the world. That smile probably had as much to do with the barely showing curve of Lady Harriet's abdomen as it did with her sense of humor.

Miranda had heard of Lord Martin Kestrel. Her aunts would be quite pleased to know that Mr. MacLeod could claim a famous, high-ranking diplomat as a relation.

"My aunts," she said, clapping a hand to her cheek. "I must inform my aunts."

When she began to rise, MacLeod pinned her to her seat with a baleful look. "Lady Phoebe has already dispatched a suitable message."

"A suitable message informing these aunts of what?" Lady Harriet questioned.

MacLeod looked at her, and his fair skin turned slightly pink. "Informing them that Lady Miranda and myself are engaged."

Lady Harriet looked between the two of them, her expression most skeptical. When she spoke, her voice took on a Scottish burr that very much reminded Miranda of the lady's uncle. "Engaged? Aye, but in what?"

Martin Kestrel rose to his feet. "Aren't you being a bit rude to our guests, my dear?" the diplomat asked his wife.

The lady turned to him and answered, "With a MacLeod, it's best to be suspicious from the beginning. Saves nasty surprises later."

He rubbed his jaw. "So I recall." He sat back down. "Carry on."

Miranda was caught by Harriet's stern gaze. "Are you, in fact, engaged to be married to my uncle?"

Miranda found herself sitting up straighter. The woman's expression and tone reminded Miranda of her governess. She supposed she should have been offended at this interrogation, that she should reply with a haughty comment that what she intended doing with Andrew MacLeod was no one else's affair. But she found herself smiling instead.

"As you pointed out, we're engaged in something."

Lady Harriet laughed. "Good answer." She glanced toward Andrew. "Never let yourself be intimidated by one of us, that's another rule when dealing with MacLeods."

"Harriet," Andrew said warningly. "Can we stay here, or not? Will you arrange that Miranda's seen in public, or not?"

"Will I go along with whatever your assignment is without asking questions?" she added for him. She put her hands on her hips. "Yes, and yes to your questions, and no to blindly going along with any scheme you and Aunt Phoebe may have cooked up. Is your life in danger?" she asked Miranda.

"Yes," Andrew answered for her.

"Yes," Miranda answered for herself. She gave Andrew a reluctantly admiring look. "He's saved me once already."

Andrew went red again, and opened his mouth, but stopped himself from whatever he wanted to say. "The bait isn't taking her danger seriously," he said instead.

"I am."

He turned a stern look on Lord Martin. "Her safety is at issue, and this is a safe place to keep her."

"Perhaps you could put me up in a china cabinet," Miranda added, rankled at the tone he took. "As Mr. MacLeod seems to be of the opinion that I am a fragile piece of porcelain."

"She's a civilian, and out of her depth."

At least he wasn't using her gender as his argument against her. "We've been through this," Miranda reminded him. "Your aunt—"

"She's no kin of mine!"

Miranda looked to Lady Harriet. "He's quite touchy on the subject, isn't he?"

"Our family history is rather complicated," Harriet answered. Lord Martin snorted. She ignored her husband, and went on. "What sort of social gatherings am I supposed to arrange?"

Andrew waved a hand impatiently. "Music recitals. Dinner parties. You decide. The most I know about these affairs is to show up wearing a black suit of clothes."

"An engagement ball?" Martin suggested.

Miranda folded her hands in her lap, the fingers lacing tightly together so as not to betray her nerves. She was shaken by the notion of pretending to the world that she really was betrothed. The last man she'd been betrothed to had died, and the last man she'd been interested in was a faraway mysterious stranger. Andrew MacLeod was a hard, cold fact.

She made herself sound bright and cheerful when she said, "That would be lovely. Wouldn't it, Andrew dear?"

He glared. And the fury in those normally cold blue eyes when they met hers sent a thrill of heat through her. She very nearly gasped at the intensity.

Oh, dear. It seemed that Dante had a rival no matter how hard she tried to fight it. She had to admit that to herself, and be wary that she didn't start to believe the masquerade. How on earth had her emotional life—sterile and dry and straightforward for years—suddenly become so complex?

Did MacLeod feel it as well? They had kissed already, she reminded herself, and there was nothing short of passion in the way the man kissed. His fury now was a thing of passion, as well. But was he simply angry at the indignity of the situation? Or, like her, did he sense danger in the mere pretense of intimacy?

"An engagement ball would be appropriate," MacLeod growled, jaw clenched.

"That's settled, then." Lady Harriet rubbed her hands together. Her brain seemed to already be racing ahead to plan a combined social event and espionage operation. "Do you expect your would-be assassin to attend this function publicly, or only covertly?"

"I suppose it depends on his boldness, and to what degree he is certain that I will recognize him," Miranda said.

Andrew relaxed slightly as he turned his attention to work. Here at least the ground was familiar, no matter how loathsome he found it. He said, "The traitor may come into our trap openly, if he hopes to determine whether Miranda knows him. In an ideal scenario, she would in fact recognize him and alert us to his identity." He frowned as he felt Miranda stiffen beside him. She was going to protest—

"I do hope our charade is successful, Mr. MacLeod, but I do *not* share your hope that I recognize the man."

Miranda's face was white and pinched. Andrew's hand started automatically to rise toward her cheek, but he forced himself to be still.

She turned to their hosts and explained, "I am in danger now because I once had the misfortune to be in the same place at the same time as your traitor. I was . . . injured . . ." She hesitated, then continued. "I have no memory of what he looks like. Nor do I wish to. I will act as bait in your trap, but that is the extent of my participation. I have no desire to relive a particularly unpleasant event."

There was a moment of silence. Miranda absently twisted Phoebe Gale's ring around and around her finger. Lord Martin watched her with a mixture of admiration and pity in his expression that Andrew knew she would hate. Then Andrew saw his niece watching him with that thoughtful expression of hers, and suddenly he couldn't stand it anymore. He stood abruptly.

"Thank you for your hospitality," he said to the air above Harriet's head. "I shall take dinner in my room, if you don't mind." He sketched a bow to the ladies, and fled.

Chapter 11

Miranda was brushing her hair when Lady Harriet startled her with a knock at the door. How long had she been sitting there, staring through her reflection? She quickly set the brush down and invited her hostess to come in. She could feel another headache building, like the oppressive atmosphere before a storm, but she was determined to carry out a civil conversation.

"The rooms are very lovely. Thank you again for allowing us to stay here."

"You are more than welcome." Lady Harriet's friendly smile seemed genuine. But could one really tell, with a family of spies?

Lady Harriet sat down and tilted her head to consider Miranda for a moment. "I suspect that Uncle Andrew really will hide in his room for the rest of the day. He knows you're safe with us." She smiled suddenly, and reached out to grasp Miranda's hand. "I've never seen him so flustered before. Did you see him bow?"

"Yes."

"It's so unlike him to be polite. He must be very fond of you."

Miranda withdrew her hand politely but firmly, and Lady Harriet's smile disappeared. "I have found that Mr. MacLeod is mostly fond of his work," Miranda said coolly. He had kept her in the dark, tried to make her remember things best left forgotten.

But then there was that kiss . . .

Lady Harriet was smiling at her again, and Miranda firmly stopped herself from reminiscing. "I have heard something of your reputation as an adventurer, Lady Miranda. I believe that you and my uncle will prove very suitable for one another. Purely in the sense of a working relationship, of course," she added, as Miranda opened her mouth to protest again. But she was further taken aback when the other woman said quietly, as if to herself, "Da will be pleased."

"Da?"

"My father. Uncle Andrew's brother. Never mind. You don't want to know more about our meddlesome family than necessary."

What a meddlesome family indeed, Miranda thought. If they were not all spies, they would surely have turned their dubious talents to match-making and gossip mongering. And it seemed that Lady Harriet's time was not sufficiently occupied with espionage.

"I appreciate your kindness," she said to MacLeod's well-intentioned niece. "This playacting at being engaged will certainly be easier if Mr. MacLeod and I achieve an effective working relationship, as you say."

She rose, forcing Lady Harriet to do the same. Darkness curled around the edges of her vision, and Miranda gripped the back of her chair in a way that she hoped appeared casual.

"I would like to rest awhile before dinner myself, if you don't mind," she announced. The pain had reached its pounding stage, becoming more and more difficult to ignore.

Lady Harriet took the hint. "Of course." Then, with an odd intensity, "Let me know if there is anything at all that you need. Anything I can do . . ." She hesitated a moment, then turned and quickly left the room.

Miranda was beyond caring whether the other woman could tell something was wrong. She was simply grateful to be left alone. As the pain reached its crescendo and her vision narrowed to nothingness, she groped her way over to the bed, cursing her helplessness.

In the last few moments before she fell into a

welcome oblivion, she found some relief in imagining Dante's comforting embrace. The strong arms were Dante's, but the intense blue eyes she imagined were MacLeod's.

"Bloody hell," she murmured, far too gone to be ladylike and polite by herself.

As darkness completely descended, she had the odd thought that perhaps it was she and MacLeod who were exchanging places rather than the spy and the rescuer.

Andrew was brooding.

He knew that it would accomplish nothing, but the habit was ingrained deep in his Scots blood. He paced the path between the bed and the door in one of Kestrel House's tasteful guest bedrooms, and knew that it was pointless to keep agitating himself like this.

He could not avoid Miranda for very long, and he would be betraying his duty if he did. But even after a few hours away from her, he found that he missed the woman. That would not do. He must fulfill his vile responsibility to cause her pain, to push her to remember things she wished to leave forgotten. She was the assignment—the *last* assignment. Once it was over he would never see her again, never need to think about her again.

He would go back to the university, where people worried about killing only on an abstract level, if at all. There were certainly some vicious rivalries among his fellow academics, but no one was likely to use a weapon more deadly than a cutting remark. That was how normal, sane people lived. His life would be wonderfully boring, with no concerns about killing, or loving, or weighing duty against either.

When had that stopped seeming like a good idea?

His thoughts were interrupted by a knock at the door. He wanted to swear at whoever was in the hall to go away, but duty was as habitual as brooding. Miranda might need him.

Harriet barely waited for him to open the door before she strode into his rooms. "What can I do for you, Lady Harriet?" he asked, still holding the door open.

His niece was a clever woman and a skilled agent. He always thought of her as being a cheeky fifteen-year-old, following him around the family estate and demanding lessons in everything from Latin to knife throwing. She was still cheeky. She gave Andrew such a long, appraising look that he almost smiled.

"I know that you have no use for advice," she said. "But I'll offer some anyway. It's obvious that you are uncomfortable with this assignment. Do you want me to take over?"

"What? No!" That rattled him, as she had obviously intended. He had been desperate enough, on the train to London that morning, to briefly consider giving Phoebe Gale his resignation. But for Harriet to suggest it . . . She had always been good at manipulating him. He shut the door and crossed over to the grouping of armchairs where she had seated herself.

He sank slowly into a chair across from her, and suddenly realized how very tired he was. He took off his glasses and rubbed his eyes, then put the specs back on. He looked at Harriet, who was still watching him patiently.

"No," he said, more slowly this time. "I will finish this assignment. I must. I . . . I owe it to Lady Miranda."

"Do you? The advice I came to give you is to evaluate carefully your emotional involvement in this assignment. You obviously care for Miranda, but you must not allow that affection to interfere with your work."

"As you yourself have so ably demonstrated," he replied with heavy sarcasm.

She paled slightly at his anger. She had ultimately married her "assignment," and that drama had been the favorite topic of family gossip, at least until her brother Kit ran off to America with an exiled princess.

Harriet had regained the MacLeods' attention now that the impending arrival of his brother's first grandchild had thrown everyone into a tizzy all over again. Though his own engagement might trump even that, for a short time.

He scowled as Harriet pressed on with her point. "I would not presume to lecture you, Uncle—"

Andrew snorted at this patent falsehood, but she persisted.

"—but as you point out, I have some small experience in this area. And I don't want you to be hurt," she finished quietly.

At that the rest of his anger drained away, leaving him simply tired again. He conjured up a weak smile. "That's kind of you, Harry."

He knew that a romantic story like Harriet's had no place in his future. The thought made the weight of his fatigue seem to double. He stood up to escort his niece out of his rooms.

She paused at the door and put a gentle hand on his arm. "I seem to be unwelcome everywhere I go this afternoon." She smiled. "But I must say one last thing." Her expression became more serious as she continued, "Uncle Andrew, we—the family—have been aware for the last year that you have labored under some burden. We are a secretive lot by nature and by training. But I hope that whatever it is you cannot share with us, you may someday tell Lady Miranda. I think she could help you in a way that none of us can." She stood on tiptoe for a moment to kiss his cheek, and then was gone.

Andrew leaned his forehead against the cool smoothness of the door once it was closed behind her. Always too perceptive was young Harriet. But she was wrong about the most important thing: Lady Miranda was the one person who must never, never learn his secret.

Chapter 12

〜⌒⊙⊂〜

The next morning Miranda and Lady Harriet had already finished breakfast and were working on invitations for the ball by the time MacLeod put in an appearance. He looked much better than yesterday, Miranda thought, more the tweedy scholar than the harassed spy. His eyes were clear, his shoulders were straight, and he seemed at ease with one hand in his pocket and the other holding a cup of tea. In fact, he looked positively civilized. Perhaps hiding in his rooms all night really had done him some good.

"Would you care to help us, Mr. MacLeod?" she asked politely. "Or were your secretarial qualifications entirely imaginary?"

"On the contrary," he told her, stalking over to the large desk where the women were seated. "My qualifications were entirely genuine. The only falsehood was my name."

"Your name, and your motives," she countered. She had not intended to start an argument. It just seemed to happen automatically.

"I am confident that I can guard your physical safety while still producing excellent handwriting, Lady Miranda." His eyes had become cold and guarded again.

"If you two are going to bicker, I shall take my work into the library," Lady Harriet announced, not even looking up from her papers. "It's not good to expose the baby to such nonsense."

Miranda opened her mouth to apologize, but MacLeod beat her to it.

"I'm sorry, Miranda. I . . ." He glanced at his niece, but she was still busily writing. "I have no wish to quarrel with you."

"Nor I with you," she replied.

"Oh, why not?" Harriet whispered, without looking at either of them.

They both ignored her.

"And we would be grateful for your help, since we have more than eighty invitations still to write." Miranda held a piece of blotting paper out to him like a formal peace offering. He accepted it solemnly, but she thought she saw a hint of a smile behind his eyes.

He took up a pen and paper and said, "So what is it we're writing?"

Miranda gestured to the small stack of completed cards. "You can copy from one of those. Here is the list of guests—" She stopped and groaned as one name caught her eye. "Not cousin Cecil!" she exclaimed in dismay. "Must we really invite that sniveling, conniving—"

"We must, if we want this engagement ball to look legitimate," Lady Harriet replied calmly, still writing.

"I suppose you're right," Miranda agreed. "At least there will be enough other people attending that I won't have to speak to him." She sighed and continued explaining the invitations to MacLeod. "The ball will be held a week from today—"

"A *week*?" It was MacLeod's turn to be dismayed. He slowly lowered his pen, and his nostrils flared, but he kept his temper. "We have to maintain this farce for a *week*?"

"You did agree that an engagement ball would be appropriate," Miranda reminded him. "Besides, we wouldn't want to deprive cousin Cecil of an opportunity to harass me." She smiled seraphically. "And I am quite looking forward to my numerous aunts taking their turn at you."

"That is wicked of you, Lady Miranda."

"But not undeserved, you must agree," she countered.

This time the smile reached more than his eyes, though only briefly. "Touché."

"We could have arranged a salon or recital in only a day or two," Lady Harriet joined in. "But they wouldn't have had nearly this level of public exposure. This will get us as much publicity as taking out an advertisement in the *Times*."

Miranda found that she was genuinely enjoying herself. "Yes," she said. "This way someone is *bound* to try to kill me."

"But you get to wear a stunning ball gown while waiting to be murdered."

"It is true that I do not have enough opportunities to wear stunning ball gowns."

She couldn't help but laugh at MacLeod's horrified stare. In his protective moods he could be adorable as well as irritating.

"Don't worry," she told him. "I'm not forgetting the gravity of the situation. I merely propose that we enjoy the ball for its own sake. And if it enables us to achieve our goals, so much the better."

"And besides, we already posted the first batch of invitations earlier this morning. There's no changing our minds now." Lady Harriet punctuated her comment with the flourish of a signature. She finally glanced up to meet MacLeod's gaze, and Miranda was startled by the deep affection she saw in her hostess's expression.

"We can certainly have a recital or a lecture or

something in the interim," Lady Harriet continued as she plucked another piece of paper from
the stack. "If Lady Miranda feels up to it." This
time her eyes met Miranda's, and her expression
was one of playful challenge.

"Of course," Miranda said, blotting an invitation of her own and placing it with the other finished papers. "Recitals and lectures are two of
the most delightful things about a visit to London."

Yesterday this would have been an all-out lie.
But she found to her surprise that with the morning sunlight streaming through the windows, and
Lady Harriet's encouraging smile, the prospect
did not seem so bad.

Or, for all that the reasons were indeed bizarre,
perhaps it was being ushered into the bosom of
Andrew MacLeod's eccentric family that was en-
ergizing. In the end this whole exercise in false romance might end up deeply bruising her heart,
but she decided to wring what enjoyment she
could out of it while it lasted.

To Andrew's surprise and relief, they passed
the rest of the morning very companionably. They
agreed to host one recital and one lecture in addition to the engagement ball. Miranda was lively
and involved, and her cheerfulness was conta-
gious. He'd suspected yesterday that one of her

headaches was developing, but an evening's rest seemed to have done her good.

The headaches had often come in the afternoons in Italy. He was glad that they were so infrequent now, but he knew that Miranda still chafed under the helplessness they brought. He hoped that they might someday cease to trouble her altogether, but that did not seem likely.

He still dreamed sometimes of cradling her to him while she slept, of the texture of her hair against his cheek. He cursed himself for treasuring memories that for Miranda must hold nothing but pain. Pain that he had caused. Her refusal to try to remember told him that she wanted to forget as much about Italy as possible.

How ironic that he remembered the time of her convalescence as a cherished interlude between long periods of violence and injustice. It would be best if he, too, could forget that time.

Andrew stopped his woolgathering with an effort. He must not allow himself to become inattentive just because this house seemed safe.

The women were making plans to go shopping once the invitations were finished. Harriet was a perfectly capable bodyguard, but he intended to go along as well. He told himself that it was his responsibility.

Besides, capable or not, Harriet was with child. Lord Martin's wrath over his wife and child's endangerment would be nothing in comparison to Court MacLeod's if even the tiniest trouble ruffled the perfection of his eldest child's maternal bliss. Never mind that Harriet was fierce as a tiger, healthy as an ox, and would relish a fight. The rules of society dictated that the norm was for the male to protect the weaker female. And the rules were going to apply today, no matter how boring shopping for frocks might be. He was going along to escort his niece and his fiancée on their outing.

It had nothing to do with wanting to spend the day by Miranda's side.

Nothing at all.

Chapter 13

The next several days were the most enjoyable Miranda had had since her return from Italy. London itself was a foreign country compared to the order and serenity of Passfair. The bustle of carriages and pedestrians crowding the streets, the explosion of color and sound spilling out of the shops, everything was busier and brighter and faster than she was used to. Last time she had come to London for a lecture, the crowds and noise had made her feel claustrophobic. Now they were exhilarating and refreshing.

Of course the air was smoky and foul in comparison to the sweet breezes of the country. And the noise and crowding and glimpses of poverty really were appalling, but this time she didn't mind them as she had in the past.

Miranda thought this must be a sign that she

was truly recovered from her long illness. She reveled in the profusion of sensory input, even sometimes the stench of a badly drained street or the din of busy traffic. It was all part of the world, and she began to think that living in the world was better than hiding from it. Perhaps.

After all, hadn't she used to be an adventurer?

And what was this masquerade but a new adventure?

Lady Harriet often had her own work to attend to, so Miranda was accompanied about town by her new fiancé, Mr. Andrew MacLeod, which was causing a barely subdued sensation among London's elite.

Miranda had never set out to be scandalous, but she didn't bother to avoid scandal, either. Her natural independence and interest in travel had made her a popular source of gossip for years. Now she, one of the wealthiest heiresses of the time, was apparently marrying a mere university professor, a Scotsman from the Highlands whose breeding no one knew anything about, and whom she had known for only a fortnight.

She was greatly entertained by the buzz of speculation printed in the gossip columns—and occasionally even whispered in the shops. It seemed that anyone who mattered in society judged that her eccentricity had almost crossed a line into madness.

Her betrothal to Malcolm had never caused this much of a stir, Miranda thought, as she dressed on the Wednesday afternoon after their arrival in London. Of course their relationship had been far more private, a simple country engagement. They'd spent more time trying to smooth her father's ruffled feathers at losing his only child than being feted and such. She'd told herself that she hadn't needed any fanfare, only Malcolm's sweet, quiet presence. They'd never had a fight, never a hint of rancor.

Unlike the verbal jousting with Mr. MacLeod. MacLeod was certainly never boring.

She felt a twinge of guilt, as if she was dishonoring Malcolm's memory by thinking that his refined qualities were somehow boring.

He had been a nice man, a good man. And he had loved her, she was certain. But she wondered now if she would have felt stifled in a marriage to such a proper gentleman.

Well, there had been a very short time when he had not been completely proper. She smiled fondly, yet found the memory of the incident far off and faded and, well, tepid.

She was not meant to be tepid.

No. Better to remain independent. Or as independent as possible, she revised the thought with a brief grimace at herself in the dressing table mirror.

MacLeod had taken it upon himself to follow her on every errand and outing since they'd arrived. His presence did make her feel safe, and she found that she quite enjoyed his company when he wasn't being sullen. To his credit, he seemed to have put aside the frustration that had driven him to his room that first night.

MacLeod was capable of being perfectly agreeable when he relaxed a little, Miranda thought. She smiled as she recalled one conversation about the impracticalities of women's fashion. It had started when they were planning today's music recital.

They were discussing the arrangement of chairs in the music room when MacLeod suddenly leaned back with a contemplative look on his face. "Lady Harriet was once quite the aspiring musician, actually," he announced.

"Oh, no! Not that again," Harriet protested, laughing.

MacLeod turned to Miranda with a serious expression and a gleam in his eye. "Oh, yes," he continued. "My darling eight-year-old niece attended a performance of the Bach Cello Suites, and was so taken with the instrument that she decided she must learn how to play."

"That's charming," Miranda commented, a little puzzled at what the fuss was about.

Harriet gave a very unladylike hoot of laughter.

"Never trust Harriet when she's charming," MacLeod said. "She begged Court and Hannah for a cello, but they wisely waited. You see, she was also working on her knife throwing at the time, and she took it into her head that she should design a split skirt that could accommodate the cello while also concealing her favorite weapons belt."

Harriet was nearly breathless with laughter now. "I pestered Uncle Andrew incessantly for weeks until he agreed to help me. He was absolutely mortified to be tailoring a girl's underskirts."

"*I* am telling this story," MacLeod said reprovingly. "The point is that Harriet got so caught up in her sewing project that she lost interest in the cello, and the rest of us have been teasing her about it ever since."

"I was only eight," their hostess protested.

"You were a terror," MacLeod declared. "You used my bedroom door for target practice at four o'clock in the morning."

Miranda and Harriet were both laughing by then. MacLeod still didn't join them, but he looked more relaxed than Miranda had ever seen him.

And now, a day later and alone in her room, Miranda laughed again just remembering the conversation. The man was obviously very fond—and proud—of his family, though he didn't often allow himself to show it. Still, even when he unwound enough to talk about them, there was an unhappiness in his blue eyes that she thought went beyond mere discontent with his current assignment.

What was it that made him feel the need to set himself apart from a loving family? Why did he feel he did not deserve love? For that was what she sensed from him—a dissatisfaction with himself that drove deep into his soul and made him set himself apart from his fellows.

She couldn't help but wonder if there was anything she could do for his pain. Oh, not that she was fool enough or arrogant enough to think that she could solve another person's problems. But talk sometimes helped, and if MacLeod could not bear to unburden himself to his family, perhaps a stranger willing to listen without judgment would help.

Not that he would want her help, she supposed. And could she listen without judgment? While it was true that they would soon part ways forever, she wasn't likely to forget the man—

"Not the way he kisses," she murmured, and refused to be embarrassed.

And she doubted he was going to forget her.

"I dare him to try," she declared.

And why on earth was she talking to herself? It was too blatant a sign of eccentricity. She might be a spinster with the bad habit of running off and having adventures, but there was no reason for her behavior to be odd even in private. Ah, well, she'd put this instance down to being Mr. MacLeod's fault, for everything about that taciturn fellow was maddening.

It was time for her to pretend to be a social butterfly, so she firmly put aside speculation on Mr. MacLeod's emotional state as she made her way downstairs to help Lady Harriet greet their guests.

Her bodyguard's happiness was none of her concern, she reiterated on the way. She would allow herself to be used as bait in his trap, and that would take care of the problem that had caused her to need a bodyguard in the first place. Her aunts would have to accept that Miranda was an independent woman and capable of taking care of herself. If Aunt Rosemary was so fond of MacLeod, she could take him on as her own secretary.

Pity, though, that he wouldn't be around to write Miranda's memoirs after all.

Her breath caught in her throat as she reached the bottom of the staircase and saw MacLeod standing in the hall, talking to Lady Harriet. If she didn't know better she'd almost think that the pang of emotion that went through her at the sight of him with another woman was jealousy.

It's probably just the tightness of this corset, she joked to herself as she stopped and stared at the man before anyone noticed she was there.

He had dressed for the recital, and the result was splendid. The dark fabric of his coat was stretched tight across his broad shoulders, and the bright white of his collar set off the clean line of his jaw. He smiled at some comment of his niece's, and delicate crow's-feet appeared at the corners of his eyes. They softened his face in a way that Miranda wished she could see more often.

Then she was at his elbow without knowing quite how she got there. Spontaneously she told him, "You really ought to smile more."

He turned to her, startled, and their gazes met with what felt like an electric shock. The smile had disappeared from his face, replaced by an intensity different from any she had seen before. Fury she was familiar with, and irritation, but this was something different, and it bore into her with diamond-hard brilliance.

Then he visibly collected himself. "Good suggestion," he said dryly. "I'm sure the traitor will be so beguiled that he turns himself in immediately."

Abruptly turning away from both women, he headed into the parlor.

Miranda resumed breathing—had it been only a few seconds since her last breath? She ignored MacLeod's habitual sarcasm and focused on a more interesting question: what had been the meaning of that inscrutable expression?

"Well, you've scared him off again," Lady Harriet laughed. "And he seemed to be doing so well yesterday!"

She took Miranda's arm and led her in MacLeod's wake, toward the gathering crowd of people waiting to hear the recital—and get a look at the latest subject of their gossip.

Miranda experienced a moment of annoyance that her hostess should make light of MacLeod's obvious distress, but she was distracted by Harriet's words. Was that it, perhaps?

Improbable as it was, had that scalding, compelling look been one of fear?

Andrew made himself stay still at Miranda's side as the pianist got herself settled at the front of the room. He tried to look at least relaxed, even if he couldn't quite make himself appear to be doting over his ladylove. He was very annoyed with himself for so far being unable to melt into the role of Miranda's betrothed. He was used to a certain amount of undercover work. He could act. Yet this time he couldn't find the distance needed to play the part properly.

Perhaps the role was too seductive.

Bah! What a foolish thought.

He wanted to be pacing, he wanted to be at the back of the room watching the audience for suspicious behavior, he wanted to be anywhere but sitting quietly here doing nothing. Sitting quietly gave his mind time to wander, and that was never good.

Why had she said he ought to smile more? She had no basis for comparison—in Italy she had often made him smile, but had been unable to see it. He really had no right to be smiling at all, considering what he had done to her then. What he was putting her through now. But their easy companionship of the last few days had lulled him into an unjustified serenity, one neither of them could afford if he was going to keep her alive.

He risked a glance in her direction, but she was blissfully engrossed in the music. He was acutely aware of her every breath, every light brush of the red fabric of her skirts against his leg. But she had no attention for anything but the nocturne. She loved music. She had told him once that music allowed mortal souls to glimpse the infinite. It still amazed him that she could lose herself in music when her outside troubles were so great.

"I love music," Miranda told him as he led her down the path toward the village. "Even before . . ." She paused, but only briefly. "Before, when I could see, I loved music. Now it means even more." She rested her head on his shoulder for a moment, and sighed.

"It sets me free," she said.

Andrew squeezed her hand where it rested on his

arm. She was so trusting, and at times like this her trust was so calm and assured that she almost made him believe. He would have given anything to deserve the confidence she had in him.

"I hope you will like the music today," he told her in his Italian-accented English. The original Dante, killed in the firefight that had injured Miranda, had spoken only Italian—and a thick rural dialect, at that. But Andrew didn't see the need to take on the bandit's linguistic limitations along with his name.

That other Dante would have laughed, to see the tough British agent playing nursemaid. But the fact was that Andrew had never felt so at home as he did here in a foreign country, caring for a woman he'd known less than a month.

"I know I will like the music, Dante," she told him. "But what about you? I know you don't often like to go to the village."

He guided her around a large tree root before responding. "I do not like the village because of the many people," he said truthfully. It was not Dante's home village, but there were still too many there who might identify Andrew as an impostor if anyone—including Miranda—asked the wrong questions. "But I will like the music if it makes you happy." And that, God help him, was also the truth.

She laughed a little breathlessly, then startled him by stopping and turning to face him in the middle of the path. Her eyes did not quite meet his, but her hand reached up unerringly to cup his cheek. She was unbearably beautiful, with a healthy touch of color starting to come back to her face and the early morning sun individually illuminating every strand of her raven hair. One patch had gone silver. It was like moonlight on dark water.

In truth, it was a sign of her mortality, a mark from her injury, a badge of survival, as well. She would no doubt hate the slash of silver if she ever saw it, but he couldn't help but find it lovely. He ceaselessly had to keep himself from stroking and touching this bit of hair. Though she was touching his cheek, he managed once again not to caress her in turn.

"I am full of hope today, Dante," she said. "Do you know why?" He shook his head against her hand, resisting the temptation to turn and kiss her palm.

"I think I'm starting to see again," she whispered, as if saying it out loud might make it less true. "I see gray shapes today where yesterday there was only blackness. Who knows what I might see tomorrow?"

Andrew smiled. "That is very good news, cara," *he said, hiding the terror at what she would soon see that came with her announcement.*

She sighed contentedly, and they continued making their way along the path.

He was delighted that her blindness might be only temporary. But with the knowledge of her returning health came a sudden melancholy. He also knew that once she had recovered, he must go back to Britain. His assignment remained unfinished; the traitor was still at large.

And, most of all, he could not risk allowing the Englishwoman to see his face.

They approached the village square from the west, and Andrew described for Miranda the bright festival decorations and the way the sun glinted on the square's central fountain. A platform had been erected at the eastern end for the musicians, and Andrew led Miranda to the back of the gathering crowd so she could rest on the fountain's marble base. Her face was flushed with excitement, but he could tell that the long walk from the cabin had tired her.

She settled gracefully onto the cool white stone and reached back to dip her hand in the water. There were no women here doing laundry this morning, but a few of the village children were splashing around, and Miranda responded cheerfully when they called out to her.

A few minutes later the musicians appeared and launched into a loud, foot-stomping, slightly out-of-tune dance piece that brought the festivities into full swing. Miranda laughed with pleasure, and before he could think better of it, Andrew grabbed her hand and her waist and swung her into the joyful dance to which neither of them knew the steps. Her scent, so close, made him giddy and light-headed. He felt laughter of his own *bubbling up from a place he'd thought long dead, and her beautiful smiling lips demanded irresistibly to be kissed.*

At that moment a heavy hand descended on his shoulder, and the next moment he had twisted the hand up behind its owner's back without even thinking.

"A message, sir!" the man said desperately. "From your aunt in Florence!"

Of course. The code meant that his superiors had something to tell him. Andrew backed off immediately, apologizing in fluid Italian to both the strange man and to Miranda, who was asking if he was all right.

"I am fine, signorina," he told her, taking her hand and turning to face the stranger. "It is only that this man surprised me. He has a message from my aunt." He waited expectantly.

The villagers continued to laugh and twirl around them, leaving a small bubble of calm around them and the fountain. The messenger was sweaty and stubbled from his journey, but he took a moment to straighten his clothes where Andrew's rough handling had skewed them. He looked uncertainly toward Miranda, but Andrew glared at him, and he quickly surrendered his message.

"A message from your aunt in Florence," he repeated the correct initiation of the code. "She's very ill and says you must come without delay. Your cousin from Venice is still two weeks away. It's most urgent."

Damn. The traitor—or his agents—knew of Andrew's existence and might find him within two days.

Phoebe Gale, who in her twisted way probably thought it amusing to be encoded as a sickly Florentine relative, was calling him back to England.

He could not stay. If they caught Miranda in his company, they would kill her immediately.

He felt the icy resolve of his trade come over him as he turned and took Miranda's other hand. He raised both her hands to his lips and kissed them gently.

She looked concerned. "Dante—" she began, but he cut her off.

"Miranda." He'd rarely used her name since she'd told him who she was. But somehow the artifice of *signorina* seemed ridiculous now. "I must go to Florence right away." She opened her mouth to say something, but he continued as firmly as he could. "It is not safe for you to come with me. I must travel fast, through dangerous places."

He watched the struggle on her face as she was forced to acknowledge her limitations. She was an intelligent woman, and offered no impractical protest. Instead she simply sighed.

"You are going to suggest that I return to England now," she stated. "I do not wish to go."

"But you know it is the wise thing to do," he finished for her. "You are well enough to travel slowly; you do not need me to care for you anymore. This man is trustworthy—he will escort you back to your home."

The messenger looked rather startled at this news,

but as an agent of Lady Phoebe he must be accustomed to doing odd jobs on short notice.

Miranda also looked surprised. "Dante, I know you think I am very adventurous, but even I cannot travel halfway across Europe with a man I only just met." She turned toward the man and said in Italian, "Please, sir, will you take me only to the British embassy in Rome?"

"Of course, miss," he replied. But he met Andrew's eyes and nodded confirmation that he would continue to follow her discreetly through the rest of her journey. Lady Phoebe employed only the best—Andrew was impressed that the man had managed to find him at all.

But if he could be found by Aunt Phoebe's people, it might not take even two days before he was found by their opposite number, and he had to put as much distance as possible between himself and Miranda before that happened.

"When must you go?" she asked in English, as if following his thoughts.

"Now. At once," he replied. "I will tell—" He realized he didn't know the messenger's name.

"Paolo," the man supplied.

Andrew nodded and continued. "I will tell Paolo—who you see can understand English—how to go to the cottage. There is nothing there that I need. You and he should both rest today, then start for Rome tomorrow. I will tell him how to care for you."

She frowned. Andrew knew she hated the dependence created by her unpredictable and incapacitating *headaches. She would rather no one knew about them, but again her practicality won out. She nodded.*

Then she ran her hands up his arms to his shoulders and stood on tiptoe to whisper in his ear. "I will come back to Italy, when I am well," she said. "I will come back and find you again."

She stood back for a moment, seeming to gaze at him. He tried to memorize every feature of her face before she turned and held out her hand to Paolo, who took it.

Andrew gave Paolo quick instructions, unnecessarily reaffirming the need to keep the lady safe. Paolo nodded his understanding, and led Miranda gently back the way she and Andrew had come so recently. It was too bad, Andrew thought, that there wasn't really time for her to stay and hear more of the music.

At the far side of the square, Miranda turned to smile and wave at him one last time, as if she could see that he was still standing where she'd left him, watching her go.

He had no doubt that she would make good on her promise. He fervently wished that he could be here when she did.

Chapter 14

❧

Miranda closed her eyes and sighed to herself as the first movement came to an end. In the pendant silence just after the last notes died, she thought how wonderful it was to have this respite from the chaos of her current life. All that existed was the music; everything else faded to inconsequence.

Except her acute awareness of the large man seated so closely beside her. She was aware of the pleasant scent of him, the warmth of his skin, the darkness and texture of his clothing. She fought an urge to lean against him and take his hand the whole time the music played. The tension between the peace brought by the music and the longing stirring in her sang through her still.

She risked a glance in MacLeod's direction. He wore a contemplative expression, and she wondered if it was because of the Chopin or if he was thinking about something else entirely.

The second movement began, and Miranda let herself be swept away in the currents and eddies of interweaving notes. Despite strong sensory awareness, she didn't spare another thought for MacLeod until the end of the recital, when they stood at the front of the room together to thank performers and audience for attending.

He was perfectly gracious, but his posture seemed stiff and uncomfortable to her. As they mingled among their guests afterward, he spoke very little. He merely nodded distractedly as she invited various guests to attend her lecture for the Ladies' Travel Society the next day. When she casually leaned toward MacLeod, he sidled away.

Well, perhaps the movement had not been so casual after all, and it was just as well that one of them remembered that their engagement was a masquerade. But weren't they supposed to be touching, and sharing romantic glances? Wasn't her behavior more correct in this instance than his? Stubborn, stiff, Scottish fool!

After everyone had left, Miranda drew her fiancé aside, into the privacy of the empty breakfast room. He came without protest, but through his fine jacket she could feel the hard, tense muscle of his arm. Unbidden, her mind provided her with an image of what that arm might look like unencumbered by jacket or shirt.

She dropped her hand abruptly and turned away to hide her embarrassment. She intended to lecture the man on behaving more believably as a betrothed couple, but that didn't mean she wanted the distraction of imagining him naked.

"Mr. MacLeod," she began, before her thoughts got away from her, "I think it is important that we be perfectly honest with each other."

His face remained physically calm, but that strange intensity from their encounter before the recital returned to his eyes.

Yes, she thought, it was fear. But what on earth was the man afraid of? This was obviously the wrong way to begin the conversation, and Miranda hurried on before MacLeod could escape again. "It is quite clear that I, or at least this *assignment*, have come to make you uncomfortable." She did not bother to hide her rueful expression when talking about herself as a pawn in his political game. "But I think that your prey would be more likely to approach the trap if you could put on a more convincing performance. I'm afraid that our guests today may have left with the distinct impression that we despise each other." She tried to lighten the statement with a laugh, but it came out as only a sad half cough.

He wasn't looking at her now, but had taken off

his spectacles and was polishing them slowly. The silence stretched out so long that Miranda thought he would rub the lenses away rather than speak to her, but he stopped abruptly and put the glasses back on. He met her eyes with the same openness she had seen when he was comfortably talking about his family.

"I'm sorry," he said simply. "I realized today that I've been . . . distracted from my duties. I have . . . enjoyed your company a great deal, these last few days, and this afternoon, I suddenly found it difficult to maintain the pretense . . ." He faltered, and his gaze fell again as he laughed ruefully. "In short, I've been appallingly unprofessional."

He knew he should be ashamed that a civilian had just called him to task for failure to do his job properly, but somehow it just seemed sadly funny. Miranda looked surprised and a little confused by his admission, but he thought she accepted its honesty.

He needed to reassure her that all this trouble, the elaborate plotting and planning, would not go to waste. More than that, she was right: he needed to pull himself together so that the plan *would* work, and Miranda would be safe.

He had hoped, a year ago, that his hasty and unusually reckless flight across Europe would lead their enemies away from Miranda permanently.

But the traitor had found her, and she was willing to risk her life to see that the man was finally stopped. Andrew could do nothing less than his best to see that the plan succeeded.

He felt as if he'd spent the last two weeks in a fog. Since Miranda had reentered his life—or, more accurately, since he'd reentered hers—he'd had brief periods of lucidity, as now. Like that stolen kiss in the forest grove near Passfair. But in between his life had swung wildly between confused periods of guilt and delight at simply being with her. It disturbed him that simple concern for a woman could rob him of his usual efficiency and acuity.

It was, as he'd said to her, unprofessional. He might be on the verge of retirement, but he was no doddering old man, rendered incompetent by emotion. He could face the world as Miranda's fiancé for a few more days—it wasn't as if she was unpleasant company! How much better it would be for him if she was.

Miranda was still staring at him. His resolve nearly crumbled when he saw her expression, a mix of puzzlement, concern, and impatience that perfectly reflected her compassionate and practical personality.

How could he pretend to only pretend his regard for her?

But, as so often, she surprised him. "I have enjoyed our time together, as well," she said. "I don't see why duty should dictate that we remain entirely indifferent to one another. I should think that some level of . . . friendship—"

Did he imagine her slight hesitation over that word?

"—would make this exercise easier, not more difficult."

"Of course you're right," he said. "It's perfectly simple."

Not as simple as she thought, but he must resist the absurd impulse to enlighten her as to the complexities of their relationship. He could behave with genuine friendliness toward her. And if he continued to feel more and more that he was betraying her by keeping things from her, well, it would make it that much easier to leave when his job was completed.

He smiled grimly, pleased with this solution, and held his hand out to her. She took it, smiling a little uncertainly in response, and he brought her hand to his lips for a quick kiss. His pulse quickened with the contact, and he thought he saw a slight blush touch her cheeks.

He offered her his arm and escorted her back out into the hallway and toward the drawing room and afternoon tea.

The fit of her body against his as they walked in step was the most wonderful feeling in the world.

Now that he was this close, could he maintain the distance for the three days until Saturday's ball?

"Don't worry," he reassured himself as much as her. "I won't let distractions get in the way of my job any longer."

Miranda didn't know what had happened to MacLeod in the breakfast room yesterday, but his previously sporadic good mood seemed to have taken up residence permanently. It was unsettling. Disturbing.

Lovely.

At least in those moments that she let herself forget it was a game. And she was very annoyed with herself for allowing that delusion to happen all too often.

At the moment half of Miranda's mind was dutifully occupied with giving a lecture about the benefits and hazards of solitary travel for women. She did not mention stray bullets in either category. The other half, of course, and regrettably, was occupied with thoughts, images and inchoate yearnings centered around the uncommonly undour Mr. MacLeod.

Blast and damn him for having a lovely smile. And eyes that could twinkle with merriment and send sparks through her.

It's not as if it is real, she thought angrily, and momentarily lost the thread of what she was saying.

Fortunately, her hesitation was apparent only to her. Her audience continued to watch her with polite attention even while she thought herself fumbling and less than brilliant. She thought that perhaps her performance was too rote, too pat, too . . . lacking . . . in any current thrills.

Was that her performance, or her life?

And how was MacLeod responsible for that? Though it was tempting to blame him for *everything*, she wasn't really childish enough to do so.

Concentrate on your duty to inform and entertain the audience, Miranda!

The small salon was comfortably full, with mostly women and a few scattered men, quite a few of them familiar faces from the recital and past lectures. The organizer, Miss Derringer, had been incoherent with delight when they arrived.

But while words continued to flow from her, Miranda's mind kept stubbornly returning to the subject of her erstwhile secretary and so-called fiancé.

MacLeod had been unfailingly courteous and cheerful since their conversation yesterday, and it made her want to smack him. She'd wanted him to put up a more pleasant public image for their performance. But it hurt her that she, too, was shut on the outside of his new façade.

And it annoyed her that she felt hurt. Why couldn't she just be grateful that her bodyguard was no longer an emotionally erratic nuisance?

Miranda concluded her talk with her favorite anecdote about Turkish baths, and as the audience applauded she saw eager smiles on many faces. Their enthusiasm was gratifying, but for all their professed love of adventure, most of the people here were probably happiest when "abroad" was as much like England as possible.

She forced herself to smile benignly on the departing crowd, letting the excited, empty babble pour over her. Not a single spy or traitor among the lot, she thought sourly.

She sighed. What was wrong with her? She used to feel exhilarated after a successful lecture. Tonight she was just tired and distracted.

She turned away from the lectern to scowl at MacLeod. He was leaning casually on the wall behind and to her right, hands in his pockets, scanning the crowd. She was pleased that she'd summoned enough willpower not to glance at the man once during her lecture. Then again, perhaps, for the sake of their masquerade, she should have stolen at least one convincingly simpering glance his way.

Now that she did look at him, she couldn't help but wonder what possible threat he could hope to find among thirty-odd twittering, middle-aged English ladies and their bored husbands. Miranda almost laughed as she mentally placed Phoebe

Gale mixing with tonight's group, like a wolf among spaniels.

She found that she was still gazing at MacLeod. She allowed herself a moment to admire the small cleft in his chin, and immediately regretted it as his eyes met hers and he raised one inquiring, infuriating eyebrow. She felt a blush rising in her cheeks, which only irritated her further, so she turned her back on him and stepped down from the small dais to chat with some of the audience who were lingering among the salon's scattered, elegant chairs.

She was having a pleasant conversation about architecture in Prague when suddenly, directly behind her, she heard a smooth baritone voice say, "*Buon giorno, signorina.*"

Her heart stopped. It was Dante. She would know his voice till the day she died. But how could he be here, in London? Had he come to find her? The thoughts skipped across the surface of her mind in the split second it took to whip her head around, his name on her lips.

But there was no one. Only MacLeod, greeting the Italian ambassador's wife. The ambassador and Mrs. Montessori had been kind enough to attend several of Miranda's lectures before, as well as the music recital, and tonight as usual they were being polite and friendly.

Miranda could hardly breathe. How could she have mistaken MacLeod's voice for Dante's?

Was it possible that her attraction to the Scotsman had grown to the point where she was forgetting her Dante's voice? She closed her eyes, focusing on the sense that had been her primary source of information during her time with Dante.

She ignored the questions of the people behind her, and *listened*.

He was there. With no trace of the Scottish burr to which she'd become so accustomed, Dante's gentle, slightly gruff Italian voice was there, not ten feet away from her, talking knowledgeably about the price of tomatoes.

She opened her eyes, and was surprised to find that she was still standing up. She couldn't feel her feet. Dante was replaced again—almost—by MacLeod, who this time had not seen her watching him.

Her mind reeled with the possibilities of what she had discovered. *Might* have discovered, she corrected herself. She still was not convinced that it wasn't some bizarre, headache-related confusion.

She nearly screamed when poor Miss Derringer startled her from behind with a high-pitched "Lady Miranda!"

But Miranda gathered herself enough to offer a sincere smile to the salon organizer and the handsome young man at her elbow. He was a gracefully dressed gentleman with a sleek head of black hair and a neat mustache, an almost comical counterpart to Miss Derringer's perpetual air of disarray.

"Lady Miranda!" she fluttered again. "That was simply *marvelous*. All the ladies are *so* pleased that you could come." Her beaded purse swung noisily as she gestured to punctuate each phrase. "And of course Sir Simon *insisted* on meeting you. Lady Miranda Hartwell, this is Sir Simon Lester, a generous supporter of the Ladies' Travel Society."

Sir Simon kissed her hand and offered a dazzling smile. "It is indeed a rare pleasure to meet a lady of your accomplishment and intelligence," he said.

Miranda was suddenly aware that MacLeod was standing very close behind her. She could sense his presence, a tense alertness almost as tangible as body heat. He was of a height with Dante, she thought. He had the same muscular arms . . .

Sir Simon had just finished saying something, but Miranda had no idea what it was. She risked a possible change of topic and said, "I cannot imagine that you are personally plagued by the concerns of a woman traveling abroad. You have a sister, perhaps?"

"Alas, it is my mother who insists on seeing the world." He sighed dramatically. "She is sixty-three years old and maintains that it is the perfect age for gallivanting recklessly across Europe. I try to encourage the most reasonable manifestations of her hobby."

"Indeed. I feel certain that she is grateful for your concern, but she sounds to me like a woman who is capable of taking care of herself."

Miranda also felt an unreasonable desire to lean back onto the support of MacLeod's tall frame. Instead she stepped toward Sir Simon, accepted his offered arm, and allowed him to escort her toward the exit.

Sir Simon was silent as they walked arm in arm, and Miranda searched for another polite topic. "Have we met before?" she asked politely. He looked vaguely like half a dozen of Malcolm's old school friends, but she barely listened to his answer.

Andrew walked a step behind, and was listening closely as Lester replied, "I don't believe we have, but I would be delighted if we had the opportunity to meet again."

Andrew had felt his hackles rise the instant he saw the young man approaching Miranda. Lester had barely concealed a leer as he complimented Miranda's intellect. Had he no sense of propriety? Andrew refrained from snatching her hand from the man's arm. A well-behaved gentleman would not interfere with his fiancée's harmless social interactions.

"A lucky thing for him I'm feeling well-behaved," he growled under his breath. Then he caught sight of his reflection in the window glass. He carefully removed the dangerous glower from his face and replaced it with something close to a secretary's general amiability.

Jealousy, he supposed, was not a good excuse for plotting an assassination.

Chapter 15

"What was the meaning of your shameless behavior at the salon?" MacLeod demanded abruptly after dinner that evening.

The Kestrels had gone to an embassy function, and Miranda and MacLeod had spent a somewhat tense meal discussing safe, dull topics. Miranda had barely paid attention, still trying to figure out whether MacLeod could really be Dante, and if he was, what in heaven's name it meant. Why had he been in Italy? Why had he taken care of her? Why was he back here now? And why hadn't he *told* her?

The one answer to all her questions might simply be that it was his job. He'd been under orders to care for her then, as he was under orders not to let her be killed now. There was apparently something to be said for the long arm of the British

Empire. And his auntie Phoebe had probably ordered him not to tell her the truth about his various identities. They'd been through all that once already.

But for some reason, after having witnessed the antipathy between Andrew and the old lady, she had trouble casting MacLeod in the role of unquestioningly obedient nephew. Of course, he wasn't Lady Phoebe's relation at all, as he'd pointed out.

But was he Dante? And how could she confront him about it? And considering how vulnerable and open she'd been with Dante, could she bear to face the man she'd made a fool of herself with if he admitted to the deception?

And speaking of embarrassing confrontations . . .

Here they were, he standing near the fireplace and she seated a comfortable distance away. She nearly choked on her after-dinner sherry when he asked his outrageous question. There he stood, tall and stiff and looking every inch the outraged suitor.

"*Shameless?*" she repeated incredulously. "Are you implying that *I* have something to be ashamed of?"

"I'm just saying that a lady of your standing should give more consideration before throwing herself at mustachioed men with titles."

It took Miranda a moment to remember which of her acquaintances of that day had worn a mustache. "Sir Simon was a perfect gentleman! He wanted to ask me about the Sistine Chapel."

"I can assure you, my girl, that is not at *all* what he wanted from you." MacLeod actually had the audacity to shake a finger at her, and Miranda couldn't suppress her laughter.

"Mr. MacLeod, I am *not* your girl! I am a grown woman, perfectly capable of interacting with civilized individuals of either gender. Have you forgotten that our engagement is merely a pretense? Your responsibility is to protect my safety, not my virtue."

Miranda paused for breath, and MacLeod took a step back, apparently dumbfounded. Only then did it occur to her that in addition to being condescending, he might be genuinely jealous. So much for his short-lived emotional stability.

Now, wouldn't that be interesting? Inconvenient and wrong, of course, but the notion certainly piqued her curiosity.

For the thousandth time that night, she returned to the idea of MacLeod and Dante being one and the same. She had to be certain. She couldn't resolve what she felt until she knew the truth.

Dante might have some right to be jealous. Ah, but if it had only been MacLeod playing a role—?

Who was more confused—should it be true—he or she?

"Playacting is not good for one's constitution," she said.

"You have no idea how true that is."

She put down her drink, stood, and took a few steps toward MacLeod, unconsciously drawn to him by the weary bitterness his tone betrayed. He was polishing his glasses again, a habit she was beginning to associate with moments of nervousness.

"I am sorry," he began. "Of course it's not my place—"

"No, I'm sorry," she interrupted, stilling the motion of his hands with one of hers so that he looked up at her, startled. She continued, "It is kind of you to be concerned."

"It's not kindness," he said, a little breathlessly. "It's just that I'm not accustomed to working in a situation where someone else makes decisions."

"That's called a partnership, Mr. MacLeod. You might someday come to appreciate the merits of such a system."

She stood very close to him now. She could see all the fine details of his face, the long eyelashes, the very beginnings of dark stubble on his cheeks, the faint triangular scar on his left temple.

Andrew felt his breathing quicken as though he'd just run a sprint. He was hyperaware of Miranda's light touch on his hands, and the faint breeze of her exhalation on his face. Her eyes were huge and dark, and he could not for anything remember which of them had spoken last.

She closed her eyes, and raised one hand to gently cup his cheek. The sense of déjà vu was dizzying, but this time he did not shake his head. He kept still, just watching her face.

This time, too, she was not blind, and when she took her hand away and opened her eyes, she only smiled sadly and walked away from him without a word. The door shut with a soft click behind her.

What was her memory of that last morning in Italy? he wondered. Her melancholy reaction to their touch showed that she still missed Dante.

But Dante was a fiction, a nonexistent man with a nonexistent clean conscience. Andrew had shot Miranda, but Dante had nursed her, and now Andrew was causing her further unhappiness because he could not compete with the memory of his own ill-conceived creation.

Andrew crossed to where Miranda had abandoned her drink. He stared into its silky liquid depths, where firelight and the cut of the glass combined to form shimmering abstract patterns. He quickly drained the sweet sherry, then went to the sideboard to refill it with dark, bracing whisky.

The crash of breaking glass jolted Miranda out of her light doze. Heart pounding, she got up from the chair where she had finally drifted to sleep and ventured out of her bedroom into the hallway.

A series of smaller thumps and grunts continued to drift up from the back of the house. The front hall lights had not been extinguished, which meant that the Kestrels were still out, but it was far too late for the servants to be working.

Miranda briefly ducked back inside her room to grab an iron poker, then crept along the upstairs corridor toward where the noises had come from. The darkened doorway leading to the back hall was now ominously silent. She tried to approach it quietly, conscious of being lit from behind by the lights of the downstairs entryway, and feeling slightly foolish. All the recent talk of spies and traitors was making her mistrustful . . .

But she found that despite being unspeakably furious with MacLeod—Dante—the maddening Scotsman—she was now worried because he had not also emerged from his bedroom to investigate the noise. Had she imagined it after all?

As she reached the doorway to the back hall, there was another muffled thump, followed by a short, sharp Gaelic curse from around the corner.

MacLeod.

His voice was perfectly recognizable, now that she was free of preconceptions about his identity. What was he doing breaking glass in the middle of the night? She could hear him muttering to himself now, but she couldn't make out the words.

She lowered her poker slightly and hissed, "MacLeod!" into the darkness.

She didn't know why she felt the need to whisper; if the servants in their basement quarters hadn't heard the crashing already, her talking wasn't going to wake them up.

All sounds from down the hall stopped abruptly. After a moment she heard footsteps approaching, and she lifted her poker again just in case.

But it was MacLeod who appeared, looking slightly disheveled and not wearing his glasses. He stood in the doorway, firmly blocking her way, and stared at her for a moment, as if trying to focus on her face.

Then he said, in a normal conversational tone, "I'm sorry I woke you."

Miranda almost laughed at the absurdity. "What is going on?" she demanded. "What was that noise? Are you all right?" She tried to see past him into the passageway, but there was still no light, and he was stiff as a monolith in the doorway.

"We must leave here," he said abruptly. "It's not safe."

When she impatiently tried to push past him, he raised one hand to the doorjamb, inches from her face, and she saw that it was dark and slick with blood. She quickly stepped back and looked up at his face in alarm.

"You're hurt!" she said.

He looked at his hand as if it belonged to someone else, and she stamped her foot in frustration. "What the *blazes* is going on?" she demanded again.

He looked down at the carpet. "I am dripping on Harry's floor," he said calmly, "about which she may or may not be upset." He considered his hand again, and continued, "I don't know if it's my blood, actually."

"Well, whose is it then?"

"You shouldn't see him," he said, still blocking her path. "I told you, it's not safe for you here anymore."

"Someone came to attack me?" Being shot at in the forest had been terrifying, but the idea of someone breaking into the house to harm her made her blood run cold. "Where is he now?" she demanded.

"I didn't kill him." MacLeod met her eyes defiantly, though the thought had not even crossed her mind. Then he dropped his gaze and whispered shakily, "I only *nearly* killed him. I seem to have lost my edge."

Miranda was shocked as much at the despair in his voice as at the admission itself.

Suddenly subtle clues of sound, sight, and scent clicked in her mind and she exclaimed, horrified, "You're drunk!"

He did not reply, but his mouth twitched in irritation and he abruptly turned and went back the way he'd come. Miranda followed, keeping one hand on the wall while the other gripped her poker.

Soon MacLeod's figure became visible again as he turned up the nearest gas lamp. Also illuminated was the source of the crash that had wakened her. Lying on its side by the wall was a six-foot-tall wooden display cabinet with now-demolished glass doors; and on the floor, the man whose head had apparently been used to inflict the damage.

There was blood everywhere.

"Are you sure he's not dead?" Miranda asked, surveying the wreckage.

MacLeod glared at her, but moved to inspect the intruder's motionless form. He knelt carefully among the broken glass by the body, and his slight unsteadiness was only noticeable because Miranda was looking for it.

"His pulse and breathing are still strong," MacLeod reported.

A thought suddenly occurred to her. "So, is he the . . . ?" She trailed off, but realized immediately that he couldn't be the traitor. If he were, she would now be completely safe and MacLeod would not be insisting that they leave.

MacLeod gave a derisive snort. "This man's no *gentleman spy*." He used the phrase with contempt, and lifted the man's limp, bloodied arm from the floor to show her its rough workman's hand. "Poor sod isn't even a professional thief," he continued, dropping the arm unceremoniously back to the carpet. "Though he did really quite well, getting this far into the house."

They considered the body in silence for a moment, and then MacLeod suddenly lurched to his feet again. Miranda was afraid he might overbalance, but he simply banged his fist against the wall.

"This was a *stupid* plan!" he shouted, now cradling his hand to his chest. "How could I be mad enough to think the man would show himself by attacking you personally? He's just going to hire every poor bloody lackey he can find until one of them gets lucky and kills you!"

His Scottish vowels were becoming more and more pronounced as his agitation grew, and Miranda wondered for the thousandth time how this could possibly be the same man she'd known in Italy. Dante would never have become drunk or raised his voice to her.

MacLeod was back to insisting that they must leave immediately. Harriet would clean up the mess, he said.

The situation was obviously getting out of hand. MacLeod drunk and dithering would be a hindrance to any sort of proper planning. She did the only thing she could think of to get him back on track.

"MacLeod!" she said sharply. "You are behaving unprofessionally. Either speak sensibly or shut up and go to bed."

That had the desired effect. MacLeod blinked in surprise, then took a deep breath and blew it out slowly.

"You're right, of course," he said.

"Of course." She nodded.

"Of course," he said again.

He seemed to pull his thoughts together while he retrieved his glasses from his pocket and put them back on.

"I believe we should leave Kestrel House, Miranda," he said, enunciating carefully, "because our enemy obviously knows where you are, yet will not reveal himself by coming in person. We are needlessly endangering you by staying."

"Shouldn't we find out what this man knows about who employed him?" Miranda asked.

"We can leave that to Harriet. Our priority is to keep you safe."

"I thought our priority was to use me as bait."

"Well, we've seen how brilliantly that plan worked!"

"That plan is not finished, MacLeod," she insisted. "The day after tomorrow we have more than a hundred people coming to this house. One of them may be your traitor, and he may still reveal himself somehow. He doesn't seem to be a criminal genius, after all. Don't throw down your cards before you see the entire hand you've been dealt."

She could tell that she was wearing him down, but he was still frustrated. "Sometimes it is better to abandon a bad plan," he insisted. "We don't need to carry it out just because we sent out fancy invitations."

"On the contrary," she said. "How could you possibly hope to catch him if we make it clear that we know what's going on? I think he still believes that you're just my secretary that I've taken a fancy to." He looked doubtful, so she pressed the point. "If he knew you were Rob Roy, don't you think he'd have sent some more competent assassins?"

He thought about that for a moment, then said, "If we didn't know what was going on, wouldn't we inform the police?"

"So let us inform the police," she replied. "We'll report an attempted burglary. We can turn this fellow over to them if you like."

MacLeod sighed, and she knew she'd convinced him. Just when had she decided she liked this plan, anyway?

"Why are you suddenly so eager to continue acting as bait?" he asked, adding mind reading to his list of infuriating habits. He nudged the motionless intruder with his foot. When there was no response, he went back over to the gas lamp, turned up the light, and began examining his injured hand.

"I can't resume my normal life until the traitor is caught," she answered as she moved to join him, careful not to block his light. "I can't just hide indefinitely and hope someone thinks of another way to draw out a man for whom we have no name and no physical description . . ." She trailed off, distracted by what she saw in the lamplight.

"It seems some of it is my blood," MacLeod said in response to her silence, his voice a little shaky.

There was one long, smooth gash down the back of his left hand and wrist, and many smaller parallel cuts. His shirt cuff was sticky with blood, and the deeper cuts were still bleeding. He wiped away some of the mess with a formerly white handkerchief.

"Hitting the wall with it probably didn't help," Miranda commented.

"It seemed like a good idea at the time," he replied, grimacing as he tried to make a fist.

"You'll need to get it stitched if you want it to heal cleanly," she pointed out.

"There isn't time," he said. "I still think we need

to get you out of the house, even if we come back for the ball. Remember what happened to the last bloke who tried to kill you? Someone is probably watching the house, keeping a close eye on him and on us." He gestured to the body on the floor. "Ring for the butler so we can secure our friend here and get going."

"There *is* time," she insisted. "If the house is being watched, wouldn't a middle-of-the-night departure arouse some suspicions?"

"Fine," he said sourly. "We'll go in the morning, when it will be easier to follow us." Miranda opened her mouth to retort, but he interrupted her. "Don't worry, we'll act innocent and come back for the damned engagement ball. But we might as well not spend the intervening time as sitting ducks."

She was about to ask if he proposed that they spend the entire day in a carriage so as to provide a moving target, but at that moment she heard the front door open as Lady Harriet and Lord Martin returned from their evening out. Miranda left MacLeod to guard their prisoner and went downstairs to greet their hosts.

Chapter 16

~~~ OC ~~~

Andrew let himself slump against the wall as soon as Miranda left. For the thousandth time he cursed his idiocy. His stupid, self-indulgent behavior had endangered Miranda and jeopardized the assignment. He'd already made good progress on the bottle of whisky when he'd heard the distinctive, stealthy noises of an intruder. He couldn't bear to think what might have happened if he'd already gone to bed by then. Drunks were notoriously sound sleepers.

It was almost worse to contemplate what might have happened if he'd killed the man. In his stupid, drunken state he had almost committed murder. Miranda might not trust him after this, but at least she still didn't know what he truly was. A highly trained, cold-blooded killer who would as easily put a man's head through a glass window as shoot him in the back from a hundred yards away.

He looked down at the hot blood still seeping out of his arm to soak his handkerchief. Interesting how wounds from glass didn't close as quickly as more jagged injuries, he thought vaguely. He was starting to feel a little light-headed, and he hoped their prisoner wouldn't bleed to death before they could patch him up and get some information out of him.

Suddenly Harriet was there beside him, tsking over his hand.

"I broke your cupboard," he told her.

"And I hear you've been standing here arguing for ten minutes rather than cleaning up the mess," she replied.

The butler and a footman appeared, and at Martin's instructions carried the intruder away toward the back stairs. The staff at Kestrel House were quite an exceptional lot, Andrew thought. But they weren't enough, even if Harry had hand-picked and trained them.

"Miranda's not safe—" he began.

"You've kept her safe enough for tonight, Uncle," Harriet interrupted him softly. "Now come down to the kitchen so we can bandage you up, then take a hot bath and go to bed. After that you can lie awake telling yourself what an idiot you were to get drunk on duty."

"How productive that will be," he complained,

as she led him in the servants' wake. "Where is Miranda? Did she tell you about the police?"

"I suggested that Miranda go back to bed, as well. The local man is on his way, and Martin will speak to his friend Inspector Gregson at Scotland Yard. The morning newspapers will report that an intruder broke into the house, was caught by the heroic Mr. MacLeod, and now is refusing to talk to the police."

Andrew groaned. "Why are you setting me up to be the center of attention?" he demanded.

"You would be anyway," she reminded him as she settled him on a kitchen chair and went to fetch supplies from the butler across the room, where their intruder was now lying sprawled on the servants' dining table.

The stitching process was extremely unpleasant, but in Andrew's morose mood it seemed only appropriate. He distracted himself by explaining to Harriet why he wanted to get Miranda out of the house until the ball, and discussing ways to avoid being followed when they left. Harriet agreed to help him, finished wrapping him up, and sent him upstairs for the promised hot bath.

He went, mostly to keep himself occupied. The energy of the fight and the subsequent argument with Miranda had long since worn off, and he could feel his body preparing to shut itself down.

His hand and his head both throbbed, and his gut was twisted with the familiar ache of guilt.

Andrew dragged himself out of the bathtub when the water had cooled to room temperature. He couldn't stop shivering as he dried himself and put on his nightclothes. He crawled into the large, comfortless bed, and lay staring at the wood panels of the ceiling. Sleep finally claimed him as the black of the sky outside his window began lightening to gray.

The only soothing thing about this long night was that in his dreams he went back to the sunny Italian garden where he had heard Miranda's laughter for the first time.

"Lady Harriet asks if you would be kind enough to join her for breakfast, my lady." The housemaid spoke quietly and retreated once Miranda acknowledged the message.

Miranda watched dust motes floating in the beam of morning sunlight that splashed across her bedspread. She was a little surprised that the maid hadn't woken her sooner. She'd expected MacLeod to be sitting in a carriage, waiting to whisk her away at dawn. Perhaps in a fit of generosity—or remorse at his behavior last evening—he had decided to let her sleep in. Or were his injuries worse than she'd thought?

Now she must venture out of her room to face the day. And face the fact that Dante was not at all the man she'd believed him to be. That was probably what was hardest about the whole situation: she'd spent so much time and energy trying to return to a man who, apparently, had never existed.

Was he entirely a figment of her imagination?

MacLeod had physically been present, obviously. But was the kind, generous, witty personality of her Italian rescuer merely an invention of her fear and loneliness?

MacLeod seemed to care for her. If he was upset at having deceived her about his identity, it might explain some of his moodiness. And he had saved her life twice now—three times, counting Italy.

And aside from everything else, she still felt an uncontrollable thrill of attraction every time she saw him. And, obviously, she thought about him far more than was healthy.

She knew she would need to resolve her feelings at some point. But it didn't look as if it was going to happen this morning. Well, if she survived this exercise she supposed she had an entire lifetime to spend back at Passfair working through her emotions.

The pang of loneliness and loss this thought sent through her was a literally physical pain, so strong that she doubled over with her arms crossed protectively over her stomach for a few moments. In that time the scents of the sun-warmed grape arbor washed over her memory. She felt the touch of a gentle hand on hers and the sound of soft laughter. Desire swelled through her, strong as wine heating her blood.

"Dante." The name was whispered in a raw, aching whisper, devoid of hope, but full of desperate need.

Her dreams were dashed. All she had was to return to the life she'd always led. She would never find him now—

But Dante was here!

She could find him again.

Perhaps. Perhaps MacLeod was a truly fine actor, but how could everything about Dante have been an act? No actor could stay in character for weeks on end, could he?

Dante *had* cared for her. Did MacLeod? Was it the role he played or the real man she was attracted to?

Both, she admitted. It was all terribly confusing, and very, very aggravating—Lord knew, Andrew was dreadfully aggravating—but her foolish attraction to him was real.

She didn't want to go back to Passfair alone though perhaps it was inevitable. It was certainly the proper thing to do. But since when did she *want* to be proper? She simply seemed to be forced into being conventional most of the time.

But could she forgive him for his ruse? Should she? Were they only separated by curtains of pride and stubbornness? Should she confront him? Or should she wait to see if he confessed on his own? Were he to admit to her about being Dante, would that not be some proof that Andrew MacLeod cared for her?

And how did one get that repressed and dutiful gentleman to admit to having feelings?

She asked herself this question as she forced the confusion and loneliness to the back of her mind. She straightened her shoulders, looked around the bedroom, sighed.

She had no idea.

She dressed methodically, and when her stomach began to growl from hunger rather than emotional upset she stopped dawdling and headed resignedly down to breakfast. Perhaps her hostess would have some information gleaned from last night's attacker.

Lady Harriet was waiting for her, along with a young woman Miranda didn't know. Lady Harriet introduced them.

"Lady Miranda, this is my sister Lucy. Lucy will be impersonating you today."

Miranda paused at the sideboard in the act of pouring herself coffee, but she finished, sat down, and then hazarded a guess. "A diversion?" Lucy nodded approvingly. "Is *everyone* in your family now involved in my little adventure?" Miranda asked.

"Well, Uncle Andrew's engaged!" Lucy exclaimed, as if that was sufficient reason to risk life and limb. "We wouldn't miss it for the world. Even as an assignment, we find it delightful." She peered closely at Miranda. "I don't suppose you'd consider taking him on as a full-time project?" she added quickly, enthusiastically spearing a sausage.

"Lucy," Lady Harriet said reprovingly. Then she ignored Miranda's blush and went on. "It will add verisimilitude to have some family attending. Just to be safe, Mrs. Swift will make sure that your aunts' invitation to the ball is . . . misplaced."

"Besides, it will annoy Uncle Andrew no end to have all of us around. That alone is sufficient reason for us to come and offer our assistance." Lucy made her comment with a perfectly straight face, and Miranda decided she was going to like this direct young woman very much.

"How many of you are there?" she asked, imagining legions of MacLeods descending on the house.

"Only three more sisters, the twin brothers, and our parents will be coming for the ball," Lady Harriet said. "They should arrive later today. Lucy and Sara were already in town, conveniently for us, and Anna lives in London."

"Our brother Kit and his wife live in America,"

Lucy added. "Kit says he makes his way as a riverboat gambler, and that Lily is doing quite well as a dance hall girl. Though the truth is they are respectably settled in somewhere called St. Paul."

"Alexander is abroad somewhere as well, but he's rarely allowed to tell us where he is. He'll come home wounded, Sara and Mum will nurse him back to health, and then he'll be off again."

Miranda counted quickly, and ran out of fingers. "Isn't it a bit . . . unorthodox, to have eleven people involved in a 'secret' mission?" she asked.

The sisters exchanged a significant look.

"This situation is somewhat unusual," Lady Harriet admitted.

"And most of us aren't actually *involved*," Lucy added.

"More just . . . observing."

"We're terribly nosy."

Miranda laughed. She was certainly entertained by this lot. She doubted any member of the MacLeod clan ever suffered from boredom or loneliness, either.

"Well, as long as you don't overwhelm the other guests, I suppose we'll be fine," she said.

"We're experts at being unobtrusive," Lucy assured her.

"Except when circumstances dictate otherwise," Harriet said pointedly, placing her napkin on the table and rising from her place. "Lady Miranda, I hope you won't mind loaning Lucy one of your dresses. You two are of similar size and build. We'll give her a nice big hat with a veil and no one will be the wiser." She stood behind her sister, hands affectionately on her shoulders. Lucy rolled her eyes a little and kept eating.

"That's fine, of course," Miranda said, feeling a little bemused.

"This way you can safely stay here all day."

Miranda wasn't sure she liked the idea of sitting trapped in Kestrel House with the MacLeod horde for an entire day, but it was probably preferable to being assaulted. Probably.

Lucy gave her an amused and shrewd look, wiped her mouth delicately, and said, "Or if you feel the need to go out, you can borrow one of *my* dresses and take the girls for a walk. Sara is adept at borrowing my clothes, and I'm sure Anna would enjoy a spot of bodyguarding."

Miranda found herself smiling again. "If only I knew which sister was which, I could ask them." She sighed wistfully, and the others both laughed.

Talk of bodyguards reminded Miranda of what she'd been thinking before discussion of the MacLeod family tree had distracted her. "And what about the unfortunate gentleman from last night?" she asked. "Was he able to tell you who hired him?"

Harriet shook her head. "He's still barely coherent. Sara did have a lovely time practicing her medical school lessons on him, though. Lucy can fill you in on what we know." She patted her sister's shoulders a final time and then headed for the door, saying, "I'm afraid I have to go wake Uncle Andrew." She shot Miranda a brief inscrutable look from the doorway, then smiled again and left.

"It sounds like you two had quite an eventful evening," Lucy commented dryly.

Miranda wondered whether Lucy knew the half of it. She was tempted to ask more about MacLeod's condition, but he couldn't exactly be at death's door if his niece was going to roust him out of bed. Besides, there were more important things to discuss.

"And so did our unwelcome guest," she said. "What more can you tell me?"

Lucy stood and went to the sideboard to fetch herself more coffee. "Well," she said, "what I saw this morning wasn't much of an interrogation." Calmly stirring four teaspoons of sugar into her cup, she returned to the table. Miranda noted for the first time that Lucy's hands were sinewy and stained; not the hands of a proper young lady, but of a working woman.

Oblivious to—or ignoring—Miranda's scrutiny, Lucy continued speaking. "His name is Dodgson," she said. "He does rough work occasionally for a man called Statler, who approached him last night with the task of killing you. We're trying to track Statler quietly, but we're afraid he may already be dead. Dodgson doesn't seem to know anything else, and he is now in the safe but firm hands of Scotland Yard."

Putting a name to the bloodied face she'd seen in the lamplight last night made Miranda feel slightly ill.

The man called Dodgson had come to kill her, not out of any personal hatred, but as a job. He probably had a brood of children somewhere, growing up to be criminals like their da. Were they destined to end up like him, beaten on the floor of a wealthy peer's back hallway, surrounded by blood and glass?

The image seemed much more gruesome against the bright white linen of the breakfast room than it had last night. She saw again MacLeod's dark sticky wound, his drawn face with its desperate intensity as he confessed how near he'd come to murder. The drive to protect her, faced with the ugliness of violence.

Suddenly the hard knot that had been residing somewhere in Miranda's gut dissolved. MacLeod and Dante. *He really is the same man*, she thought. *I just didn't have the chance in Italy to get to know him properly*.

And now what? Did she have the right to confront him? He was still on assignment, as he must have been a year ago, though he seemed to be handling this one with notably less aplomb. Was he troubled because he wished to tell Miranda the truth and could not? Or because he feared she would discover it? Perhaps it wasn't stubbornness and pride between them, but fear.

Lucy was regarding her calmly. How much did MacLeod's numerous relatives know about the events in Italy? Miranda suspected from their behavior toward her that it wasn't much. She had to talk to MacLeod alone. She felt her breath come a little quicker as she resolved to confront him with what she knew, whether she had the right or not. It wasn't as if she were the government operative on assignment. Bait or not, she was a civilian, with the right to pursue her own agenda. Which happened to be Andrew MacLeod.

Though she was still confused about just how much she wanted to pursue him.

"Why must Lady Harriet rouse . . . your uncle?" she asked Lucy, as casually as she could after her long silence.

"He has to come with me," Lucy replied. "After all, he's barely left your side all week."

"Of course." Miranda grimaced at the irony, but logically she knew that a few more hours' waiting would make no difference.

Or perhaps she could catch him before they left . . .

Lucy gently interrupted her thoughts. "If you're finished eating, Lady Miranda, we could go see about our costumes," she said.

"Of course," Miranda said again, and rose to follow her companion out of the breakfast room and upstairs. There was no sign yet of MacLeod.

Chapter 17

❧ ⌒◯◯⌒ ❧

Miranda gave Lucy a suitable day dress, which was just slightly tight at the hips and short at the ankle, but not obviously so. Lucy produced a horrible gray walking dress, assuring Miranda that its very lack of fashion acted as its own sort of camouflage should Miranda absolutely *have* to leave Kestrel House.

When they emerged, Lady Harriet met them in the front hall with the nice big hat.

"Uncle Andrew's just having his coffee, but he'll be ready in a moment," she reported, gesturing to the breakfast room door. Miranda thought her cheerfulness looked a bit forced.

The three of them together managed to get Lucy's hat and veil fixed in place. Miranda turned toward the breakfast room, intending to join

MacLeod, but the door opened and her fiancé emerged. So much for a private chat.

He looked haggard. One eye was genuinely bruised and the other had the dark smudge of sleeplessness beneath it. He carried himself stiffly, and kept his left hand in his jacket pocket as he walked toward them.

These are the results of drunken brawling, Miranda reminded herself. Even if the brawling was with a man who'd come to kill her, the drunken part was not to be encouraged. She sternly suppressed the urge to give MacLeod a hug and send him back to bed.

He bid them all good morning but managed to avoid meeting her gaze. He turned to Lucy, taking in her costume with one long, sardonic gaze. "Shall we make our escape before the vandal hordes descend?" he suggested.

"Mr. MacLeod—" Miranda began, not sure if she should ask him for a private word now or simply wish him a pleasant day.

He forestalled her decision by interrupting her. "Lady Miranda, please—" he said in a rush, sarcasm temporarily abandoned. He paused and took a deep breath before continuing more slowly, addressing a point somewhere below her left elbow. "I most profoundly apologize for my behavior last night. It was unforgivable for me to expose you to danger as I did."

Finally he looked up, and in the liquid blue depths of his eyes she recognized a hopelessness that she had never thought to see, either in Dante or in Andrew MacLeod. With a jolt she understood that indeed he would never forgive himself.

How very melodramatic.

As he tore his gaze away and took Lucy's arm to escort her to their carriage, Miranda felt a wave of anger wash through her. The man was obviously miserable, and yet he *still* refused to take her into his confidence. She, who was to all appearances the source of his unhappiness, he kept ignorant and isolated while he invited his entire extended family to participate in this increasingly painful charade.

Her resolve to confront him strengthened: she must force him to either let down his guard with her, or at least to fortify it against everyone else. Preferably both. His moping about looking like a beaten puppy would do no one any good.

Miranda needed the day to pass quickly. She composed herself to be pleasant and turned to Harriet. "I would enjoy taking a walk with your other sisters when they arrive," she said, "if indeed they fancy a bit of bodyguarding."

Harriet chuckled. "I'm certain they will, if only to get the chance to talk with you. They can be maddeningly inquisitive."

"I am not surprised." Miranda smiled and felt herself relax a little.

"They'll be rudely banging on your door within a few hours, I'm certain."

"And I will be happy for the distraction."

She could easily occupy herself for a few hours, she thought, writing in her long-neglected journal.

True to Harriet's prediction, the rest of the MacLeod clan arrived mid-afternoon. They made such a great racket that Miranda thought the neighbors three doors down were probably aware of their arrival. She had been dozing, her head pillowed on her arms and her ink bottle left open to the air. She shook her head at her foolishness. She had written only a few awkward sentences before deciding to take a "brief rest."

There had been a vivid dream, of course, involving a mad chase with MacLeod from an unknown enemy through countryside that switched back and forth between the gentle geography of Kent; the twisting, crowded streets of London; and craggy Italian hills. True to all the other frustrations plaguing her, there had been no end to this dream. Even as she woke, she nursed a bleak hope of at least getting kissed in her dream. It did not help that she woke suffering from improper physical frustration that was almost worse than her mental state.

Now she busied herself with needed activity, and had just finished tidying her things away when a maid appeared to courteously inform her that the MacLeod ladies were going for a stroll and would be glad of her company.

Good. Yes, definitely good. A brisk walk was certainly a help for subduing restless female energy into acceptable channels, even if exercise was no real cure. She didn't know if there was any cure that didn't involve "scratching the matrimonial itch," as her aunt Rosemary put it.

She thanked the maid and dismissed her with a message that she would be ready shortly. She belted and tucked herself into Lucy's plain gray dress and put on her most practical walking shoes.

Miranda had never thought herself overly proud of her station, but looking at her reflection, she decided that her taste for elegant and well-tailored clothing was not a frivolous one. The dress itself was not abhorrently ugly, but it was drab and shapeless enough that she was confident that no casual observer would identify its occupant as Lady Miranda Hartwell. She looked more like a middle-aged governess. And with her flamboyantly gray-streaked hair covered by a snood and a bonnet, her one recently distinguishing mark was completely covered.

The front hall was bustling with activity when Miranda descended from her room a few minutes later. Enough luggage for a royal entourage was processing through, and she suspected as much again was making its way through the back hallways, as well. It appeared that the MacLeods traveled in style.

Lady Harriet barely blinked when she saw Miranda in her costume.

"Most of what you see is only my mother's luggage," she said as she saw Miranda's amazement. And then she cheerfully introduced the three young women waiting with her.

Sara, obviously the youngest, shared a clear family resemblance with her sisters Beatrice and Harriet. The third newcomer, introduced as Anna Gale, was the one blond in the group, and had their aunt Phoebe's high cheekbones and steely eyes.

"I'm sorry if I've kept you waiting," Miranda said once introductions were finished.

"Not at all!" Sara said cheerfully. "We have absolutely nothing better to do."

"Shall we go before we lose the light?" Anna suggested. She smiled and led the group out into the bustle of the Mayfair afternoon.

The rain of the previous week was gone, at least for the moment. London was enjoying that rarest of pleasures, a day both cool and clear. Miranda found that aside from the weather, she also enjoyed the novelty of anonymity. As she strolled among her better-dressed "sisters," no passersby sought to meet her gaze. No one called out to her from the shops. In fact, no one seemed aware of her at all, aside from her companions. It was very refreshing.

The girls themselves were delightful. Sara, being seventeen, was even less circumspect about her curiosity than Lucy had been earlier. But even she did not press past where Miranda was comfortable talking. Miranda spoke of some of the places she had seen and people she had met, and found it pleasant just to talk about her ideas without feeling any expectations from her audience.

Her companions displayed a wide range of knowledge on eclectic subjects. Beatrice surprised her by inquiring ardently about Miranda's impressions of the Basque language, and Sara told them in eager detail about her recent exploration of the anatomy of frogs. As they all absorbed that, a little queasily in Miranda's case, they entered a green park nestled among several gated embassy estates. The white gravel path wound among stone benches and primly manicured trees, bushes, and flowers.

"This is where we first met Lily!" Sara exclaimed abruptly. They had come upon a pair of benches beneath a large tree. The shade had prevented the day's moisture from dissipating, so there was a small puddle on one bench, and the earth visible between them was black with damp.

Miranda thought it looked a singularly uninviting place to meet someone. But since Sara seemed about to burst, she inquired dutifully, "And who is Lily?"

Sara opened her mouth, but Beatrice spoke first. "Lily is our brother Kit's wife," she said a little sternly.

"Ah, yes, Lucy mentioned a Lily and Kit living in America. Somehow I assumed that Lily is American."

"Oh, no!" Sara exclaimed. "Lily is the princess in the family."

"And unfortunately that is all we ought to say about her at the moment," Anna said. This was pointedly directed at Sara, who grinned shamelessly. Anna shook her head at the others, but Miranda thought she saw a half smile, quickly suppressed.

So. Andrew MacLeod wasn't the only one in his family accustomed to keeping secrets. Miranda smiled with her companions, but felt herself drawing back from them. Over their time together she had occasionally allowed herself to imagine that she and MacLeod shared a true bond, a regard for each other that could withstand everything they were going through. Now, as they continued walking and left the park, she wondered if she'd ever even glimpsed his true self.

She startled when Anna took her arm companionably. They had arrived back in Mayfair, and were just a few doors down from the Kestrels' town house. The street was still bustling, but the sky had clouded over again, and a brisk breeze stirred the delicate feathers on Beatrice's hat.

Anna leaned toward her, smiling. "Turn your face toward me, and laugh as if I've said something funny," she said softly in Miranda's ear. Miranda froze for a heartbeat, then did as she was told.

"Do you see someone?" she whispered, trying to maintain her inane smile.

Anna patted her arm affectionately and laughed at some imagined comment. "He's not paying attention to us, but we don't need to flaunt your profile as we go by."

She raised her arm to straighten Miranda's hat, blocking the sightline between them and the street as she did so. Miranda's breath quickened a little. Was someone watching? Would they notice Anna's charade? Suddenly Miranda's simple disguise did not seem remotely adequate.

Then they were at the house, up the front steps, and safely through the door into the warm, lamplit interior. Anna squeezed her arm once more before releasing it.

"Don't worry." She grinned. "He didn't give us a second glance."

Come to think of it, her companions had skillfully kept themselves between her and the street on their way out of the house. She hadn't given it any thought at the time, but it would have mostly shielded her from any observer.

"So there is still someone watching, even though Lucy and . . . and Andrew are gone?"

If Anna noticed Miranda's stumble over the name, she gave no sign. "There may be some rationale behind it," she said. "Or perhaps they're just halfheartedly attempting to be thorough. I can tell you with certainty that no one followed us after we left the house. Nevertheless, perhaps one of us should stay with you in your room tonight, if you don't mind."

Miranda nodded agreement. As they went their separate ways to dress for tea, she reflected that there had been nothing halfhearted about last night. She wondered how long they'd all have to wait until the next attack, and whether Andrew and Lucy might not have had to wait at all.

Andrew sank gratefully into the welcoming leather of the armchair. He'd seen Lucy safely back to Kestrel House before seeking the refuge of his club. It was a useful place to hide out occasionally—no one asked questions, and the staff was paid well for their complete ignorance about its members. The lighting was comfortably dim, and the loudest sounds in the room came from a fellow across the room fluttering the pages of a newspaper. Andrew's chair sat in a corner close to the fireplace, and the fire was just warm enough to combat the increasing chill of the damp evening. It had begun to rain again just as he arrived.

Andrew closed his eyes briefly. At the moment he simply wanted to enjoy the quiet for a little while. Lucy and he had performed their task well, and Miranda was as safe for the evening in the company of his extensive family as she would be with him.

Probably safer, he reflected sourly.

He winced internally, for the hundredth time that day, at the thought of his performance last night. He'd become so caught up in his pathetic personal crisis that he'd let down his guard against the very physical threat to Miranda. He didn't know which was worse: that he'd made such a botch job of protecting her, or that she knew he'd been neglecting his duty.

He desperately wanted to recover both her trust and his own crumpled self-assurance. This purgatory of old and new guilt was going to either drive him crazy or get him killed, if not both.

But the only way out of it was to tell Miranda everything, which was not only against his orders but would probably drive her away from him. This business of hiding his feelings for her was nearly intolerable, but the thought of never seeing her again was even worse.

He'd had the occasional dalliance over the years, but he'd always been aware that physical and emotional intimacies were often emphatically unrelated. His brother Court seemed to have stumbled on the perfect combination of the two with Hannah, but Andrew had been only a boy when Hannah and Court came together. He was still mystified by the process of their falling in love, especially with the problems they'd had between them. How had they contrived for love to happen to both of them simultaneously?

And what the hell was he supposed to do when being in love simply wasn't a reasonable course of action? So far his attempts to stop it had been miserably unsuccessful. Every time he thought he had his feelings under control, Miranda would laugh, or smile, or simply look at him, and he would disintegrate.

And his physical attraction was almost harder to control than the emotional one. He wanted. He simply never stopped *wanting*. That was the most dangerously maddening, hard-to-control part of this onrushing debacle. If he lost control—

Andrew slowly relaxed fists he hadn't realized were tightly bunched, and felt the combined weight of moderate injury, a sleepless night, and a full day's activity begin to settle on him. It was an immeasurable relief to sit peacefully for just a few moments, listening to the patter of rain against the window glass. It felt like the eye of the storm: eerie stillness amid a chaotic bluster of activity.

He wasn't aware of falling asleep, but he startled awake at some small noise, real or imagined. He was perfectly alert in an instant, nerves tingling as he reoriented himself to where he was. A glance at his pocket watch confirmed that he was late for supper, and he headed out in search of a cab. He felt vaguely nauseated from lack of sleep, but Harriet would scold if he missed the meal entirely.

Harriet had acquired far too many governesslike habits during her stint masquerading as a governess. She had gotten so far into the role that she'd come to deeply love her charge, Lord Martin's daughter, Patricia, who was now away at boarding school. She'd also fallen in love with Martin Kestrel, the man she was assigned to protect. How well Andrew now understood the predicament she'd gotten herself into. At least Kestrel had returned her love, and all was now well. It was a good thing that she would soon have a child of her own to practice her maternal skills on.

Harriet had been remarkably reticent last night, he reflected sourly. He must have been a pathetic sight indeed, for her to treat him so gently.

And Miranda . . . He had no idea what she must

think of him at this point. Lucy had said that Miranda might spend the afternoon with the rest of his nieces, and only God knew what they might have told her.

Chapter 18

Miranda was more frustrated than amused at the irony that, since deciding she *wanted* to talk to MacLeod in private, she had not been near him without at least five other people in close proximity.

He had not returned with Lucy, only reappearing hours later, when everyone had just finished eating. He greeted his family politely, apologized for being late, and obediently disappeared downstairs when Harriet told him to go get something to eat.

Miranda had found dinner quite pleasant, despite her mild anxiety about her fiancé. The MacLeods were all intelligent and entertaining companions, and skillfully included her in their conversation. It was her first chance to get to know Sir Ian Court and Hannah MacLeod, progenitors of the family business.

Court was Andrew's brother and patriarch of the clan, but it was Hannah who had the blood connection to the infamous Aunt Phoebe. Miranda did notice that the conversation was always subtly steered—by various family members—away from matters of intelligence work. That was understandable, though. For all their easy acceptance of her, she was still an unknown quantity in most ways.

Andrew rejoined them not long after they had all settled in the drawing room after dinner. Miranda was painfully aware of him as his nieces took turns reading from Sara's copy of *Jane Eyre*. Everyone else—Court and Hannah, Harriet and Martin, even the handsome young twins Gabriel and Michael—sat around the room in quiet enjoyment.

Andrew alone seemed restless, picking absently at the bandages on his hand. She caught him looking at her once, but he turned away immediately, a quick flush rising from his collar to his hairline. Miranda felt her own pulse quicken in response, and marveled again at the idiocy of their relationship, even as she struggled to focus on the sounds of Brontë's smooth prose. That wasn't much help, though, because of course Jane was tragically in love with the unattainable Mr. Rochester.

Desperate for a distraction, Miranda turned to observe Court and Hannah where they sat together on a low settee. They both seemed completely at ease, content to sit among their children and listen to a good story. How had they managed to produce this astonishing collection of people?

Miranda had never given much thought to having children; even when she had planned to marry poor Malcolm the issue had rarely emerged from the back of her mind. The question of how one could fashion a coherent and responsible adult from the traditional squalling infant was more than she felt able to contemplate at the moment. She was still struggling with the mechanics of reconciling two existing adult personalities.

Unaware of Miranda's scrutiny, Court MacLeod reached over to his wife's hand and gently entwined his fingers with hers. She smiled in response, and leaned her small, tidy head briefly against his shoulder.

For no discernible reason, these subtle gestures of affection brought a lump to Miranda's throat. She clenched her teeth and looked back at Andrew. He was watching Harriet read now, his brother's daughter, not much younger than he and glowing with the promise of the next generation inside her. He looked tired, Miranda thought, and tried unsuccessfully to dredge up her righteous anger against him. At the moment she felt merely confused, and hurt, and desperately in need of his comforting hand in hers.

When Harriet reached the end of a chapter and declared that it was late and past time they all go to sleep, Miranda thought she might have the chance to speak with Andrew alone. But he avoided her gaze and left, speaking in low tones with Court and Hannah. Miranda felt her jaw clench again, and deliberately relaxed before she responded to Michael's—or was it Gabriel's?— polite good night. Then she set her mouth in a grim line and resolved again to corner MacLeod the next day, whether he liked it or not.

Andrew frowned as, for the dozenth time, he checked to see that the library windows were securely shut. The house was asleep—he could hear the ticking of the ornate grandfather clock in the front hall. He shut the library door behind him and padded silently past Miranda's rooms again.

He knew he was being foolish. He was ruefully aware that part of him wanted to make up for last night's debacle with extra vigilance tonight. But life didn't work that way; the damage was done, and he was damned lucky it hadn't been any worse. The shallower cuts on his hand were itching abominably, and pacing through the quiet house was not helping to distract him.

He was still staring at Miranda's door. Anna was comfortably established on a cot in the bedroom, and she was probably aware of his presence. In fact, she was probably rolling her eyes at him at this very moment. He sighed and turned toward his own rooms, trailing his fingers lightly across the smooth wood of Miranda's door. He knew he ought to get some sleep. He would do no one any good by being overtired tomorrow.

Miranda set her teacup down with a clatter and a barely suppressed sigh of frustration. Harriet glanced at her from the other side of the tea service, but returned without comment to listen to Anna's speculation about some upcoming cabinet appointments.

The whole family was present, except for Court, who had yet to return from some errand or other; and Andrew, who was simply absent. There were several animated discussions occurring simultaneously, and periodically someone would try to include Miranda in one of them. But she found it difficult to concentrate on any one topic, and her companions seemed to sense and accept her disinterest, because they mostly left her alone.

Miranda wondered if Andrew had an opinion on such mundane political concerns as the appointment of cabinet ministers. If he'd had the courtesy to show up for tea, she could have asked him. But he had disappeared. Again.

The day had passed in a blur of activity in preparation for the ball, and every time Miranda had turned around, Andrew MacLeod seemed to be just leaving the room. And now here it was, nearly evening, and she had never quite contrived the opportunity to take him aside privately.

She'd been intermittently aware of him all day, was even beginning to wonder if he was deliberately checking in on her. But he hadn't spoken to her, and the time never seemed right for a confrontation—she certainly had no desire for this particular scene to be played out in front of a large audience of MacLeods.

How would she even broach the subject to begin with? *I know you've been lying to me, in addition to all the lies that you knew that I knew about . . .*

And now guests would be arriving in a few hours, and she still needed to bathe and dress. Well, this was an engagement party, after all. At least he wouldn't be able to evade her while they were dancing.

Abruptly the drawing room door opened a crack, and her dancing partner appeared, hesitantly, around it.

"His Grace deigns to join us!" Harriet observed dryly. "Anna, offer Uncle Andrew a sandwich."

"I . . . I beg your pardon," Andrew said. "May I borrow Lady Miranda?" He turned toward her. "Miranda? It's a bit urgent."

Miranda excused herself with perfect politeness and joined him in the hallway, carefully shutting the door behind her. He turned to lead the way up the stairs, but she grabbed at his sleeve, forcing him to stop.

"What are you playing at?" she demanded. "I've been trying to talk to you for two days, and you've done nothing but run away and hide. And *now* you decide to speak with me?"

His eyes widened. "I'm sorry, I don't . . . I have . . ."

She waited expectantly, wondering if she'd already doomed this conversation to end in disaster. But could she really hope for anything else? Their companionship over the last couple of days had been distinctly uncomfortable.

Andrew finally collected a few of his wits and repeated, "I'm sorry. Whatever you want to talk about, of course I want to hear—" *I may dread it, but I ought to hear it anyway*—"but Court has just come back. He says he has news from Phoebe."

Miranda's hand still rested on his sleeve, so he took it and led her up the stairs as he continued. "We've got to hear what he has to say before the guests start to arrive."

The sensation of Miranda's hand in his overwhelmed all his other senses on the short journey to the sitting room where his brother waited. It felt as though he had a direct link to her through the warm, smooth skin of her palm. He could feel her knuckles with his thumb, and allowed himself to remember, fleetingly, the gentle caress of her hand on his face.

He reluctantly released his grip as they entered the room and sat down. Seated behind an ornate writing desk, Court was shuffling papers, which was his way of organizing his thoughts, even when they weren't written down. Court's broad frame and wide shoulders dwarfed the feminine size of the gilded desk. His blunt-fingered soldier's hands would look more natural holding a saber or a rifle than engaged in paperwork. Andrew thought that the silver mingled with his brother's dark blond hair seemed a bit thicker at his temples than he remembered. It certainly added to his air of distinguished gravity.

"Thank you for joining us, Lady Miranda," Court began. "What we are discussing obviously concerns you intimately, but of course you understand that otherwise it must remain completely confidential."

Except for you and a dozen other MacLeods, Miranda thought.

Andrew was not as polite. "Is that why Phoebe Gale talked to you and not directly to me?" he asked. "You are not *officially* part of the service anymore," he reminded his brother.

Court smiled. "She claimed you'd be too busy

for the next few days to come see her personally. I rather think she wanted to avoid telling you her news face-to-face."

Andrew snorted.

Miranda tried to imagine Lady Phoebe *hiding* from anything, and said distractedly, "Of course I understand the delicacy of the situation. Please do go on."

Court took a deep breath and dropped his news like a boulder into a calm lake. "She's had a short list of suspects for your traitor for two months."

Miranda heard herself say, inanely, "What?"

Andrew just stared for a moment, then forced his thoughts into order, and asked the more important question: "Who?"

"First, it's important to remember that there's no more evidence for one of these than the others, so don't go jumping to conclusions," Court warned.

"I haven't lost all capacity for rational thought, despite what Phoebe may have told you," Andrew snapped.

Court gave a small shrug. "Very well," he said. "Then in no particular order, they are Cecil Hartwell, Sir Simon Lester, and Ambassador Montessori."

"Cecil?" Miranda asked incredulously.

At the same moment Andrew said, "Lester!" That lout had had his eye on Miranda all week.

Andrew thought it would be extremely gratifying if Lester turned out to be the villain.

Then his brain took over again. "Montessori is Italian," he pointed out. "We were told the traitor worked for the foreign office."

"Hartwell and Lester don't, either. You were misinformed."

"So why them? And *why*, in the name of Saint Margaret, was I not kept informed?"

Court, an ordained minister of the kirk, frowned at Andrew's use of such a Papist declaration, but let it go. "To answer the second question first, officially your job now is to protect Lady Miranda, not pursue the traitor. Unofficially, I think the higher-ups have only recently acquired some real evidence, no matter how long Aunt Phoebe says she's had her suspicions."

"And the evidence?"

"I don't know all of it. It's widely known that Hartwell is roaringly in debt and his legal actions against his cousin are failing." Miranda nodded at this, and Court continued. "Aunt Phoebe knows he was in Europe, thinks he might have followed you to Italy, my lady, and speculates that he undertook the political intrigue to finance the trip.

"As for Lester, he's been under the eye of the home office for some time, but now he's up for a cabinet position, and the consensus is that he wouldn't balk at selling secrets or killing someone he considers an obstacle on his road to power."

"And an inconvenient woman tourist able to identify him as a traitor would certainly qualify as an obstacle," Miranda observed. Then she reddened. "Oh, dear," she said. "I think I told him he looked familiar, when we spoke after my lecture. I was only being polite, but if it *is* him, if he thinks I saw him . . ."

"And Dodgson came later that night," Andrew finished.

Court nodded grimly, leaning forward again as he warmed to his topic. "It's a possibility. But I understand the ambassador also attended the lecture. And Montessori, it seems, has an embarrassingly expensive mistress to support and some very helpful friends in our foreign office."

"Not much to choose among them, is there?" Andrew grumbled.

So much new information all at once! He took off his glasses and polished the lenses as his brain furiously sorted through all the new data, comparing them to other bits of knowledge and slotting them in where they fit. He had yet to meet Miranda's Cousin Cecil, but the other two men had both turned up recently.

Andrew was determined not to let himself be biased by the fact that he'd found the Montessoris to be pleasant and Sir Simon Lester repugnant.

Pleasant people had turned out to be villains before now. He wondered if in this case Montessori would technically be a traitor to the Italian government, or if perhaps his superiors there would be grateful for whatever secrets he stole from Britain. Or perhaps he was a freelance agent, selling information to the highest bidder.

Another thought occurred to him. "So why all the fuss over Miranda now?" he asked. "Why didn't our man try to kill her months ago?"

"Aunt Phoebe speculates that it just wasn't worth the trouble before," Court said. "It was hearing rumors of both Cecil's looming debts and Sir Simon's possible cabinet appointment, as well as Lady Miranda's return to semipublic life, that prompted her to send you along to Passfair. Apparently there are some very important people who are rather glad of these assassination attempts."

Andrew started to protest angrily, but Miranda spoke over him. "Of course. Without these attacks we'd have no earthly way of pursuing the traitor."

"We'd be at a dead end," Court agreed.

"Well said, Court," Andrew growled. "It'll be terribly comforting for Miranda when she finds herself dead one of these days."

"Lady Miranda agreed to help us," Court pointed out sharply.

"She hardly had a choice! And you'd have kept

her in the dark if she hadn't gone to Phoebe and forced your hand."

Court's voice dropped to a menacing rumble. "As you pointed out, Hannah and I are *officially* retired. I had very little to do with this case until I received a certain engagement notice. And from what I hear, you weren't running to enlighten her yourself."

Andrew stood abruptly, nearly tipping his chair over backward. Court rose more slowly, until they were nose-to-nose across the tiny desk, the older brother's face a slightly more thickset, fairer version of the MacLeod family features.

"The point is," Andrew ground out slowly, "she's a civilian in danger. We can't put her out like a lamb for the slaughter."

The tension between the brothers was palpable, like static electricity. Miranda was desperately curious to hear more, since they seemed to have forgotten her presence. But she was afraid they might actually come to blows, and they had a meeting to finish.

"Really, it's all right," she interjected. Andrew and Court both turned to her, startled, and she refrained from smiling at their twin expressions of mingled surprise and chagrin. She continued speaking calmly as they resumed their seats. "I can't say I like it, but I'm starting to get used to it.

And tonight we can narrow our focus to these three men, rather than casting about randomly among all the guests."

Court seemed both pleased and relieved as he resumed talking about the ball. He knew as well as she did that as much as the two of them might argue around her, it was ultimately her choice whether they continued their operation.

At first Andrew sulked silently. Miranda could almost hear the gears clicking over furiously in his brain, trying to formulate an argument that would convince them to abandon the whole business.

But she and Court were in the right, and she sensed the tiny settling of Andrew's shoulders as he finally accepted it. He joined in the conversation shortly after that, the brothers resuming their camaraderie as if they had never argued.

Court outlined his plan for keeping their suspects under surveillance all evening. It involved the discreet circulation of his many offspring throughout the house, and the ways Miranda should communicate with them if necessary.

At that point there was a knock on the door, followed quickly by a smiling Harriet. "When you three are done with your plotting," she said, "don't forget that Lady Miranda still has her engagement ball to prepare for."

Court consulted his pocket watch and nodded.

"We're just about finished here. Would you let the family and household staff know we'll have a briefing in the drawing room in twenty minutes?"

Harriet nodded and disappeared. Andrew muttered something that might have been "Friends, Romans, countrymen . . ." and started to rise, but Court stopped him.

"Actually, I'd like to speak to you for a moment alone, please." He turned to Miranda to say, "Thank you again, my lady, for all your help. Good luck this evening." And with that, she was dismissed.

She frowned, but left obediently. Andrew watched her go, wondering what it was she'd so urgently wanted to talk to him about.

Chapter 19

Court interrupted his thoughts by sitting down in the chair Miranda had just vacated. "I apologize for what I said earlier. You look rather horrid," he said conversationally.

"It's been . . . trying," Andrew admitted.

"Phoebe says you can't cope with being in love."

"Phoebe Gale is an interfering old besom," Andrew snapped.

He scowled. That had come out with more venom than he'd intended. He'd always tried to keep his dislike of Hannah's beloved aunt somewhat in check.

Court quirked an amused eyebrow. "A statement uttered by few and refuted by none," he said. "But she can also be quite perceptive. And she is kinder than you believe, as long as kindness doesn't interfere with protecting queen and country." He paused and leaned forward, hands clasped between his knees. "I only bring it up, you see, because we've all been a bit worried about you. Even Phoebe, cold-hearted as she frequently is. It might be helpful to talk about it."

"There's nothing to talk about," Andrew said firmly.

Court sat back. "I see," he said. "I'm sorry. I had hoped, once this was all over . . ." He paused, then started again. "Everyone thinks she's delightful, Andrew." He smiled a little, clearly hoping the conversation might still go somewhere.

Andrew sighed. His brother had practically raised him, and Court's attitude still sometimes teetered toward the fatherly. Generally Andrew didn't mind, but right now it was just tiresome. He didn't feel like being coddled.

"Your concern is touching," he said acidly. "You and Lady Phoebe and Miranda's aunt Sibelle should set up shop together as matchmakers. You'd terrorize the countryside."

"Ah, but we'd manage results, and results matter, in defense of the country, or in matters of the heart. You and Lady Miranda might make a fine match, you know," Court added. He sounded like the kindly minister he was when he added, "Two weary hearts could heal each other, lad."

"So Harriet has told me."

"So I am telling you. You should listen to me, brother."

"Because you found your happily-ever-after? You deserved it, man!"

"As do you. You've always been too hard on yourself. Think of the woman if you won't think of yourself. It could be that she wants and needs you. If you want to protect her properly—"

"Enough."

Andrew stood and looked down at his brother, who didn't move. The suggestion was utterly ridiculous. And utterly catastrophic, if he allowed himself even for a moment the hope that such things could be true.

He needed this conversation to end. "Reprimand me if you like for my behavior the other night," he growled, "but don't preach a sermon just now. If you've nothing useful to add, I should really go get ready for my engagement party."

"Very well," Court said. He rose and returned to the position behind his desk, standing with his big hands splayed across its delicately gilded surface. The abrupt chill in his voice made it clear that the time for fraternal sympathy was over. "You know that your behavior two nights ago was inexcusable. After tonight, your public role in this operation will be finished and you may consider yourself relieved of duty. You will return tomorrow to Skye Court, and Anna will take over protecting Lady Miranda until things here are completely resolved."

Andrew felt his mouth fall open, and snapped it shut. He hadn't expected this. And yet how could he not? He'd left Court no choice, and it was too late now for apologies and explanations. Besides, Court wasn't the person to whom he owed those things.

Court had returned to shuffling papers, though Andrew knew the nonverbal dismissal was only a postponement of their argument.

He retreated to his own rooms, feelings of disorientation resolving quickly into a surprising sense of clarity. Now that he was confronted with the order to leave Miranda behind, he knew he could never obey it. He had no choice. Somehow he would have to catch the traitor here, tonight, so that tomorrow he would be free to tell Miranda everything.

It would be better to let her reject him, aware of the truth about himself and her beloved Dante, than to abandon her in ignorance again.

Miranda felt a brief twinge of guilt as she surveyed the colorful crowd before her. After all, she'd invited them here under false pretenses.

On the other hand, most of the guests were far

more interested in impressing one another than they were in whether Miranda Hartwell might be getting married. There were many significant glances at her fiancé and his spectacular bruises, and gleeful discussions of his physical prowess. But Miranda knew that if they hadn't come here tonight, they'd have happily gone to some other event. That was the nature of the Season in London.

And the MacLeods, who arguably had an interest in her hypothetical nuptials, seemed to be enjoying themselves regardless. Gabriel and Michael were tall, handsome young men, and were flirting shamelessly. Harriet and Martin were circulating independently through the crowd like the professional diplomats they were. She knew that Lucy, Anna, Sara, and Beatrice were all somewhere about as well, but she couldn't see them from where she stood among the crowds of cheerful, chatting people. The guests laughed, and twirled, and glittered, and had no idea that matters of international politics were being played out under their very distinguished noses.

I used to know these people, Miranda thought. A few years ago she'd been one of them. Not shopping for a spouse like some, but enjoying the trivialities of the social season every now and then nonetheless. Now she felt detached, awkward. She wasn't up on the latest gossip or in on the latest jokes. And she had trouble rousing any interest in either.

Someone pressed another glass of punch into her hand. She smiled, and half of her brain produced small talk while the other half contemplated poison. People kept graciously offering her food and drinks, but she didn't feel safe consuming any of it. They were hoping to flush out her would-be murderer, after all. She mimed taking a sip from her glass, and discreetly deposited the whole thing behind a china vase on the mantel. She'd already put one sandwich in a potted plant and two other drinks behind the large bronze multiarmed statue of an Indian god on the other side of the room.

Andrew was mostly silent by her side, and occasionally wandered off to consult with another MacLeod. If possible, he seemed even broodier than usual, though, oddly, also more physical. He stood very close to her, and she often felt the backs of his fingers brush against her own. Miranda wondered what Court had said to him after she left their little meeting.

It was during one of Andrew's brief absences that Miranda perceived a head of sleek black hair making its way toward her through the crowd. Sir Simon.

"How perfectly charming to see you again, Lady Miranda." He beamed, bending over her hand before presenting her with the inevitable glass of punch.

With his neatly trimmed mustache and his exquisitely tailored evening coat, he seemed—he might *be*, Miranda reminded herself—perfectly harmless.

"Charming," she agreed vacuously. How to make small talk with someone who might want to murder you?

"Congratulations and all that. Splendid party, splendid food," he continued cheerfully.

"Thank you," she replied, politely pretending to sip from her glass. She licked her lips afterward, catching a faintly sharp taste mixed with the fruity sweetness. She dredged her brain for information from their conversation at the lecture. "And how is your mother?"

"Oh, she's well, very well."

Was it her imagination, or was he gazing at her with more intensity than their exchange warranted? Or was it simply the natural obsequiousness of an up-and-coming politician? This whole business was making her suspicious of everyone and everything.

Andrew chose that moment to return from his perambulations. He casually took the glass from Miranda's hand and slid his left arm possessively around her waist. She leaned into him almost without thinking. She could feel the heat of him through the boning and fabric of her dress, and the layers of cloth between them suddenly seemed stifling.

"Sir Simon, isn't it? Good of you to come," Andrew said, shaking hands heartily. Andrew MacLeod as scholar and social misfit in full force.

Sir Simon's smile remained cemented in place. He said he'd heard about the attempted robbery at Kestrel House, and announced that the criminal classes were getting out of hand.

Andrew replied, but Miranda found it difficult to concentrate on his words. His thumb was very slowly rubbing up and down her back, just at the base of her rib cage.

She suppressed a shiver of pleasure, and watched with relief as Sir Simon melted back into the crowd.

"Well, he's not *acting* very guilty," she said.

"You need a conscience to feel guilty," Andrew replied sourly. He toasted her briefly with her punch glass. "You didn't drink any of this, did you?"

"Of course not. You can put it in the coal scuttle or somewhere."

He turned to look behind them, his arm dropping from her side. Her skin tingled in the void where his touch had been.

"I should give it to Lucy," he said, continuing to scan the room vaguely.

"But I rather like Lucy," she protested.

That earned her a brief smile. "Lucy adores poisons," he explained. "She'll pour a noxious potion in this glass and tell us whether there's anything in it besides the punch."

"Yet another useful MacLeod skill."

"Hard evidence is quite useful, yes. I don't suppose Ambassador Montessori has offered you anything to drink this evening?"

"It's in the piano bench."

"Excellent."

"But other than that he seems to be avoiding me."

"Hah. I spoke to him earlier. Already quite drunk, and his wife was trying to convince him to leave."

"That's promisingly suspicious."

"Could be," he agreed.

"There's Lucy," Miranda said, spotting the other woman over by the west doors. She was talking to Sir Simon, who looked somewhat alarmed. "She seems to have made a conquest."

"She's probably quizzing him on top-secret cabinet politics. Better leave her to it."

At that moment Harriet appeared on the dais with the musicians, clapping her hands to get everyone's attention. She thanked the guests for attending, formally presented Andrew and Lady Miranda, and invited them to take the first dance.

Miranda froze for an instant. Harriet's beaming

introduction brought home once again the magnitude of the deception they had created. For a moment Miranda had an absurd impulse to march up to the front of the room and explain everything. The charade was becoming too complicated: she wasn't marrying MacLeod, or Dante . . . but suddenly she couldn't imagine dissolving their engagement, either.

She didn't *not* want to get married.

Which was ridiculous, she knew, because she was angry with him and didn't know if she could trust him and now everyone was staring at them, waiting for them to start the dancing.

She reached across to grab Andrew's unbandaged right hand and pulled him out onto the parquet, smiling defiantly at all the staring faces around them. He hurriedly set her glass down and followed.

Then the music started.

Sometimes, in the months after her return to England, she had imagined this very scene. Not the fear or the hidden sandwiches, of course. But she had occasionally allowed herself the fantasy of dancing again in Dante's arms.

To her surprise, the reality was even better than the daydream. Andrew was a solid, vibrant, perplexing presence whom she perceived now with both sight and knowledge greater than she'd had a year ago. His gaze wandered the room more often than it met hers, no doubt communing with her other bodyguards. But his touch on her hand was light and sure, and his occasional fleeting grip on her waist made her want to linger in his embrace. Despite his claims of social ignorance, he was an elegant dancer. Lithe, quick, and confident, his movements were those of an athlete, if not a musician.

Miranda was still aware of feeling frustrated and confused, but the simple physical joy of the dancing overrode her more intellectual concerns. This was her party, however bizarre the circumstances, and she began to enjoy herself despite everything.

Over time, her partner gradually loosened up as well. Once, during a breathlessly fast reel, Andrew grinned at her with such boyish enthusiasm that she knew he'd temporarily forgotten why they were there. She grinned recklessly back.

By the end of that dance, Miranda had almost convinced herself to drag Andrew upstairs then and there for a long . . . talk. They needed to talk. But Court came to claim her for the next dance, and the moment passed. He and Andrew exchanged a cool look as she passed from one brother to the other, but neither offered her an explanation.

Court did inform her that the guests who'd arrived so far were only those they'd invited; if there were any more hired assassins about, they weren't easily identified.

"Very comforting," Miranda muttered.

Past Court's rather broad shoulder, she saw Andrew finally catch hold of Lucy. He gestured, and she nodded and quickly left the room. Apparently she was going to get a head start on her chemical testing. Miranda was grateful, though she doubted anything would come of it. Her enemy had so far put some effort into avoiding any public attacks. He'd chosen quiet, isolated times and places to strike at her. Andrew had been the only other person present on both occasions, while tonight she was surrounded by a hundred highly respected witnesses. Hardly the most convenient environment for murder.

"Miranda," a reedy voice drawled in her ear.

She stumbled to a halt as the dance came to an end. Court gave her an inquiring look, but she ignored him and spun to face the gratingly familiar man who'd addressed her.

Chapter 20

❦

"Congratu-bloody-lations," Cecil Hartwell, Baron DuVrai, continued.

His voice rang out clearly in the brief silence between songs, but the musicians quickly launched into their next piece. The other guests pretended to stop listening eagerly, though gasps and whispers about the man's use of vulgarity sped through the room.

"Cecil," she acknowledged warily.

He looked Court up and down with a sneer. "I say, Miranda, you really have gotten desperate to keep my money from me. Whoever heard of marrying a *secretary*?"

Miranda felt a brief wave of dizziness and nausea as she responded automatically, "It's not your money, Cecil." *I am* not *going to faint*, she thought. *Not now. I haven't had a headache all week!* She didn't have one now, but the dizziness was ominous. Out loud she continued, "And you have just insulted Sir Ian Court MacLeod, not my Mr. MacLeod. Well done."

"Well, one Scot's much like another, I expect. But I must say—MacLeod, is it?—you might be almost civilized, wearing trousers and all."

"Aye," Court drawled. "A pity the same canna be said of yourself."

Miranda heard a snigger from somewhere in the crowd. Cecil must have heard it, too, because he scowled and changed tack. "So where is the lucky gold digger himself? I want to meet my future cousin-in-law."

Andrew had heard Cecil's initial greeting and was elbowing his way through the crowd around the dance floor, trying to reach Miranda's side. He couldn't hear her at the moment, with the music and babble drowning out their conversation. But Court had a dangerous look on his face, and Miranda wasn't much better. She looked furious, and far too pale.

"Mr. MacLeod!"

The voice came from behind him, and Andrew spun to face it, furious at the interruption.

It was the butler, looking uncharacteristically flustered.

"There's a man here claiming to be a Mr. Statler,

sir," he explained, drawing Andrew delicately away from the crowd and toward the door. "He says he won't speak to anyone but you. He's waiting in the library."

Andrew thought quickly. It was just conceivable that the man who'd hired Miranda's would-be killer had developed a genuine desire to talk to him. It was even possible that he had coincidentally chosen tonight to make his overture. But it was also possible that Court might burst into song and start juggling teacups, and Andrew wasn't about to place any wagers on that.

Which meant that Statler—or whoever was in the library—was probably waiting to attack him. Or had come simply to create a diversion while the architect of the scenario made another attempt on Miranda.

He was tempted to simply ignore the situation, but he couldn't risk it. Statler might have something useful to say—whether or not he had planned to say it.

"He may be here just to get me away from Lady Miranda," Andrew told the butler. "Inform my brother and Lady Harriet. Whatever's going to happen, it may be soon." The man nodded and slipped away, invisible as only servants could be.

Andrew drew that same casual inconspicuousness around himself like a cloak. He left the ball-room with the body language of an uninteresting person with an uninteresting destination. He thought perhaps three people had noticed him go, all of them family.

He made his way to the library, mentally preparing himself for the task ahead. The man would probably have to be physically subdued, and then interrogated. Andrew carefully, laboriously started to gather that core of ice within himself that would allow him to do the job. It would seal off the inconvenient, weak, nagging, doubting parts of his mind; silence them long enough for him to complete his task.

Hard to believe that barely fifteen minutes ago he'd been *dancing*. He never danced. It was a form of expression he found difficult to control, and that made it dangerous. He was much more comfortable with the everyday dangers of spying and killing.

He paused, breath held briefly, at the thick oak doors of the library. Lamplight leaked through the microscopic crack between them. He couldn't hear or see any movement inside, but that wasn't really surprising. The man might be waiting for him with a knife, or a pistol, or he might not be there at all. The walls of the room were lined with bookshelves; the only decent cover within the room would be the single large writing desk toward the northern wall.

If I were staging an ambush, he reflected, *I'd lock one of these doors and hide behind the other one.*

Andrew took one deep, silent breath. Cheerful sounds from the ballroom wafted through the house, but his immediate surroundings remained deadly quiet.

He fished his pistol out of its cleverly tailored holster and shifted it to his left hand. He crouched slightly so as not to enter the room with his head at its usual height, and prepared to open the right-hand library door. Then in one powerful burst of movement, he turned the knob, shouldered the heavy door open so that it slammed all the way to the wall, and swung around to his left to cover the rest of the room.

Nothing happened.

Andrew always felt vaguely foolish at times like this, being over-prepared for such mundane activities as entering a library. But being prepared had saved his life more times than he cared to think about, so he wasn't going to stop.

The dead man in the chair apparently hadn't been prepared for what came to him.

Andrew did a quick circuit of the room to make sure the killer wasn't still lurking. He found nothing behind the door as he closed it, except a slight dent in the wall. He would like to have locked both doors, but the key was gone.

He turned his attention to the body. As dead

bodies went it was fairly tidy, with no gaping wounds or pooling blood. Just some flecks of bloody spittle, and an agonized rictus. Andrew hadn't had much exposure to natural death, and he wondered if the results of a seizure or nerve attack would look like this.

Even if they did, though, he knew instinctively that this man had not innocently wandered into Kestrel House just to die of natural causes. He needed to fetch Lucy down here at once. All their talk and precautions about poisons had only been standard procedure, until now.

The dead man had nothing in his shabby pockets to confirm or deny that he was the infamous Mr. Statler, though the simple fact of his death made it seem likely. The traitor didn't like live witnesses to his identity. Statler did have a pistol, and, deep inside one waistcoat pocket, a tiny screw of paper with "Andrew MacLeod" scrawled on it.

Andrew wondered if the man was meant to have killed him before neatly expiring. Like a poorly laid fuse, Statler had fizzled out before fulfilling his purpose. But he'd still taken with him all knowledge of his employer, who was most likely also his murderer.

There were clues here: the poison, the gun, even the incongruously new shoes on Statler's feet might eventually lead to finding the man they sought. But all of that would take time, which Andrew absolutely did not have.

It was maddening.

He was more convinced than ever that they'd been going about everything wrong. Phoebe Gale's misplaced sense of discretion had cost them weeks of wasted energy and had needlessly endangered Miranda. Ten minutes in an interrogation room with each suspect, and Andrew knew he'd have some answers.

Politics, he thought disgustedly. *Can't go around harassing innocent peers and politicians just because there's a dangerous traitor on the loose.* The traitor's very existence was probably a great embarrassment to somebody or other.

He abandoned the library, wishing again that he could secure the doors without wasting time with picklocks. He'd have to trust that no guests would develop a sudden yen for literature.

He reentered the bright chaos of the ballroom and began searching for Miranda. He saw Cecil, chatting up a young thing in an emerald gown. Michael and Gabriel seemed to be observing him, and Anna was dancing competently with Simon Lester. The Montessoris were nearby, standing in a corner looking rather miserable. And there were Court and Hannah, mostly observing young Sara, who seemed to be enjoying herself.

But Miranda, with her stunning midnight-blue

ball gown, pale skin, and silver-streaked raven hair, was nowhere to be seen.

Where was she? Andrew fought down an irrational panic as he searched the crowd again. Harriet and Martin, dancing. Neighbors, acquaintances, family, but no sign of the one person he wanted. Needed, he corrected himself reluctantly.

But it was a large house: she might have stepped out of the crowded party for a few minutes. Even if that was true, though, he wasn't about to sit around and wait for her to come back.

He made his way quickly over to his brother. "Where is she?" he demanded. He hated that he sounded out of breath.

Court glanced at him coolly—this afternoon's argument was far from forgotten. "Lady Miranda stepped out for a moment. Bea is with her. It's none of your concern now."

That should have satisfied him, but he felt compelled to seek her out, to be near her. The evening was taking on a surreal quality: first the dancing, then the body, and all of their suspects within reach but agonizingly untouchable. He needed the reassuring stability of Miranda's presence. When he was with her, the world somehow always seemed a more comprehensible place.

He would try looking in her rooms first. He was three strides beyond where Harriet and Martin were dancing when he remembered, went back to them, and said, "There's a dead body in the library. You might want to have someone keep an eye on it."

He left them trying to decide what question to ask him first, and broke free of the ballroom once again.

He took the side stairs three at a time and came to a halt next to his niece. Beatrice looked amazingly like a younger version of Hannah. At the moment the girl was trying to hide a very relieved expression.

"Did Da send you up?" she asked in a rush. "She said she'd be right out, but it sounds like she's sick and she says she doesn't want me to come inside." She was twisting an ornamental fan between her hands so that the feathers were completely flattened.

Andrew once again silently cursed the circumstances that had led to this ill-conceived, hastily thrown-together operation. As the family cryptographer, Bea should not have to do guard duty with all of her backup halfway across the house.

But it wasn't just the circumstances. It was his responsibility. His bad decisions had led to this point as much as anything.

And here he was brooding about it instead of acting. He knocked quickly on the door. "Miranda?"

"Go away." The command from within was faint, but firm.

"Are you ill? It may be poison after all. There's a dead man in the library." Not a very clear explanation, he thought, but he heard Beatrice give a small gasp of alarm.

There was a slow shuffling sound inside the room, and then the turn of a key and more movement. When nothing else happened, he turned the knob and stepped into the darkened room.

The light from the hallway showed that Miranda had gone back to the bed and curled on her side. Her eyes were closed tight.

He shut the door behind him, and stood for a moment to let his eyes adjust to the darkness. A crescent moon was just rising, but it did little to add to the meager light of the gas lamps filtering in from the street.

He moved to the bedside. "Miranda?" he ventured again.

"I thought it was another headache," she gritted. "But they haven't been like this in months."

He recognized the careful, shallow breaths of nausea, and the faint smell of bile coming from the back room. He placed a hand gently against her forehead. It was cold.

He quickly pulled the bedspread and blankets up and tucked them around her body. Her gown

was designed to expose her slim shoulders and ex-
quisite collarbones. Her skin there was cool, too,
where he brushed against it as he arranged the
blankets.

"Thank you," she whispered.

"You're welcome, *cara*," he replied. "I'll be right
back. Don't go anywhere."

Her lips quirked in a little one-sided smile. He
wished he could stay here to hold her and comfort
her, as he had so many times. But back then all he
could do was try to make her comfortable until the
worst of the pain had passed. This time there was
something else he could do.

Miranda listened as his near-silent footsteps
crossed the room, and heard the door open and
shut. Then she was alone again, and her awareness
narrowed to the discomforts of her own body. And
the memory of one little word.

She tried to hold herself perfectly still, barely
breathing. She wished now that she had eaten
more than a single biscuit at teatime. There was an
ironic advantage to having something in one's
stomach when the stomach decided to purge itself.

She clenched her teeth against another wave of
nausea, and wondered abstractly if she was dying.
She didn't *feel* as if she was dying. She felt sick and
dizzy and irritable, and her head was starting to
pound, but there was none of the terrifying weak-

ness she remembered from the first days after her injury in Italy.

But maybe that's how it would be. One moment here, the next gone. No warning, no time for dramatic good-byes. *Should I tell Andrew I love him, out loud, before it's too late?* Absurd thought. Besides, it would be selfish of her, and not do him any good at all.

She was distracted from this train of thought by the much more pressing and practical question of whether it was worth the energy to try to reach the back room again. She'd never thought, with the new plumbing systems, that she would miss chamber pots as they had back at old-fashioned Passfair Castle.

She had almost built up the resolution to try sitting up when she heard voices outside her room. The door opened and shut, allowing the light from the hallway to briefly stab through her eyelids again. Poison-induced or not, this headache was building momentum.

Lucy's voice was saying something about garlic.

"Miranda?" Andrew's voice this time.

She opened her eyes.

Lucy knelt down beside her with a heaping spoonful of black powder. "Swallow this," she said. "It'll taste like charcoal because that's what it is. It's good for absorbing any bits of arsenic you might not want."

Andrew helped her sit up and steadied her hand on the spoon as she brought it to her mouth. The charcoal did taste bad, but worse was the greasy-gritty texture between her teeth after she'd swallowed.

"Arsenic?" she asked. "How? When?" She had shared tea with the family . . .

"It must have been within the last hour or so," Lucy explained. "Uncle Andrew told me you haven't eaten anything, but did you even touch any food or drink to your lips before putting it down?"

"The punch glasses . . ." Miranda sighed ruefully. "I wanted to be polite."

"This is good," Lucy said. "You must have tasted only a tiny fraction of the intended dose. The poisoner probably spilled powder on the rim of the glass." She frowned. "I hope the bastard licks his fingers."

Andrew couldn't bring himself to chastise Lucy for her language. He felt the same way.

And they wouldn't know for certain who the bastard was until Lucy had time to test all those glasses. Or until it was discovered that Miranda hadn't died, and the killer made yet another attempt.

Court would say that after tonight it was no longer his problem.

"Court can go to blazes," he muttered. Both women looked at him sharply. He turned to Lucy and asked, "How long before Miranda recovers? Will she need more doses of charcoal?"

"Probably a few, over the next day or so," she replied. "But I'm hoping that there was such a small quantity of poison that the effects won't last too long."

"I hope so, too," Miranda agreed wryly.

She still looked pale and unwell, and she still leaned most of her weight against him as they sat together on the bed. But she was definitely conscious, and lucid, and Andrew thought her breathing was already steadier than it had been. He made a decision.

"Right," he said. "Miranda, how would you like to get away from all this?"

She raised one elegant eyebrow. "What, now?"

"Now," he confirmed. "We'll sneak away, put about word that you've taken ill, and let the MacLeod family circus take care of things here. You've done enough." He heard his voice roughen as he finished, and quickly cleared his throat. She *had* done enough; she'd been through more than enough, more than anyone could be expected to tolerate.

And if he didn't take her with him now, he might never see her again.

Lucy scowled. "I said I hope she'll recover soon. I didn't say you could take her trouncing about the countryside with impunity." She pursed her lips thoughtfully. "How are you feeling, Lady Miranda?"

Miranda shifted her weight against him, and Andrew settled his arm in a more comfortable position about her waist. He was close enough to smell the perfume in her hair, and longed to bury his face in the thick black coils.

"I'm feeling better than before," Miranda said cautiously. "Not well, but not truly awful. I wouldn't mind getting out of here."

"Then I suppose it might be better for your health for you to disappear for a while," Lucy conceded. "I suppose you'll be wanting a diversion?" She cocked her head at Andrew, and he wondered just how much Court had told the family about the intended change in the duty roster.

"Yes, please," he said meekly.

She smiled mischievously. "Well, we have plenty of material, with a dead stranger in the library and our guest of honor struck down by a *mysterious illness*." She intoned the last two words like the title of a new penny dreadful.

"I need to put on something more practical before we leave," Miranda said.

A wholly inappropriate part of Andrew's mind suggested that he should offer to help her change clothes, but he ignored it. Instead he maneuvered himself off the bed, making sure she was steady on her own.

"I'll go secure some transportation," he said. "Meet me at the servants' entrance as soon as you can."

Miranda was already explaining to Lucy which clothes she wanted as he made his way back out into the hallway. Beatrice had obviously been eavesdropping, because she grinned at him as he emerged.

So his nieces were eager to send the two of them off alone together, were they? Well, better that than have them running to tell their father. He'd deal with Court later, after this was all over.

In the meantime, he knew where he wanted to go, but not how to get there. Miranda was in no condition to ride, so it would have to be carriage. Or train. Could he trust Court not to look for them? They would certainly be traceable going by train, but it might be even worse if he tried to commandeer a hansom for such a long journey at this time of night.

He stopped in his own rooms long enough to change his jacket and collect the rest of his weapons. He had a little money, enough for train fare and some food once they arrived. The cabin in the woods near Fort William was almost as rudimentary as Dante's hut had been. But it was well built, and remote, and the anarchists who'd been using it until a few months ago were now residing in prison.

He slipped silently out the back door and went to hail a cab.

Chapter 21

❝**A** journey of a thousand leagues begins with the first step," Miranda said. It was the first time either of them had spoken for several hours. MacLeod didn't act as if he'd heard her. He kept looking out the train window of their private carriage. Though it was dark out and Miranda wondered what he was staring at.

Perhaps his own dour reflection, she supposed. The man was so handsome when he smiled. So she suspected he deliberately tried not to. She'd dozed off and on for a while, undisturbed by the raucousness of the engine or the rattling of the car on the sometimes rough tracks. And always when she woke he was looking out the window. The train sped on, and he just sat there. A small lamp mounted near the door shed a little light, highlighting the lines of his face and emphasizing his brooding expression.

Though he might pretend to be a statue, Miranda felt the need to talk to the man. Though they were together, she feared that they had never been more apart. At least if he was allowed to have his way.

"A thousand leagues," she repeated, speaking a bit louder this time. "Do you know the expression?" She was determined to get his attention, thought she didn't know why. Perhaps because breaking him out of his broods was a challenge? Though why she wanted a challenge right now she did not know. After all, the last hours—and days—had been trying. Maybe she just wanted a diversion from thinking about how harrowing her latest adventures had been.

Or perhaps she hated seeing Andrew MacLeod so very withdrawn.

"A thousand leagues," she said again. Louder this time. "The first step!"

"I'm not deaf, woman," he finally said. "Though I will be if you keep shouting."

"I was being emphatic," she responded. "Do you know the saying?"

"No."

"It is Chinese, I believe. Have you ever been to China?"

"No."

"Nor I."

"I would like to travel in Asia. Have you traveled in any part of Asia?"

"No."

"Not even India?"

"My brother—" he began, then cut himself off.

"So Court has been to India. As a missionary?"

MacLeod sighed, and finally turned his gaze from the window to her. "As a soldier."

"I see. But you did not accompany him? He raised you, did he not?"

"He was in the army in India when our parents died. He was seriously injured in action at the time he met Hannah. He came home to recover, and was left to deal with a lad who'd spent months running wild in the hills of Skye." He stopped speaking abruptly, and pressed his lips together in a thin line. He looked quite annoyed for having opened up even a little about his history.

"You are too used to keeping secrets, man," she complained. "You know much about me." *Too much.* "But you try to stay a closed book to me. That is not fair."

"Life is not fair. As you are well aware," he added, with slightly less asperity in his tone.

"I do not ask for, nor do I expect, life to be fair. I am no child, MacLeod, expecting the world to be perfect."

"You deserve it to be!"

His intensity stunned her, and it touched her very, very deeply. Still, she answered, "Villains should get what they deserve. For the rest of us . . ." Miranda made a small gesture. "We should be grateful if we manage to get what we need. What do you need?" she couldn't help but ask.

For a long time he didn't answer, or look at her. Finally he turned a very intense gaze on her. "Perhaps I will get what I deserve," he said softly. "Because I am certainly a villain."

"Oh, bother!" she muttered under her breath. Then her annoyance got the better of her, and Miranda shouted, "Your sense of melodrama has gotten out of hand, sir! What on earth could you have done to make you so miserable and guilt-ridden?"

"Well, for one thing," he replied in his much more normal, phlegmatic tone, "I have spent most of my life being a professional assassin."

This was not the answer Miranda expected at all. If she'd expected anything, it was that he'd declare that he'd deceived her and was her Dante, and his brooding was from a sense of guilt over the masquerade. But—an assassin? This confession quite floored her, and sent her world reeling out of control yet again. She didn't want to believe him, but she'd seen the truth in his haunted eyes, in his matter-of-fact tone.

Then she remembered something he'd said after he'd fought the man who'd broken into

Kestrel House. *"I only nearly killed him. I seem to have lost my edge."* That was how he'd put *not* killing the intruder.

"Oh," she sputtered. "Oh."

He offered her no further explanation. In fact, he went back to tensely staring into the darkness outside the window.

Her head began to throb, her stomach to churn. And she wasn't sure if the taste in her mouth was charcoal, or if she was tasting ashes as her image of MacLeod went up in flames once more.

Miranda closed her eyes and turned her face toward the rough fabric of the upholstery. She prayed for darkness to descend on her. And in a way her prayer was answered, for it wasn't long before she once again fell asleep.

He should not have told her. Of course he had known that even as he spoke, but the words came anyway. For a man used to keeping secrets, trained to it, conditioned to it, he came close to being a babbling fool whenever Miranda pressed him on any subject.

Fortunately for the sake of the Empire's security, Miranda Hartwell was on the side of the angels. She would not betray any secrets he told her—but he should not be telling her anything in the first place. He should not even be tempted.

The woman had been his downfall from the first

instant he laid eyes on her. She made him weak, vulnerable. And the worst part was, he liked these soft feelings far too much. It was such a temptation to let his guard down, to relax with her as he never could with anyone else. Even with his family he felt bound to maintain the persona of capable, coolheaded agent at all times. Miranda somehow stripped him of pretense, as if by sheer force of being herself she induced echoes of sincerity in him.

But telling the truth had proved dangerous, just as he had expected it would. For Miranda had not spoken a word to him throughout the rest of the journey. And it was not a short journey to their hiding place. They had had to change trains in Glasgow, and it had been more hours until they arrived at the station in Fort William. Then they'd had to hire a driver to bring them to this isolated two-story house set in a thickly wooded glen.

Not a word from Miranda. Not a glance. She sat beside him, stiff, unyielding, wrapped in silence. The only time they touched was when she allowed him to help her off and on trains and carriages. Now she waited beside him on the front steps, with her hands folded before her as he opened the door.

He should have been relieved. But instead he was very near the point of begging her to speak to him. For now he allowed the damning silence to continue as he stood back for her to enter, and then followed her inside.

The first thing she did, without bothering to look around the room, was turn to him, lift her chin defiantly, and say, "Thank God we have real privacy at last! Now, tell me all about it."

Andrew was completely taken aback by this. "Tell you all about what?"

"About being an assassin, of course. We couldn't very well discuss it before, but now I want to know how a nice man like you came to— to your profession."

"*Killer*," he said. "That is the word you want. Or perhaps *murderer*."

"That is a harsh word."

"I judge myself harshly. I have that right."

She eyed him critically, but not with the revulsion he deserved, the revulsion he'd been certain he'd seen in her when he first told her. Apparently she had thought over what he'd told her, and come to some romantic conclusions about the type of man he was.

"Whatever you have done has been in the service of your country, has it not?"

Her question confirmed that she was trying to excuse his past. "I know a sin when I commit one," he told her. "Don't try to excuse the taking of life by making it into a patriotic gesture."

Miranda took a deep breath for a retort, then she forced her lips together and let it go for now. The man had been carrying a grave weight on his shoulders for a long time. A few moments of her telling him *There, there, it's all right* wasn't going to make it right with him. The sort of healing he needed would take time and patience and a gentle touch. Only she wasn't sure if she had any of those qualities. Time, especially, was her enemy. She was certain the man was bound to be rid of her as soon as he considered her out of danger.

Well, MacLeod could want what he wanted, but that didn't mean he had to get everything his way, now did it?

She smiled.

"What's that look for?" he asked immediately.

Miranda chose to ignore this and finally have a look at their surroundings. She walked through the ground floor, finding that the only other room was a kitchen, with no provisions in the cupboard or wood for the stove. The main room held a fireplace full of old ashes. A narrow staircase to the left of the front door led up to a pair of small bedrooms. Andrew did not follow her on her round of inspection, but waited for her to return to the sitting room.

"Primitive, isn't it?" he asked, rising from the sagging sofa when she came back.

"Quite. I live in a castle, Andrew," she pointed out. "With more servants than I need. I am like the lilies of the field who neither reap nor sow." She folded her hands before her. "I have never, nor do I intend, to roll up my sleeves and cheerfully offer to do housework for you."

Though even as she said this, she remembered how Dante—MacLeod—had taken care of every small detail of household management for her comfort. Perhaps she should make some effort to repay this domestic generosity. She would be glad to, actually.

"We need to hire at least one maid and a cook, and possibly a manservant for heavier work. My treat," she told him.

A smile crept over his usually stern features. "My lady, you are impossibly spoiled."

"And I intend to stay that way. About the servants?"

"I have already made arrangements. I sent a note back with our driver to the owner of a small hotel I stayed at the last time I was in the area. I asked her to send back a meal from her kitchen this evening, and to arrange for some help to arrive in the morning. While we are in hiding from your would-be killer, we are not completely in exile." He gave a small, only faintly mocking, bow. "Amenities shall be provided without anyone in London being the wiser."

"How delightful," Miranda answered.

And once again looking around their isolated surroundings she couldn't help but wonder what else could occur at a place like this without anyone else having to be any the wiser.

She had some thoughts on the subject.

Chapter 22

◦◦◦◦◦◦

They managed to find some candles, and Andrew scrounged enough dry fallen branches from the nearby woods to light a fire in the hearth. The flames sputtered and crackled, but they added warmth as the evening grew cooler. The basket of food that was left at the front door provided ample supplies for several meals. And the innkeeper had sent along a couple of bottles of wine to go with the food, and plates, glasses, and cutlery as well. They brought a quilt down from one of the bedrooms and spread it out for added comfort on the braided hearthrug.

"What a lovely picnic," Miranda said after they'd divided up plates of food and settled before the fire. She lifted her glass and studied the flames through the rich, red curtain of the wine.

Then she sneaked a teasing glance at MacLeod. "And, dare I say it, romantic?"

As expected, his expression was as stern as ever, but she was certain the twinkle she saw when he looked at her was in his eyes, and not merely a reflection of firelight off his glasses.

"You may say whatever you wish, Lady Miranda. And I daresay you will."

She took a sip of the wine. It was not very good, but she still appreciated the warm glow it sent through her. Or was the warm glow a response to having MacLeod looking at her? And she had him to herself. At last. She had a few notions about what to do with this situation, but was a bit puzzled at where to start.

She took another sip of wine while he continued to look at her, and her temperature rose some more. "Wine is quite healthy, you know," she said, though she felt herself flush all over.

"Aye. So I hear. Unlike whisky," he added.

"Oh, that's good for one as well. If one does not overindulge. I'm sure you do not approve of overindulgence in anything. Oh, dear, I didn't mean—I'd forgotten—" She reached out and touched him on the arm as she recalled his recent lost bout with a bottle of whisky.

She half expected him to draw away, but he put his hand over hers instead. "You've definitely almost seen me at my worst."

She noted the *almost*, but didn't inquire about it, even if that was what he expected her to do. Oh, yes, he was looking for excuses to put her off, to disgust and frighten her with his awful history. How did one tame a MacLeod? she wondered.

"You know, I am just as tough as any of your female relatives," she told him. "Mentally, at any rate. Oh, I'm not going to shoot at anyone, or steal enemy secrets, or anything like that. But I am not at all squeamish, and I can be fairly bloody-minded." Her hand was still on his arm, and she squeezed, feeling hard, tense muscle beneath her fingertips. "You said something about what I deserve earlier. What I think is that I should be the judge of what I deserve."

She knew she wasn't putting this at all well, or quite the way she wanted.

"Woman, I have no idea what you are talking about," he said, confirming her own confusion. He moved away from her touch, and turned his gaze toward the fire.

They sat in silence for a long time, eating plates of cold meat pie, bread and cheese, and gingered peaches. Miranda finished her one glass of wine, but had no more. Andrew didn't have any.

Finally, in frustration, she poured him a glass and thrust it into his hand. "It won't kill you. You don't have to remain completely clearheaded all the time."

"It might kill you if I don't" was his quick answer.

"We're safe now," she insisted. "*We're* safe. We're both well away from the intrigue and the danger. We don't have to go back. Not to any of it. Don't you see that? You're a free man! Don't you want to be a free man?"

"Do you think I have a choice?" he asked her, voice raw. "I've tried to walk away, but I can't escape the past."

"Well, of course you can't," she agreed. "But there is no reason to wallow in it."

"Wallow?" His indignation filled the whole room, although his voice had been deathly quiet. "Madam, wallowing is for amateurs."

Miranda threw back her head and laughed.

Andrew enjoyed the sound of her laughter. He found it far more intoxicating than the wine she had offered. But not to disparage her hospitable intent, he accepted the glass from her and took a drink.

"I have had much better," he said, and just barely managed not to add that he had tasted the best vintages of his life in Italy.

He looked at her smiling face, saw the mirth shining in her eyes. And he saw more than mirth there. There was warmth, affection. Desire?

Or was the desire only on his side? It burned in him, hard and hot, and more difficult to control all the time.

"Being alone with me is a mistake."

Miranda shook her head. "I've made mistakes before, Andrew."

"This was my mistake. I—"

"I agreed to come here."

"You were ill. And—"

She put her hand on his cheek, leaning close to do so. The scent of her was intoxicating. "Are you afraid of compromising my virtue?"

He put a hand over hers. "Afraid?" Oh, yes, he was afraid of that. And of many other things.

"It is *my* virtue," she pointed out.

"What an odd woman you are, Miranda."

"You do know how to flatter me, Andrew."

He had to tell her. Now. Before this went any further. Before he lost control. And he was so close that he was trembling with the effort to hang on. His body was tight with need. Desire burned at his sanity.

"My sweet Miranda," he whispered. "There's so much. So much you don't know."

"I know that you are a good man."

He shook his head wildly. "No! No."

"Who does not like things he has done."

She had somehow moved closer to him, or perhaps he to her. All he knew was that the empty plates were shoved aside and the quilt was bunched up around them. The candlelight gave a golden glow to her pale skin. They sat in a small pool of light, a refuge that held only Miranda and him. The rest of the world did not exist, and the shadows around them invited intimacy.

It invited the sharing of secrets.

If he did not tell her the truth now, he never would. And if he told her the truth, how long would this intimacy last? He wanted her, needed her. And he was damned if he did and damned if he didn't when it came to telling her the truth.

"You deserve—" His voice caught in his throat. It was a harshly rasped whisper when he continued. "The truth."

She waited in silence, though he'd expected her to speak. She stroked his face, and brushed her fingers through his hair. The touch was gentle, encouraging. Her expression was full of tenderness, and alert curiosity.

She was so—so very beautiful. Heart, mind, soul, body, every part of her. He did not know when his hands had settled on either side of her slender waist, but he drew warmth from the touch. Heat, sustenance, need.

He could not bear this, and closed his eyes. But that sort of cowardice would not do for his Miranda.

Andrew made himself look her in the eyes, and said, "You need to know this. I cannot ask you to forgive me. Perhaps someday you will understand." He took a deep breath, and finally got it out. "I am Dante."

"Yes, I know," she answered.

"What?"

He tried to pull away, but her hands were tangled in his hair with a strong, hard grip. He barely noticed the pain.

"And if it isn't perfectly all right," she went on, "it's not so bad as all that."

Before he could think, before he could say another word, she pulled him to her and kissed him.

The moment his lips touched hers, Andrew was completely lost.

His tongue delved into her mouth and found the kiss as intoxicating as any wine.

Her hands roamed over him as they kissed, and before he knew it she had his jacket and shirt off him. Her touch against his bare skin drove him mad. It was as if she found every scar on his torso by instinct and caressed it in a way that both aroused and comforted.

He kissed the scar on her temple and silently prayed her forgiveness for the one secret still between them. He could not tell her now. Now he had to kiss her, taste her bare flesh, touch it, arouse her as she aroused him.

He helped her undress from her upper garments, as quickly as he could with his hands shaking like leaves. He was like a raw lad who'd never touched a woman before. His body screamed for him to hurry, but he couldn't be all rough and thoughtless and hard with her. She was tender and vulnerable and so very, very dear to him. For a moment he forced himself to gaze upon her lovely breasts with their lovely pink nipples, and her slender waist, and her shoulders and throat framed by the dark length of her unbound hair.

He must go slowly, carefully, explore every inch, make her his in every way.

His hands covered her breasts, and Miranda's nipples were instantly hard and aching. She strained against him, as first his palms stroked her, then he rolled the nubs between his fingers.

Then, just before his mouth closed around the tip of her left breast, he whispered, "Tell me what you like. I'll do anything you like."

The sound of his desire-roughened voice, the promise of pleasure, the pure pleasure that arced through her, these things were all maddeningly exciting.

"I . . . like that," she told him. And he moved from one breast to suckle the other.

Then he kissed her all the way down, from her chest to her belly button, and managed to deftly strip off even more of her clothing as he went. Skirts and petticoats and stockings joined the mixed pile of their clothing.

When they were both completely naked, Miranda scuttled backward and rested on her knees. She took her time to study him. He was as hard-muscled and perfectly proportioned as any statue she'd seen in Italy.

"And so alive," she said. "So real. Really here, with me." The words came out almost like a prayer.

He held his hand toward her and she took it, letting him draw her forward. She stroked her hand up his arm, then across his shoulders, down his chest, and across his flat belly. His erection fascinated her.

"May I?" she asked, but touched a fingertip to the soft head of his member before he could answer. His gasp of pleasure was all the permission she needed. She stroked the length of him several times, slowly, urged on by his moans and the look of almost painful pleasure on his face.

"Stop," he whispered, voice raw with need.

"Am I doing it wrong?" she asked.

His eyes came open with a glance that told him he was aware that she was teasing. He licked his lips. "Woman, I'll have you on your back for that."

"Oh, yes, please," she answered with a throaty, eager laugh.

And she did it herself, lying slowly back, and bringing him with her. He settled between her widespread legs, and his fingers found the core of her, stroking her inside and out. His touch stimulated her in ways she'd never felt before. Fire skittered through all her senses, but the coiled heat of need was centered deep inside. Inside her, where he needed to be.

"Andrew," she begged, her hips lifting against his hand. "Please."

"You're sure?" He shifted position. She could feel the tip of his penis poised at her opening. "Certain?"

She knew very well how difficult it was for him to wait, to even speak. For she was at the place where need had driven them as well. She rolled her head back and forth against the quilt, fought for coherence when all she wanted was sensation.

"Y-yes," she managed. "You won't hurt me," she reassured. "Not unless you . . . leave me now. Now!" she repeated. "Please!"

He came inside her then, slowly, gently. She rose to meet him, aware of being filled, of the perfect fit of male and female coming together in the most basic, fulfilling way.

She pulled his head down for a long, demanding kiss. Then Miranda was lost to the details as the spasms of pleasure began to ripple through her. Each strong, ever quickening stroke brought her to a higher and higher level.

She was sleek and hot inside, soft as satin, surrounding him as he filled her. The small, subtle contractions of her sheath as orgasms took her drove him mad, drove him on, drove him into a hard, driving rhythm he was powerless to stop.

When she cried out as the strongest spasm yet took her, he was there with her. The climax broke over him like a tidal wave, washing him away, drowning him in utter, ultimate release, ultimate completion.

Only Miranda could do this to him.

"Only you," he murmured, and collapsed on top of her.

Chapter 23

One by one the candles were going out, and the fire had died down to a cherry glow. Wrapped in quilts, cuddled close to Andrew's warm bare chest, with his arm around her, Miranda was as warm and comfortable as she had ever been. And the happiest.

Oh, there were some muscles she wasn't used to exercising that were going to ache in the morning, but a little stiffness was a small price to pay for such a sense of completion, for such . . . joy.

She sighed, and turned slightly so that she could look up at Andrew's face. How the shadows suited his austere features.

"I love you." She thought he was asleep. Which she thought was just as well, as the words were likely to send MacLeod running like a rabbit. He was a dangerous man, but that word, that word *love* was even more dangerous. It was so full of . . . implications. So full of obligations. He was a man who understood duty, but did he understand—

"I really wish you hadn't said that."

He opened his eyes after he spoke, and what she saw in them wasn't the absolute terror she'd feared. Nor was there the mask of indifference that would have been even worse. What she saw was . . . wonderful!

"Because now we will have to have a discussion, and I am very tired, lady mine. Tired, in a very satisfied way," he added.

"Well, it had to be said sometime," she answered. "By someone."

He tucked her closer in his embrace. "And you assumed Hades would freeze over before you get such a declaration from me."

She sighed. And waited for a while, and eventually asked, "Will it?"

"It is complicated."

She wasn't to be deterred, or ready to allow any hurt to enter this. It was time for conversation rather than confrontation.

"Coming together is complicated," she said. "Do you want to be with me?"

"Do you want it?"

"I do not give myself lightly, MacLeod. What we just did was wonderful, but would not have happened unless I was committed in my affections."

"I see." The silence stretched out again, and his expression went from soft, to puzzled, to stern. She watched him, and was certain that she followed his thoughts.

"Lady Miranda," he said finally. "You were not a virgin."

"I did tell you not to fear hurting me."

"Yes. But." He sighed. And gave her a look of disappointed reproach. "I . . . am . . . I do not know what to say. I fear I am not as sophisticated about this as you think I should be."

"This?" she asked, trying very hard not to take offense.

He clearly did not want to make specific statements, and this from a man she admired for his precise language.

"Yes, I am sexually experienced," Miranda said. "And I am not ashamed of it one bit."

"But . . . I did not expect such impropriety from you."

"With anyone but you, you mean?" she questioned, letting her temper get the better of her for a moment.

"Yes," he snapped back, equally annoyed. "I thought you virtuous, pure, untouched. That you gave yourself—"

"Freely," she cut him off. "And with love. You are not going to play the hypocrite with me, are you, Andrew? Is the pot calling the kettle black here?"

"Are you saying that a spy and an assassin has no right to a sense of propriety, morality?"

"No. Of course not. What I meant is that you are sexually experienced. Or so it seemed to me."

"A man is allowed a certain . . . experience," he pointed out.

"Why?"

"Because that is the way of the world."

"It shouldn't be. I believe that what is good for the goose is good for the gander."

"Society does not agree. A woman should practice—"

"Why should a woman practice abstinence until her wedding night, and it be acceptable— expected—for a man to do as he pleases with any woman he can, and consider the women he has congress with whores, besides? I loathe such conventional hypocrisy, Andrew. And expect better of you. Even if you were not a virgin."

Andrew was quite flabbergasted by Miranda's declaration. There was a part of him that strained to be indignant at discovering that he was not Miranda's first lover. But was that not just vanity and, yes, conventional hypocrisy? This was Miranda Hartwell, a woman of integrity, of convictions. And, yes, virtue. She would not give herself lightly, or to just anyone.

He noticed that despite this latest argument his

arm was still around her and her head was resting on his shoulder. To let her go was impossible.

"I have no right to ask," he said. "You have no need to explain."

"Malcolm," she said easily. "We were betrothed, and both too young. We were . . . romantics of the worst sort."

"Worst?"

"Completely melodramatic. We knew each other all our lives, but our fathers feuded over some silly property matter. So they disapproved of our being together. We acted like we were Romeo and Juliet. There were poems, and secret meetings in the woods, with all my aunts knowing exactly what was going on. It was really mostly quite proper, until Malcolm was diagnosed with consumption."

"Oh, dear. I am sorry."

"He was dying, and I thought my life was over. I seduced him. I had to. He wouldn't marry me once he knew the prognosis. Said he didn't want to leave me a widow." She made a soft but rude sound. "As if women are not left widows every day. Well, we were lovers for a while. I think it was in secret, but with my aunts I've never really been sure." She sighed. "He died. And for years I kept up the melodramatic nonsense of thinking I'd given myself to the only man I could ever love."

She lifted her head to look him in the eye. "By the way, I was quite recovered from that girlish nonsense by the time I met you."

"By the time you met Dante," he corrected.

Her lips thinned in a hard line, and her eyes snapped. "And perhaps I went off on another romantic fantasy there," she said. "But I do not think so. Dante was kind and charming and lovable."

"Unlike myself."

She pressed a hand over his heart. The warmth of it seared him. "Yet here we are," she said. "You, and Dante, and I." Then she looked around before bringing her gaze back to his. "No, I only see one man here. You have actually been overshadowing Dante in my thoughts for some time now," she admitted. "Though I've been . . . rather emotional since I realized you are one and the same."

"Dante is nicer. Dante is a figment." Before he could vilify himself any further, his curiosity got the better of him. "How long have you known? Why haven't you confronted me?"

She laughed. "Confront you? How? When there is an army of MacLeods surrounding you at any given moment! Until we arrived here it was impossible to get near you. And that guard you keep up when you are on a high horse doesn't make it easy to talk to you. No one does dudgeon quite as well as you, my dear."

"You rarely stop talking, my dearest," he

pointed out. He ran a hand up and down her bare back, and cupped her lovely round behind. "You are certainly near me now."

"Aye," she agreed, and slid down his body in a most erotic fashion. His member rose at her movements, and she grasped it in her hand, and stroked it to complete hardness.

Within moments, she had him flat on his back with the coverings stripped away from him, and was straddling him in all her naked glory, holding herself just over his erect penis.

"Is this punishment for having deceived you?" he asked, though he was panting with need, and could barely talk.

"Aye," she agreed. "And reward for saving me."

He didn't deserve reward, but he did desperately need her. "Now," he pleaded.

Then she lowered her body slowly over his. She let him fill her, plunging slowly into soft, tight heat.

Everything then was pleasure. Everything burned away but what she and only she gave him. And then there was release.

"I have been thinking, Mr. MacLeod," Miranda said, putting her fork carefully beside the empty plate on the kitchen table.

"You seem to make a habit of it," Andrew said, turning from the stove, holding in his hands the teapot he'd just filled with hot water. He placed the brown earthenware pot in the center of the table, between the pair of mismatched cups already there. "What have you been thinking?" he inquired once he took a seat close enough so that he could take her hand.

Just as Dante had always taken her hand, she thought, and smiled, for she realized how much of Dante was Andrew's true self. He was a gentle man, and very physically affectionate when he let his barriers down. Those barriers had been coming down more and more for several days now. It was not just that they'd been making love, but they'd also been making peace. Though they hadn't talked about it.

"We haven't been talking much at all," she said. "It's been nothing but sex, sex, sex, hasn't it?"

He frowned at her. "Lady Miranda, you have a crude way of expressing what has been a beautiful, fulfilling—"

"But you have to admit we've spent most of our time in bed." And how she craved to spend more time there soon.

Right now it was conversation she craved. He had let himself go in this private time. They had laughed, and made love, and cuddled together quietly before the fire, and in bed, and held hands as they did now. They had shared warmth, as well as the burning heat of intense passion. But she dreaded that he would turn back to his stiff, self-recriminating ways once this holiday was over. She didn't intend to let that happen. Hence the need to draw him out, to reinforce that they were friends as well as lovers.

"We went for a walk at some point," he reminded her.

"And I watched you fish earlier today."

"You could have joined me."

"Wade in a cold trout stream? No, thank you."

He gestured at their empty plates. "Wading in that stream provided our meal."

"I quite enjoyed watching you cook." He was indeed a man of many talents, and quite at home with domesticity. More so than she was. "And you made a fine secretary as well." She straightened her shoulders and tried to look as prim and stern as possible. "As I stated earlier, I have been thinking."

"And you are about to reveal your thoughts to me." He looked faintly worried at her sudden stiff demeanor. "On what subject?"

"On our professional relationship, Mr. Mac-Leod."

He looked definitely worried now. "And . . . ?"

"I'm afraid I must terminate your employment with me," she told him.

He stared at her, looking quite flabbergasted. While she tried hard to hide her amusement.

"After all, it is most improper to carry on the

sort of intimate relationship we have with an employee. It is certainly unfair to the employee—and I will not be accused of taking advantage of one in my service. I did leave you a letter to that effect before we left for London, but since you never read it I suppose it wasn't effective. Therefore, you are released, with full wages owed, from my employ."

She ended this speech with a stiff little nod, then sat back to wait for his reaction. She did not know if he noted that she had said nothing about releasing him from their engagement. She was still wearing the ring, and they were sharing a bed in the way of a man and wife, after all.

After he gazed at her in dumbfounded surprise a moment more, Andrew's shoulder began to shake. Then his expression cracked into a wide, boyish grin. Behind his spectacles his eyes shone with mirth. And then he threw back his head and began to laugh.

The sound filled the room, and Miranda's heart. If there was one thing Andrew MacLeod surely needed, it was a good laugh. And so did she. The sound was infectious, and she laughed with him. It was not long before he swung her up out of her chair, and around the room in a wild dance.

Then he swung them both from the kitchen into the front room and down on the sagging sofa. And there he kissed her with such fervor that she was soon as excited as she was giddy and breathless.

"Oh, you had me going for a moment, lass," he told her. "You did indeed. But what am I to do now that I'm at liberty?"

"Perhaps you could be a travel guide," she suggested. "Taking tours around the Italian countryside perhaps?"

"That's a thought," he agreed. Then he grew serious. "For I have no intention of returning to my previous profession."

"As an academic?"

"No, the other one." The words came out as a disenchanted growl.

Miranda stroked his cheek. "It is time you rested from that world, I think. Surely being— what do you call it, a field agent?—should not be something a person spends their whole life doing? I can see that there would be a danger to a man's soul if—"

"A very grave danger," Andrew concurred. He turned to her and took her hands in his. "Lass, I'd reached my limit before—the day we met. I thought I was finished once you were safely back in England. I resigned."

"Good for you."

"But if you had not still been in danger we would not have met again."

"You came back to protect me."

He blushed, and his gaze shifted from hers for a moment. "I owed you that."

"Now you owe it to yourself—and to me—to stop."

"Protecting you?"

"No. You may do that as long as you like."

He kissed her hand. "A pleasure."

"But it would be best if you no longer partook in your family's odd hobbies—" Curiosity struck her, and Miranda could not help but ask. "How did you come to be in that village? I mean, what long road was it that led a scholar and thoroughly upright man into the life you've led? Or has your family always been in the spying game?"

"Not my side of the family," he answered. "The MacLeods have always been country gentry, soldiers mostly, and university men. We led normal lives until Court was posted to India and met Hannah Gale. She was a spy and he a soldier, each doing their duty. He didn't know what she was doing in that wild part of the world, but he protected her while they were caught in an Afghan rebellion. It ended badly then. They thought each other dead, you see. He came home and took the cloth, and took me off to a wild island in the Orkneys. He mourned and did his duty, and one day Hannah showed up with her brood."

"Brood?"

"Lucy and Kit, her adopted children. And Harriet. There was no doubting that Harriet was Court and Hannah's love child."

"That might prove embarrassing for a man of the cloth."

"Not Court. It was as if the child brought him fully back to life, though Hannah was the spark, and the enduring flame."

"Quite a love story."

"Oh, you don't know the half of it. It was Phoebe Gale who sent Hannah to Court, but it wasn't completely out of the goodness of her heart. The old woman had a job for the pair of them.

"Court wanted no part of it, but Hannah held the trump card. He insisted on marriage, as was right and proper. She wouldn't marry Court even to legitimize their child unless he helped her serve our country. He was furious, but he went with her.

"I've never known what that mission was. But when they came back he'd found his true calling, and his true love. He gained his knighthood out of it. He took us all back to Skye, fathered many children, and took over most of the Gale family business, with Phoebe happy to have him.

"And Hannah. Dear, ruthless, motherly, brilliant, tough, and tenderhearted Hannah." He sighed, and there was a dreaminess to it that spoke of a faraway, wonderful time. "She changed all our lives."

A melancholy expression crossed his face, and Miranda guessed, "You loved her, didn't you?"

He nodded slowly. "As a lad, yes, though I

knew it was wrong." He took her hands again, said reassuringly, "It was a lad's first infatuation, and long since faded to proper appreciation of my brother's wife."

"And it was this infatuation that sent you into the secret service, wasn't it?" she guessed. "You went off to serve your country rather than stay and pine for the one you couldn't have."

He grimaced. "Aye. I was a damned fool romantic then."

"I understand, none better. What with Malcolm and all."

He nodded. "Youth is embarrassing in retrospect. You can probably guess that it was scheming Phoebe Gale who used love to snare another servant for the Crown."

"She recruited you, not Court?"

"Aye. She had missions in mind for a lad of my skills that Ian Court MacLeod would not approve of. I was always skilled with weapons, you see. She had those skills honed by the best of the best. The training was fun, but the fieldwork . . ." He shook his head. "I won't pretend it wasn't exciting at first. And I had the salve for my conscience that everything I did was for a good cause. Of course, I came to realize that the men I killed felt the same about their causes."

"The world went from black and white to dirty gray," she said.

He nodded. "Precisely. And that gray seeped like gritty smoke into my very soul. But I drifted on from assignment to assignment. It was Court who cornered me one day and preached a two-fisted sermon about what I was becoming, and how I didn't belong in his family if I kept it up. It was the catalyst that made me determined to quit. In fact, I had already turned in my resignation that day I found myself holding a rifle on that hillside, with only one man left to kill before I was done with it for good and all."

Miranda listened to his tale with deep, loving sympathy and growing affection.

Then he reached the part about standing on the hillside with a rifle in his hands.

"Oh, good Lord," she murmured. And it came back to her in a horrific flash. The sunlight was warm on her face, the scent of olives and dust was in her nostrils. She caught brief glimpses—of men on the road, of men on the hill.

"Sir Simon," she whispered.

There was the sound of buzzing bees in the air. But they were not bees at all, but bullets. The men on the hill were firing—

The men—

She looked at Andrew through the haze of memory. Saw the truth in his bleak expression, in the anguish in his eyes.

"You."

He was standing across the room from her now, but she had no recollection of his moving away from her. His hands were behind his back, and he was as stiff, expressionless, and tense as he had ever been. More.

"Me," he told her.

Andrew wanted to scrub his hands across his face. He wanted to turn and run for the door. If he did as he wished, the look of betrayal on Miranda's face would be the last thing of her he would ever see. It would haunt his memory. And though he deserved that torture, he did not think he could bear it.

"I meant to tell you," he told her. "I truly did."

"When?" she asked, rising slowly to her feet. "Before or after our silver wedding anniversary?"

Wedding anniversary? The words made no sense to him. "I know you cannot want me, now that you know the truth."

"You shot me." She took a small step forward. Her hands were bunched into fists at her sides. She closed her eyes for a moment. "All that pain . . . The weakness, the fear . . . The headaches that still trouble me. It was you. You did this to me."

"It was an accident. A horrible, tragic accident."

"An accident that would not have happened had you not been there to kill a man."

He bowed his head. "Yes."

"On the other hand," she couldn't help but state, "the man would not have needed killing if he had not sold other lives to the devil." She hated that she could see several sides to what had happened. It made the visceral hatred of Andrew MacLeod harder to sustain.

"I will never forgive myself. I don't beg your forgiveness, because I do not deserve it. But I am truly, truly sorry."

"Is that why you nursed me? Was it out of guilt?"

"You needed nursing. I had the skill. But I had to keep our presence secret. That is why I assumed the identity of the bandit leader killed in the fighting."

Miranda was fully aware that he hadn't answered her question. Looking at him, she could see his anguish, his guilt and shame. That he was sorry.

"But do you love me?" she asked.

"Of course I love you!" he responded promptly. He looked surprised. She didn't know if it was because she'd asked it of him, or because he had spoken the words at last.

"But do you love *me*? Or is it some alabaster angel's image of me that you've persuaded yourself you love to make up for your guilt?"

Andrew drew himself up proudly, and glared at her through narrowed eyes. It was a familiar look, and oddly comforting.

"Woman, I've come to know the hellion you are, and there is nothing of the angel in you. Fragile you seem, but with a core of steel beneath. You are spoiled and snappish and altogether too willful for any sane man's peace of mind. Yet I love you with all my heart. Not that I expect anything to come of it," he added. "Now that you know the truth."

"Truth you should have told me sooner."

"I've said as much."

Yes, he had. Blast and damn him to eternal perdition! Her heart was raw and her head was spinning. But he loved her. Oh, bugger!

"Wait a moment," he said suddenly. "Did you say Sir Simon?" His hands were on her shoulders. "You remember?"

"Yes."

And now the agent was back, brisk and efficient and focused. How did she deal with him? Well, she didn't want to.

"And now I suppose you'll be off to send a telegram while I wait here stewing over all I've just learned."

"I—" He put a hand to his forehead. "I should."

"Fine," she said. "I'm certainly not going to stop

you." She gestured toward the door. "I want to be alone. I need to be alone." She truly, truly did.

He gave her a worried look. "Miranda, please believe how sorry I am."

"Oh, I believe you. I just don't—please go, Andrew."

She twisted the ring on her left hand. Now she felt numb, all the emotion boiled out of her. Confusion remained, but it was almost as if someone else experienced it. Possibilities piled up on top of possibilities, and the future was suddenly nothing but chaos.

"Go," she repeated. "You have no idea how much I need to think."

Even as he moved to pick his jacket off the rickety coatrack by the door, a tread sounded on the outside stairs. Andrew threw open the door. He expected to find someone from the inn preparing to knock.

He was too agitated to be surprised when he saw that it was one of his nephews on the doorstep.

"What is it, Michael?" he demanded.

"It's over" was the lad's prompt answer. "The traitor's found out. It's—"

"Sir Simon."

Andrew and Miranda spoke the name the same time as Michael.

"How did you know?" the young man asked,

sounding disappointed to have his good news anticipated.

"Lady Miranda finally remembered," Andrew answered. "Just now." He stepped back to let Michael enter the sitting room. "Report," he said once Michael was inside.

The insouciant MacLeod twin grinned instead. "Can I have a cup of tea first?"

"No."

"Oh, very well. It was Lucy who caught him, of course. It seems that he'd run out of accomplices and in desperation made another try at Lady Miranda himself. Only, of course, it was our Lucy sitting in Lady Miranda's room calmly combing her hair. She threw some sort of toxic powder on him when he snuck in through the window and tried to take her from behind. There were four of us hiding in the room, and we jumped out while he was writhing in agony. Only the fool didn't have the sense to give up peacefully. He managed to pull out a gun. Even blinded by tears he managed to put a bullet in Da's shoulder."

"What?" Andrew and Miranda demanded together.

"A scratch, no more. And you know Da. Anyway, there was a struggle, which Sir Simon did not survive. He's dead, Lady Miranda," Michael assured her. "He can never harm you again."

Miranda was glad of the young man's sympathy, but it was an effort to hold her tongue over the fact that the man who had hurt her the most was standing right here in this room. Besides, was that exactly true? Andrew's actions *had* been an accident, and Sir Simon's deliberate. And Andrew had protected her. It was all so confusing.

"Thank you," she managed to say to Michael. "You can go home now."

She sighed. "Perhaps I'd better pack then."

"There is one other thing," he said before she could turn away. He dug an envelope out of his pocket. "From your solicitor. The messenger who brought it said that it was urgent."

Miranda stared at the envelope for a moment in disgust. She loathed that her normal life was suddenly resurfacing. But then perhaps that was for the best. Even if her normal life included nasty intrusions from her stupid, greedy cousin. For surely that was what this was about. Another lawsuit, more legal complaints.

She opened the envelope and read the contents. Yes, of course. No surprises here. But this time Cecil's solicitors requested that she meet with them in their offices. It was all very urgent and irregular, but this sort of thing came up occasionally, and must be dealt with. Cecil insisted. And he was the Baron DuVrai, after all. The date set for this important meeting was the day after tomorrow.

Miranda swore under her breath, then said. "I must return to London. Right now."

Chapter 24

"**I** don't see why you have to come," Miranda grumbled. How was she supposed to think when he was near?

"Yes you do," Andrew sighed. "We've had this argument three times already."

"Well, it hasn't been concluded to my satisfaction," she snapped. Her nerves were tight as a drum, and while bickering with Andrew did not make her feel better, it did pass the time even as it took the place of conversation.

What sort of conversation would they have? Once she made up her mind? Meanwhile she took comfort in his being with her. She did not think she should, not until she made up her mind, and possibly not then.

"Being with you has become a habit," she complained.

The gray light of early morning had a firm grip on the countryside that rushed past their compartment window. The weather reflected her mood, oppressive and charged with an impending storm. Even the sheep looked on edge as the train rattled by.

"I'm afraid I cannot speak to your habits or your *satisfaction*," Andrew growled. The emphasis he placed on the last word was simultaneously insulting and tantalizing. Miranda didn't know if she wanted to slap him or throw him down on the cushions and satisfy herself right there.

"A bad habit."

She compromised by turning her back on him and glaring out the window.

She heard him take a deep breath and let it out slowly. She felt a brief twinge of sympathy—he'd had as little sleep as she.

When he spoke again, it was more conversational. "Cecil's solicitors wouldn't call you in over a trifle," he said.

"I know," she agreed tiredly.

"And you'll need a witness there who's on your side."

"I know." He was right. They'd been over this several times. There was neither reason nor time for her to go to the trouble of finding a different companion. Even young Michael MacLeod had come along, but he'd settled in another train compartment to give them the privacy Miranda wasn't sure she wanted.

"And besides, I'm still your secretary," Andrew spoke up after a few minutes.

That was a new one. He must have been saving it.

"No you are not," she reminded him, still staring fixedly out the window. She wondered if he could see that she was watching his reflection. "I dismissed you from my service."

"But you did not make it an immediate termination. I owe you at least one month's service, or until you find a replacement."

"Well, consider yourself dismissed as soon as we're finished this afternoon."

"But you did clearly state that I could protect you as long as I like."

"I did say that," she conceded. She remembered well the moment he'd spoken those words, and they melted her inside.

There was a pause as Andrew took off and polished his spectacles. When he spoke, his voice was gentler than she expected. "Do you really think this will be the end of your troubles with Cecil?" he asked.

"Of course not," she said. She kept her gaze set on the passing scenery. "Usually Cecil's solicitors meet with mine and fight things out among themselves. But every so often something requires my personal attention, and I waste a day dealing with it. It's tiresome, but not tragic."

They lapsed into silence, neither companionable nor antagonistic. She was aware of him as he fiddled with his glasses, watched his reflection as he put them back on and fished a small book out of his jacket pocket. He read for a time, and eventually he slouched down far enough to put his feet up on the seat opposite. As the light outside grew and the interior of their compartment began to fade from her window glass, she heard his breathing deepen into the slow rhythm of sleep.

She turned to look at him then, in spite of herself. Like her, he was wearing clothes Michael had brought; in his case a gentleman's weekend tweeds. He had complained that they made him look like a Yorkshire gamekeeper, but put them on anyway. The jacket was bunched up now where he slouched, and his head had fallen forward, which was sure to result in a stiff neck when he woke.

The slim book leaned open against his chest, its title embossed in tiny Greek letters along the spine. The book and the hand that had held it rose and fell gently with his breathing. She remembered the feel of that hand in hers, the weight and strength of it against her skin as they made love.

She brutally cut short that train of thought, turning back to stare intently out the window again. Sheep, hedgerow, barn, more sheep. Andrew's assignment was finished. Whatever penance he'd felt he needed to do for getting her into this mess was well over with. His successes and failure in the apprehension of a traitor to the Crown would go as publicly unrecognized as the treachery itself, but she at least felt safe now.

And despite her anger at his layers of deception she still felt a nagging sense of gratitude and admiration.

Gratitude and admiration, along with feelings of affection that she couldn't quite bury, were a dangerous combination. They left her dreading his departure when she ought to be celebrating her freedom from him. Of course, she was still thinking about that.

So she bickered irritably, and found herself looking forward to a nice bitter confrontation with Cecil.

Andrew woke with a start as the train rattled over some points. A quick look outside told him they were in the outskirts of London. His neck was sore, and he rubbed at it, somewhat embarrassed at having fallen asleep. Miranda's immediate need for a bodyguard might be gone since Sir Simon's demise, but it still wasn't like him to fall asleep with someone else around.

He trusted her too much—that was the problem. Trusted and loved and needed. And could never have. Unless—unless she somehow found it in her heart to forgive him. He didn't suppose she would, but he couldn't help but find a faint hope within himself. And that was odd, for he had pretty much given up hope of any chance of salvation or happiness. And yet Miranda brought hope out in him.

She had said she had to think. She hadn't yet said good-bye. And she could easily have sent him on his way instead of letting him come along and continue their usual bickering ways.

She was still staring out the window, apparently ignoring him, when she began to speak softly.

"Does it feel odd, for someone else to have caught your traitor?" she asked. She turned back to him, finally, searching his face.

He nearly gave a flippant answer about getting the easy part of the job for once, but then he reconsidered. She was asking a serious question, and deserved a serious answer.

"It's a bit odd, I suppose," he offered slowly, looking at the scuffed toes of his boots. "On a long assignment it is easy to get—possessive—about one's target." He risked a look at her, but she let the comment pass unquestioned. "But mostly it's just a relief to have it over with. I can look forward to a quiet, scholarly Oxford retirement."

You could join me . . . he almost said. But she still

needed her space to think. He would not presume to pressure her. Then again, perhaps she would welcome pressure? Women were so hard to fathom.

They spent the remainder of the journey in silence.

The offices of the Baron DuVrai's solicitors were tastefully opulent. Their gleaming dark wood and exotic ornamentation exuded wealth and power in a very calculated way. Cecil must have inherited the firm from the previous baron, Andrew thought giddily. Miranda's cousin would have chosen somewhere much more gaudy if left to his own devices.

He was demonstrating his appallingly poor taste at the moment by holding a pistol to Miranda's head.

Andrew's thoughts whirled uncontrollably. His icy professionalism had completely deserted him. He'd allowed Miranda to enter the building a full two strides ahead of him, and now he stood paralyzed just inside the door, for fear that her captor might actually pull the trigger.

He was barely aware of the whisper-thin coolness of the knife blade against his own throat, except to wonder about the identity of Cecil's accomplice.

The Baron DuVrai was talking, though Andrew found it difficult to focus over the rushing sound in his ears. His own breathing was painfully loud, his heartbeat pounding fast.

He knew he should be watching Cecil, calculating how to disarm him, but his gaze was convulsively locked with Miranda's. Her hazel eyes were wide with alarm, her face pale and taut with fury. And there was an air about her that demanded of Andrew that he *do* something.

". . . should have thought of this a long time ago," Cecil was saying.

Miranda closed her eyes briefly and cautiously drew breath to speak. She kept her voice as light as she could, fighting the impulse that was screaming *Run!*

"Cecil, you are being an absolute toad," she said. As if they were children at Passfair and he had stolen her plaything. "Stop being an ass and tell us what you want."

The cold metal of the gun's muzzle pressed uncomfortably into her flesh, terrifyingly near to her existing bullet scar.

There would be no reprieve this time, no glancing blow to recover from. She could feel Cecil's muscles starting to quiver from the strain of holding his arm up at the angle required to push the pistol into her temple.

Perhaps if they just stood here long enough, he would get tired and go away.

"Why are you doing this?"

"I want you *gone*, cousin," Cecil said, shattering her brief fantasy. "It's all I've ever wanted, and I finally realized that I just have to make it happen myself."

"So that you can go to jail. Or perhaps be hanged?" Andrew said. "You certainly won't get away with it."

"I won't have her married to you. I won't let her have heirs to pass on my fortune to," Cecil said. "You're dead too, MacLeod."

"Oh, I seriously doubt that," Andrew answered calmly.

Cecil must have signaled to his partner then, because the other man nodded and began to steer Andrew down a back hallway, toward the servants' entrance. She was surprised that Andrew allowed such manhandling. Her heart cracked with fear for him as he disappeared.

He'll be all right, she told herself. *He has to be.*

"Let's go," Cecil said, and they followed a few paces behind. He pushed so close behind her that their stride became an awkward shuffle. At least she had Andrew within sight in a few moments.

As the other pair had turned away from them, Andrew had looked at her with the most agonized expression she'd ever seen, fists clenched tight at his sides. *Good Lord*, she thought, *he probably thinks this is somehow his fault, too. Dolt.*

She hung on to her anger like a shield; she knew that she could not afford the luxury of fearing for his safety. She suspected that if he were alone, if he didn't have to worry about her, he would already have disposed of both assailants.

But then, if he were alone, he wouldn't have had to. He would have retired quietly to Oxford weeks ago, and never heard of half-witted Cecil and his half-witted schemes.

There was something naggingly familiar about her cousin's accomplice. He was dressed slightly too well to be one of the baron's meager household staff, she thought. As they stepped into the shadowed daylight of the back alley, and the man carefully maneuvered Andrew ahead of him into a waiting carriage, the answer finally popped into her head. He was one of Cecil's card-playing cronies, whom she'd successfully banned from visiting Passfair years ago.

So this was about some kind of *gambling debt*? A welcome wave of indignation coursed through her, bolstering her determination. At least Cecil wasn't turning out to be yet another of Sir Simon's accomplices. It was good for the DuVrai name that he was only an idiot, and not a traitor.

Cecil urged her into the roomy, darkly curtained carriage, and now climbed across to sit on her left, eyes and aim never leaving her face. The crony was directly opposite her, with Andrew on his right.

As the carriage started forward—was the driver another creditor, she wondered, or merely a servant minding his own business?—Cecil tediously started in again on how Miranda's well-being depended on Andrew's good behavior. Andrew's face remained expressionless as he allowed the crony to bind his hands, but his eyes were blue fire now, boring lethal promise straight at Cecil.

Stupid Cecil, she thought. *Kill me and you've sealed your own death.*

And in that event, she was more worried about Andrew than Cecil.

"Stupid Cecil," she said out loud. Andrew's eyes snapped back to her, demanding silently to know what she was doing. She wasn't sure, but she plowed on anyway. "You're lucky no one saw us back there," she continued. "And just where are we going? I thought you wanted me to sign something."

"Hah!" Cecil exclaimed triumphantly. "That building is empty. The solicitor's on holiday, and I gave his staff the day off. No one even knows you were there."

Except the entire MacLeod clan, not to mention the cabbie that had driven them from the train station. But Miranda wasn't about to correct him, yet. Her plan was beginning to coalesce: get Cecil gloating, and something was bound to turn up.

He barely required any prompting. "It's been ridiculously easy," he said, casually shifting his weapon's pressure point from her temple to beneath her jaw. "Why settle for some trifling allowance when I can have it all just by killing you? Poor Lady Miranda." He sighed theatrically. "Robbed and murdered and dumped in the river with her scandalous secretary."

"Scandalous fiancé," she corrected.

"Just so," Andrew agreed. "You will immediately be suspect, you know. Especially since you were so rude at the party."

Cecil ignored Andrew. He leaned close to her, his breath hot on her face as he spoke. "Do you know that it was one of your own bloody party guests who suggested it to me? I could hardly believe my ears." He giggled a little then, and for the first time she felt a cold knot of certainty in her stomach. Stupidly manipulated or not, he genuinely meant to kill her.

But his admission had given her one great advantage. She now knew she had nothing to lose.

"It was Simon Lester, wasn't it? At the party?" she asked, her voice barely wavering.

That got him to sit back. "What if it was?"

"Stupid Cecil," she said again.

So Sir Simon was involved after all. Would she never be rid of the man? Well, she would be soon one way or another, depending on whether they ended up dead or alive.

She let all her pent-up venom into her voice. "Lester is a traitor to the British government. He wanted me dead because he thought I could identify him. You presented yourself as a convenient tool, and he used you."

"That doesn't make him any less right," Cecil declared. But she felt the pressure of the gun against her neck ease up ever so slightly.

"Of course it does," she persisted. "Lester doesn't know or care about my financial arrangements. The truth is you'd have to kill half the population of Passfair before you inherited any Hartwell money."

Only a half truth, really, but it had the desired effect. She heard the man opposite growl low in his throat, the first sound she'd heard from him throughout this whole fiasco. And, in his uncertainty, Cecil's gun drew back another quarter inch, and he looked away from her to his coconspirator.

Without pausing to think, Miranda threw herself sideways into Cecil. His gun arm slid past her neck as he fired, the explosion a deafening six inches from her head.

Cecil was not a small man, but neither was he fit. Still, she wasn't in peak condition herself, and she needed all her weight, strength, and fury combined to press him to the wall of the cab, trapping his left hand beneath him. She had managed to brace his right arm above their heads, which was good because she did not think she could spare either the muscle or the attention needed to take his gun away.

Andrew and the crony were grappling furiously on the other seat, and she could feel Cecil's feet slithering for purchase beneath her. He was literally spitting invective into her left ear, which seemed to be functioning slightly better than her right. Her own breathing was desperate and ragged, while Andrew fought with deadly silence and the third man maintained a steady stream of grunts.

Andrew managed to land a solid double-fisted blow with his bound hands that sent his assailant hurtling to the other side of the cab. The carriage rocked wildly as the man hit the wall. Andrew straightened to come to her aid, but the driver must have finally decided to get involved. The carriage suddenly slowed, which threw Andrew back onto his seat and put Miranda off her balance enough to allow Cecil to bring his gun down, hard, onto her shoulder.

She grunted in pain and squirmed around to grip his arm again, knowing that their one chance was in not allowing Cecil to take aim. She knew very little about guns. Was his the sort that fired two shots? Or six?

The carriage finally lurched to a halt, which sent her rolling uncontrollably onto the floor, Cecil on top of her. She had both arms braced against his one now, but their fall had freed his left hand. He gripped her by the hair, and she could see in his grotesquely enraged face that he was quite prepared to beat her head against the floor until she released her grip.

Now who's stupid? she berated herself. *What an undignified way to die.* She heard the distant call of a police whistle, and wondered what the officials would make of this mess. Just one more scandal . . .

Andrew practically fell on top of them, barreling into Cecil so suddenly that he released both her hair and the gun. Her head hit the floor with a painful thud, and she heard the gun clatter to the seat next to the struggling men.

The third man was pulling himself to his feet in the confined space, and Miranda threw herself madly across the compartment to reach the gun before he did.

But he was not aiming for the gun. He pushed roughly past her, and she saw the knife in his hand in one horrified instant of clarity before he buried it to the hilt in Andrew's side. He didn't let go, but pulled the blade out again, slick and red.

An inarticulate scream ripped from her throat.

She raised the pistol from the seat where it lay, and fired at the man standing not two feet in front of her. The weapon bucked in her hands with startling force, but the man staggered and crumpled.

Too late, too late.

Cecil was staring at her with a mixture of horror and awe. She swung the gun around to point at him and he blanched.

Must have more than two shots, then, she thought distantly.

"Please, no, please don't hurt me . . ." he babbled. Her aim did not waver. It was just like him, she thought inanely. Utterly selfish.

Andrew had been half on, half off the seat, and the man she'd shot had fallen mostly on top of him, dragging him to the floor. Their two bodies were tangled in the gloom of the carriage, and the tears streaming down her face did nothing to improve her vision.

Her stomach did a backflip when Andrew's voice emerged from the heap, faint but unmistakable.

"Miranda. I'm all right. Don't shoot him."

Barely two minutes had passed since her first insane, impulsive move against Cecil. It felt like a year, but the shrill whistles of the constabulary were still blocks away. Summoned by their alarmed driver, no doubt. They were utterly alone for a few more seconds, and Miranda seriously weighed the merits of shooting Cecil now, in cold blood.

She could do it, she decided.

She chose not to.

She spoke to her cousin, who was still cowering in the corner of the bloodied carriage seat. "If you move before the police arrive," she told him, "I will kill you." She trusted he would believe her, because she meant it.

She carefully placed the pistol on the floor behind her. Finding that she could not remove the knife from the death grip of its owner, she simply shoved him to the side with all her strength.

Andrew was sprawled underneath, right elbow clutched convulsively to his side. He offered her a tentative smile, but she was alarmed by the whiteness around his lips. She picked ineffectively for a moment at the thick cord still binding his wrists, then gave up and grabbed the dead man's knife—hand and all—to cut the rope.

Once he was free, Andrew immediately tried to lever himself up onto the seat. She had to help, and kept supporting him when it wasn't clear whether he could stay sitting up on his own. Everywhere she touched him came away sticky, and she was terrified that his very life was leaking away under her fingers. She kicked open the door behind her, flooding bright sunlight onto their grisly scene.

"You will not die," she ordered. "I will not allow it."

Andrew's eyes widened in dismay when the light hit her. She looked down at herself—her once-pristine traveling blouse was rucked, torn, and mostly red.

"My God," he breathed. "You're hurt! Where is it . . . ?" He reached with his left hand to pluck weakly at her shirt.

"It's your blood, you idiot!" She was crying again.

"Oh, lassie," he said softly. His gaze lost focus, then his eyes fluttered shut as he gradually began to slump sideways. She grabbed his hand as it started to drop away from her.

She was sobbing now, black despair reaching up to swallow her as she eased him down onto the seat. All her anger at him seemed ridiculous now; the pride that had seen him as a threat to her independence melted away at the prospect of this ultimate loss. She brought her hand up to his face, to caress the too-prominent bones and trace the laughing and frowning lines that suddenly seemed so precious to her.

"Don't leave me, please don't leave me now," she choked.

But he didn't answer.

Miranda was almost frantic enough to scream when a face appeared at the window of the coach.

"Stay calm," Michael MacLeod said. "Help is on the way."

How could she stay calm? The man she loved was dying!

"Well, it has certainly taken you long enough."

Andrew heard the stern voice, recognized it, loved it. But he wasn't sure what Miranda was talking about.

"To wake up," she explained.

Had he been asleep, then? At an inappropriate time, perhaps? He had some vague memories of train and coach rides. Those could certainly put a man to sleep. Had he dozed off in the middle of an important conversation? That was hardly like—

A stab of pain lanced across his side, completely dissipating his rambling thoughts. He remembered now.

"Ah, yes," he murmured. "I was stabbed."

"Indeed you were," Sara's voice came from across the room. "I've had valuable practice helping Dr. Abercrombie fix you up. You nearly bled to death. It was very interesting."

Andrew managed to open his eyes to search for his niece. He found her standing by the door. "You are far too clinically inclined some—"

"She was as worried about you as the rest of us," Miranda cut him off. "She's merely practicing being phlegmatic at the moment."

"I'll go tell the others," Sara said. "You are going to make a full recovery," she added. "So stop lazing about."

The moment the door closed, his gaze went to Miranda. "You're here."

"Where else would I be?"

He realized that she was holding his hand. The smile she turned on him was warm and encouraging.

"You sounded phlegmatic yourself a moment ago," he told her.

"It was my way of helping you wake up. I thought the tone was appropriate for a MacLeod."

"Ah, well . . ." He settled his head on a soft pile of pillows behind him. "Yes." He cleared his throat. Miranda used this as an excuse to put a glass of water to his lips. His head reeled while he took several sips. His reaction was not from fever or disorientation. Not of the physical sort at any rate. It was joy that made him dizzy.

He was alive! More importantly, Miranda was at his side.

"I had to wake you up," she said, putting the glass on the bedside table. "I have something important to say to you."

His left hand gripped hers weakly, filled with a sudden sense of desperation. "I don't want . . ." He paused for breath and began again. "I'm sorry for all this. But please don't send me away."

"Where would I send you?"

She sounded genuinely incredulous. This stirred hope in Andrew he hadn't realized was there.

"Shall I take you to Oxford?" she asked. "To the Isle of Skye? Passfair?"

"Anywhere," he answered, desperately, urgently. He caught her gaze and held it, and squeezed her hand as hard as he could. "Just so long as you don't send me packing. Please. I'm so sorry for—"

"I won't, of course I won't," she answered. "I'm sorry, too. I love you. Just don't try to die on me again, damn it!"

That elicited a smile and a sharp exhalation that might have been a laugh had his side not hurt so much. "Language," he said faintly.

"I'll swear as much as I bloody well like," she said, and laughed. "And stop apologizing."

He couldn't help but respond, "Yes, ma'am."

She nodded. "It's good to have that settled."

She bent and kissed him on the forehead. Then his cheek. And finally on the lips. She let the kiss go on for a long while, until Andrew began to think that perhaps he had a fever after all. She still moved away sooner than he would have liked.

"I'm dizzy," he said. He smiled at her. "It must be from love. I like it."

They gazed at each other for a few long seconds. She brushed her fingers through his hair. "How could I ever have contemplated a future without you?"

"Or I you," he admitted. Maybe he didn't deserve her, but live without her? Never.

"It's my turn to tend to you," she told him. "Though I have a bloody dreadful Italian accent."

This drew a faint smile. "English will do," he murmured as she stroked his face.

"I've decided that I will take you home to Passfair. And we'll get married as soon as you can stand."

"I could take my vows from my sickbed," he offered.

"Fine."

He heard footsteps in the hall. His family on the way to interrupt a perfect moment. "We're going to Passfair," he said. "As soon as possible. Let's not honeymoon in Italy," he added.

She laughed again, and kissed him soundly as the door opened to admit a cloud of MacLeods.

Who wants to be cold anyway? Start the new year right with these sizzling new romances coming in January from Avon Books . . . and you'll be feeling the heat in no time.

An Unlikely Governess by Karen Ranney

An Avon Romantic Treasure

Beatrice Sinclair, forced to accept a post as governess, never expects to be tempted by the seductive pleasures Devlen Gordon offers her. While she strives to draw her young charge out of his shell, she must also confront the passion she soon feels for Devlen . . . but is he her lover—or her enemy?

Sleeping With the Agent by Gennita Low

An Avon Contemporary Romance

Navy SEAL Reed Vincenzio must eliminate Lily Noretski . . . by *any* means possible. Lily is as beautiful as she is dangerous, and in possession of a devastating weapon. He must win her confidence, find the weapon . . . and put everything on the line for a woman he soon loves but cannot trust.

The Bride Hunt by Margo Maguire

An Avon Romance

Lady Isabel Louvet is a kidnapped bride, stolen by a Scottish chieftan to warm his bed! But she is rescued by a feared warrior of legend—the brave hearted Anvrai d'Arques. Isabel's fierce spirit stirs his passion, her touch makes him wild. And her love will set him free . . .

A Forbidden Love by Alexandra Benedict

An Avon Romance

The Viscount Hastings is the most scandalous man in all England! So when he discovers Sabrina, a Gypsy in danger, he spirits her away to the most *unsafe* place in the land . . . his bed. He longs to join her there, but instead vows to uncover the secrets this beautiful woman hides . . .

DISCOVER CONTEMPORARY ROMANCES at their
SIZZLING HOT BEST FROM AVON BOOKS

Avon Romantic Treasures

Unforgettable, enthralling love stories, sparkling with passion and adventure from Romance's bestselling authors